HICKOK & CODY

MATT BRAUN

St. Martin's Paperbacks

HICKOK & CODY

Copyright © 2001 by Winchester Productions, Ltd.

ISBN: 0-312-97875-8

Printed in the United States of America

St. Martin's Paperbacks edition / May 2001

St. Martin's Paperbacks are published by St. Martin's Press, 175 Fifth Avenue, New York, NY 10010.

10 9 8 7 6 5 4 3 2 1

"You have something I want," Richter said. "I'm willing to pay quite generously for an exchange. Enough to put you and Cody on easy street."

"What makes those kids worth so much? Why you after 'em anyway?"

"I'm not at liberty to say."

"Guess that's your tough luck."

Hickok grabbed Richter by the collar and the seat of his pants and bodily threw him off the train. Richter hit the roadbed on his shoulder, tumbling head over heels, and rolled to a stop in a patch of weeds.

The conductor slammed open the door. "What in God's name happened?"

"That feller hadn't bought a ticket. He was so ashamed, he just up and jumped off the train."

The conductor gawked. "Why on earth would he jump?"

"You know, it's funny, he never said. Some folks are mighty strange."

PRAISE FOR SPUR AWARD-WINNING AUTHOR MATT BRAUN

"Matt Braun is one of the best!"
—Don Coldsmith, author of the Spanish Bit series

"Braun tackles the big men, the complex personalities of those brave few who were pivotal figures in the settling of an untamed frontier."
—Jory Sherman, author of *Grass Kingdom*

To

Macduff

Who gave of himself unstinting loyalty and
unconditional love.

AUTHOR'S NOTE

A WRITER and historian once observed, "When fact becomes legend, print the legend."

Hickok & Cody is based on historical fact. The Grand Duke Alexis of Russia actually traveled to America for a buffalo hunt on the Western Plains. There was an Orphan Train operating out of New York, carrying street urchins to adoptive homes in the West. All of this happened.

William F. "Buffalo Bill" Cody appeared in stage productions long before the advent of his Wild West Show. The plays were written by Ned Buntline and presented at theaters in New York and other Eastern cities. The success of the plays ultimately convinced Cody that "the show business" was the life for him.

James Butler "Wild Bill" Hickok did, in fact, go East to appear in Cody's stage productions. One season on the stage convinced him that acting was a sham, false heroics for the gullible masses. He discovered as well that Eastern cities left him longing for the endless skies and grass-scented winds of the plains. He returned, all too gladly, to the West.

All that is true, and all the rest is legend. In 1872, the Grand Duke Alexis and the Orphan Train converged with Hickok and Cody on the Western Plains. Heroic in fact as well as legend, Cody and Hickok became the paladins of desperate orphans. Their quest took them to New York, and the Broadway stage, and a murderous confrontation with underworld czars. New York was never the same again.

Hickok & Cody is fiction based on fact. A story of knights in buckskins who brought their own brand of justice to the streets of New York. A tale of mythical feats by legendary plainsmen.

Allegory in which West meets East—with a bang!

HICKOK
& CODY

CHAPTER 1

A BROUGHAM carriage clattered along Irving Place shortly after midnight. The driver turned the corner onto Twentieth Street and brought his team to a halt. The horses snorted frosty puffs of smoke beneath a cobalt winter sky.

The brougham was a four-wheeled affair, with the driver perched on a seat outside. A gas lamppost on the corner reflected dully off the windows of the enclosed cab. Otto Richter shifted forward inside the cab and wiped condensation off the window with his coat sleeve. He slowly inspected the streets bordering Gramercy Park.

The park was a block long, centered between Lexington Avenue on the north and Irving Place on the south. Darkened mansions lined the perimeter of what was an exclusive enclave for some of the wealthiest families in New York. The whole of Gramercy Park was surrounded by an ornate eight-foot high wrought-iron fence.

"Looks quiet," Richter said. "Let's get it done."

Turk Johnson, a bullet-headed bruiser, followed him out of the cab. Richter glanced up at the driver.

"Stay put till we get back."

"I'll be waitin' right here, boss."

Richter led the way along the sidewalk. A few houses down, he mounted the steps to a three-story brick mansion. Johnson was at his elbow, standing watch as he halted before a stout oak door with stained glass in the top panel. He took a key from his overcoat pocket and inserted it into the lock. The door swung open.

A light snow began to fall as they moved into foyer. Johnson eased the door closed, and they waited a moment, listening intently for any sound. On the left was an entryway into a large parlor, and on the right was the family sitting room. Directly ahead, a broad carpeted staircase swept grandly to the upper floors.

The silence was disturbed only by the relentless tick of a grandfather clock. Richter motioned with his hand, stealthily crossing to the bottom of the staircase. They took the stairs with wary caution, alert to the creak of a floorboard underfoot. Their movements were wraithlike, a step at a time.

A single gaslight burned on the second floor. Still treading lightly, they paused to get their bearings at the stairwell landing. Neither of them had ever before been in the house, but they knew it well. There were two bedrooms off the head of the stairs and another along a hallway to the right. The master bedchamber, which overlooked Gramercy Park, was at the front of the house. The servants were quartered on the top floor.

Richter nodded to the doorway on their left. "Careful now," he whispered. "The old woman's a light sleeper."

The remark solicited a grunt. Johnson was burly, robust as an ox, his head fixed directly on his shoulders. He grinned around a mouthful of teeth that looked like old dice. "Whyn't fix her wagon, too?"

"Quiet!" Richter hissed sharply. "Try to keep your mind on the job."

"Whatever you say, boss."

"Come along."

Richter turned toward the front of the house. A moment later, they stopped outside the master bed-chamber. He gripped the doorknob, twisted it gingerly, and stepped inside. Embers from the grate in the fireplace faintly lighted the room. He moved closer to the bed.

A man and a woman lay fast asleep. The man was strikingly handsome, the woman a classic beauty, both in their early thirties. Her hair was loose, fanned over the pillow, dark as a raven's wing. He snored lightly, covers drawn to his chin.

In the glow of the fireplace, Richter's features were hard and angular. He was lean and wiry, with muddy deep-set eyes, and a razored mouth. He stared at the couple for an instant, his expression implacable. Then he pulled a bottle of ether from his overcoat pocket.

Johnson moved forward with two rags. Richter doused them with ether, quickly stoppered the bottle, and returned it to his pocket. He took one of the rags from Johnson and they walked to opposite sides of the bed. Neither of them hesitated, Johnson working on the man and Richter the woman. They clamped the rags down tight, covering nostrils and mouth.

The man arched up from the bed, his hands clawing at the rag. Johnson grabbed him in a headlock, immobilizing him with brute strength, and forced him to breath deeply. The woman's eyes fluttered open and she gasped, inhaling raw ether; she struggled only briefly in Richter's arms. Hardly a minute passed before they were both unconscious, sprawled on the bed.

Richter stuffed the rag in his pocket. He removed the pillow from beneath the woman's head and placed it over her face. Johnson, working just as swiftly, buried the man's face in a pillow. There was no resistance from the couple, for they were anesthetized into a dreamlike state, incapable of fighting back. The men slowly smothered them to death.

When it was over, Richter arranged the woman's head in a comely pose on the pillow. Johnson followed suit, and they stepped back, admiring their handiwork. "Well now," Richter said with a note of pride. "They look quite peaceful, don't they?"

Johnson grinned. "Damn good way to kick the bucket. Never felt a thing."

"Yes, all very neat and tidy. Let's see to the children, Turk."

Richter hurried out the door. At the staircase landing, he once again saturated the rags with ether. Then they separated, Johnson moving to the bedroom on the right and Richter proceeding along the hallway. Some moments later they returned, each of them carrying a child bundled in a blanket. Richter gave Johnson a sharp look.

"Everything all right?"

"Went off smooth as silk."

Johnson was holding a boy, perhaps nine or ten years old. The girl in Richter's arms appeared to be a year or two older. She was a mirror image of her mother, just as the boy favored his father. They were both unconscious, breathing evenly.

"Time to go," Richter said, darting a glance at the other bedroom door. "Take it easy on the stairs."

Johnson trailed him down the staircase. They moved quietly through the foyer just as the grandfather clock chimed the half hour. Richter paused outside the house, juggling the girl with one arm, and locked the door. The snow was heavier now, thick white flakes swirling across Gramercy Park. They turned upstreet toward the waiting carriage.

One at a time, the children were loaded into the

cab. Richter was the last to clamber aboard, signaling the driver to move out. The horses lurched into motion, heads bowed against the squalling snow. The carriage rounded the corner at the far end of Gramercy Park.

"Whatta night!" Johnson said, motioning to the huddled forms of the children. "Who are these kids, anyhow?"

"Augustus and Katherine."

"They got last names?"

Richter permitted himself a thin smile. "Not anymore."

The carriage trundled off toward the Lower East Side.

Manhattan was an island. Some two miles by fifteen miles in mass, it was connected to the outside world by railroad bridges along the northern shoreline. The only other outlets were ferries that plied the Hudson River.

The settled part of the island, more commonly called New York City, was a five-mile stretch at the southern tip of Manhattan. With the population topping a million, there were a hundred thousand people for every square mile, a teeming cauldron of humanity. Worldly men called it the Bagdad of North America.

Delancey Street was located in the heart of the Lower East Side. There, in tenements wedged together like rabbit warrens, the working class of the city struggled to outdistance squalor and poverty. New Year's was just a week past, but the people of Delancey Street found no reason to celebrate 1872. Their days were occupied instead with putting bread on the table.

The brougham carriage halted at the intersection of Delancey and Pitt. A faded sign affixed to the building on the southeast corner identified it as the New York Juvenile Asylum. The two-story structure was worn and decrepit, a battered wooden ruin much like the rest of the neighborhood. It was a warehouse for the flotsam of the city's young.

The driver hopped down to open the carriage door. Richter emerged first, carrying the girl, followed by Johnson with the boy. Heavy wet snow clung to their greatcoats as the driver hurried to jerk the pull-bell outside the entrance to the asylum. A pudgy man with wispy hair and dewlap jowls opened the door on the third ring. He waved them inside.

"I was getting worried," he said. "Thought maybe something had gone wrong."

"Nothing went wrong," Richter replied. "Just this damnedable snow, that's all. The streets are a mess."

"Hardly the night for an abduction, hmmm?"

"Your mouth will be the death of you, Barton. Let's hear no more about abduction."

Joseph Barton was the director of the Juvenile Asylum. He was a man of small stature, and corrupt to the core. He spread his hands in a lame gesture. "No harm intended. I was just making talk."

"Don't," Richter warned. "All the talk stops tonight."

The anteroom of the asylum was warmed by a potbelly stove stoked with coal. There was a tattered sofa and a grouping of hard straight-back chairs meant for the infrequent visitor. The children were placed on the sofa, still wrapped in their blankets. Richter took a moment to check the pupils of their eyes.

"Marvelous invention, ether," he said with some satisfaction. "They'll be out for at least another hour."

"I'd hoped for longer," Barton said in a piping voice. "The train's scheduled to depart at eight. What if they make a fuss when they wake up?"

"How many brats do you have in this sinkhole?"

"At the moment, probably five hundred or so. Why do you ask?"

Richter stared at him. "You ought to know how to handle hard-nosed kids. Get them some clothes out of your stockroom, nothing too fancy." His gaze shifted to the children. "Turn 'em into regular little orphans."

"Yes, but—" Barton hesitated, undone by his nerves. "What if they resist being put on the train?"

"I'm sure you'll think of something clever. That's what you're being paid for."

There were hundreds of men and women in New York who devoted their lives to homeless children. Most of them were affiliated with religious organizations, or charitable foundations. There were, as well, men without scruple or conscience who looked upon indigent children as a means of lining their own pockets. Joseph Barton was just such a man.

The opportunity for graft stemmed from the fact that youngsters under fifteen represented one-third of the city's population. At any given moment, upward of a hundred thousand homeless children were roaming the streets of New York. Some were orphans, their mothers and fathers dead from the ravages of disease and overwork. Others, children of the poor, were simply turned out by their parents to fend for themselves. To survive, they raided garbage bins and learned to live by petty crime.

The crisis brought swift action by the state legislature. The Truancy Law, enacted at the close of the Civil War, authorized police to arrest vagrant children ages five through fourteen. Some were brought to the

House of Refuge, operated by a coalition of religious concerns. Others, particularly the troublemakers, were packed off to a secular facility, the Juvenile Asylum. The latter institution was dedicated to discipline, instilling the virtue of daily toil. The children were then indentured as apprentices to tradesmen.

Those youngsters considered beyond redemption were shipped West on the Orphan Train. Farmers and ranchers on the distant plains welcomed them with a mix of Christian charity and a profound belief in the values of hard work. All of which nicely solved the problem of delinquents and mischievous street urchins. The Orphan Train departed New York's Grand Central Station every Friday.

"I'll certainly do my best," Barton said now. "None of the children especially like the thought of being sent West. We're sometimes forced to restrain them until the train leaves."

"I don't want them harmed," Richter told him. "The whole idea is to get them adopted. The farther West, the better."

"Oh, yes, I understand completely."

"Make sure you do, for your own good."

There was a veiled threat in Richter's tone. He pulled out a wad of greenbacks and started peeling off bills. "There's the thousand we agreed on," he said stiffly. "A thousand more once they're adopted."

Barton thought it unwise to count the bills. "How will I satisfy you the adoption has actually taken place?"

"You've no need to worry on that score. I'll know."

"Very well, just as you say."

"One last thing," Richter said. "You'll likely read about some missing children in tomorrow's papers.

Don't try to put two and two together and get four."

"How could I not put it together?" Barton asked guilelessly. "Were there all that many children abducted tonight?"

"Pretend you're deaf, dumb and blind. Otherwise . . ."

Richter motioned casually to Johnson. The bruiser fixed Barton with a cold, ominous look. Barton quickly averted his gaze.

"Otherwise—" Richter went on, "Turk will pay you a visit some dark night. I doubt you'd recover."

"There's no reason to threaten me. I'm quite good at keeping a confidence."

"Then I predict you'll live to a ripe old age."

Richter walked to the door. Johnson gave Barton an evil grin, then turned away, closing the door as he went out. On the street, the two men crossed to the curb, where Richter paused before entering the carriage. He looked up at the falling snow.

"I'm afraid we'll have to sleep fast, Turk."

"Why's that, boss?"

"We have a train to catch."

Otto Richter was a man who left no stone unturned.

CHAPTER 2

THE CAMPSITE was something on the order of a bivouac. Tents were aligned with military precision, forming a boxlike square fronting the waters of Red Willow Creek. Cavalry troopers stood guard at the cardinal points of the compass.

Wild Bill Hickok and Buffalo Bill Cody stood with a group of army officers in the center of the compound. Cody, with a flair for showmanship, was resplendent in pale buckskins, a crimson shirt worn beneath his fringed jacket. Hickok wore a stained buckskin jacket, his woolen trousers stuffed into the tops of mule-earred boots. A brace of Colt Navy pistols, carried cross-draw fashion, were wedged into a wide belt around his waist.

The weather was uncommonly mild for January on the Nebraska plains. Though the mercury hovered around forty, patches of snow still dotted the landscape from a recent storm. The campsite was located some forty miles south of Fort McPherson, headquarters for the Fifth Cavalry Regiment. Among the officers present were Lieutenant General Phil Sheridan, Major General George Armstrong Custer, and four brigadier generals. The officers were attired in field dress, their gold braid sparkling in an early morning sun.

A burly Russian Cossack snapped to attention as the flap opened on the largest tent in the compound. The Grand Duke Alexis, son of Alexander II, Czar of all the Russias, strode from the tent. He was tall and stout, with dark muttonchop whiskers and a regal bearing. He wore a fringed buckskin jacket, ivory in color and elaborately decorated with quillwork and shiny beads. The jacket was a gift, presented to him by Sheridan only yesterday.

"Good morning," he said, addressing the group in a heavy accent. "Excellent day for a hunt, is it not?"

"Excellent indeed," Sheridan replied. "I trust you slept well, Your Highness."

"Oh, yes," Alexis beamed, favoring Cody and Hickok with a broad smile. "You gentlemen will teach me how the buffalo are killed. *Da*?"

"Yessir, we will," Cody assured him. "You'll get the hang of it in no time. Won't he, pardner?"

"Why, shore he will," Hickok agreed. " 'Specially with you to show him the ropes. You're in good hands, Duke."

The Grand Duke chose to overlook his truncated title. He was fascinated by the similarity between the two men. They were both solid six-footers, ruggedly handsome, their hair spilling down to their shoulders. Yesterday, when they met his train in North Platte, he'd been surprised to find Hickok in the party. From conversation, he gathered that Hickok was between jobs as a lawman and had been invited along by Cody. He felt fortunate to have them both on the hunt.

The Wild West was all the vogue with European nobility. Every year, royal sportsmen crossed the Atlantic to hunt buffalo on the wind-swept plains. The hunt for the Grand Duke had been orchestrated by the State Department in concert with the army brass. Russia was a friendly power, having aligned itself with the Union during the bloody turmoil of the Civil War. Five years ago, in 1867, the Grand Duke's father had ceded the territory of Alaska to the United States, further cementing the relationship between two great powers. All of which accounted for six generals in attendance on today's hunt.

Phil Sheridan motioned to where troopers waited with saddled horses. "You're in luck, Your Highness," he said with an expansive gesture. "Cody insists that you use his personal horse, Buckskin Joe."

"Finest buffalo horse on the plains!" Custer interjected, ever eager to display his expertise. "I can truthfully say I've never seen his equal."

"I am honored," Alexis said, looking at Cody. "How did you arrive at such an unusual name for your horse?"

"Well, don't you see, he's a buckskin. I just tacked on 'Joe' to give him a handle."

"A handle?"

"Yessir, a handle . . . a name."

"Ah, of course, now I understand."

The men walked toward the horses. Cody got Alexis mounted on Buckskin Joe, and the nobleman told himself he'd made a wise choice. Through the Russian ambassador, he had requested that Buffalo Bill Cody act as his personal guide. Cody was hailed by the press and the public alike as the most formidable buffalo hunter on the Western Plains. In 1867, while working as a contract hunter for the Kansas Pacific, he had killed 4,280 of the shaggy beasts. The tracklaying crews, grateful for the bounty, tagged him with a sobriquet that stuck. He became Buffalo Bill.

Wild Bill Hickok was no less a legend to the Grand Duke Alexis. On and off a scout for the army, Hickok's greater fame stemmed from his years as a lawman. His notoriety had little to do with buffalo and everything to do with Western desperadoes. His name was known on the steppes of Russia just as it

was throughout the capitals of Europe. The world
doted on his adventures, awed by tales of his speed
and deadliness with a pistol. There was, in the lore
of the West, only one Wild Bill. He was the most
renowned mankiller of the day.

The hunting partying rode south from the Red Willow Creek camp. They were trailed by a troop of cavalry, acting as escort in the event they encountered a
hostile band of Sioux. An hour or so out, with Cody
and Alexis in the lead, they topped a low rise on the
rolling plains. Spread out before them, grazing on the
umber grasses of winter, was a herd of some three
hundred buffalo. Alexis was determined to take one
of the great beasts with his new pistol, a Smith &
Wesson .44 presented to him before he entrained from
New York for the West. Cody explained how to place
the shot from horseback.

Hickok and the generals waited on the knoll. Cody
led the way onto the prairie, approaching the herd at
a sedate trot. He cut out a woolly-coated cow grazing
at the edge of the herd, and forced her into a lum-
bering lope. Then, twisting in the saddle, he motioned
Alexis forward. The Grand Duke spurred Buckskin
Joe into a gallop and bore down on the cow. His arm
extended, he fired six shots from the Smith & Wesson, raking the cow with lead. She swerved away,
seemingly unfazed, and rejoined the herd. A moment
later she went back to cropping grass.

From the knoll, Hickok grunted with mild amusement. Sheridan cursed, and Custer shook his head,
and the other generals held their silence. They
watched as Cody took Alexis aside for a short lecture
on the craft of hunting buffalo. Finally, with Alexis
nodding, Cody pulled a Springfield .50 rifle from his
saddle scabbard. Like his horse, he had named his

rifle, and he fondly called it "Lucretia." The name derived from a Victor Hugo drama entitled *Lucretia Borgia*, the story of an ancient Italian noblewoman noted for her venom. The rifle was as deadly as its namesake.

Cody selected a mammoth bull from the herd. He rode off to the left of Alexis, urging Buckskin Joe into a gallop with a hard swat across the rump. The bull snorted, whirling away from the horsemen, quickly separated from the herd. Alexis kneed Buckskin Joe alongside, matching the bull stride for stride, the reins in one hand, the butt of Lucretia pressed to his shoulder. The rifle boomed and the bull went down headfirst, his horns plowing furrows in the dark earth. Alexis vaulted from the saddle, tossing the rifle to Cody, and pulled an evil-looking knife from his belt. He cut off the bull's tail, thrusting it overhead with a jubilant shout.

Before the day ended, the Grand Duke of all the Russias killed six times more.

The regimental band played a lively air. A celebration was in progress, with the royal party seated in the dining tent. Waiters in white jackets scurried around lighting coal-oil lamps as a vermilion sunset slowly faded into dusk. The menu for the evening featured buffalo hump aux champignons.

"A toast," Sheridan said, raising his wine glass. "To the Grand Duke Alexis. Seven buffalo in a single day!"

"Hear! Hear!"

The men were seated around a long table covered with white linen. They chorused the toast in loud voices, quaffing wine from crystal goblets. Alexis, who was savaging a slab of buffalo hump with the exuberance of a man who reveled in the kill, accepted their praise with regal modesty. He raised his own glass.

"I, too, make a toast," he said in an accent thickened by wine. "To Buffalo Bill, who must surely have Russian blood. A man among men!"

"Hear! Hear!"

Their shouts rang out across the compound. Fully five hundred men were camped along the banks of Red Willow Creek. There were four troops of the Fifth Cavalry, the regimental band, and a train of sixteen wagons to haul provisions. Major engagements against hostile tribes had been fought with fewer men and no supply train at all. But the troopers encamped by the creek found no fault with the royal hunt. Tonight, they feasted on buffalo as well.

The guest of honor insisted that Cody and Hickok be seated at his end of the table. He was aware that Sheridan, commander of the military division, and Custer, the fabled Indian fighter, felt somewhat slighted. Yet he'd been feted by generals since childhood, for he was, after all, the successor to the Russian throne. He wanted to learn more of the plainsmen, the storied heroes of the frontier.

Hickok, he discovered, was the mentor of Cody. At thirty-five, Hickok was nine years older and already a legend before they met. In 1867, a New York journalist traveling the West wrote an article for *Harper's New Monthly Magazine*. The article dealt with Hickok's exploits during the Civil War, when he'd infiltrated behind Confederate lines, operating as a Union spy. The journalist proclaimed, with attendant gory details, that Hickok had killed over a hundred men. He anointed him "The Prince of Pistoleers."

Other publications jumped to follow Hickok's adventures. He worked as a scout for the army, serving under Custer in the Seventh Cavalry. Then, after a stint as a deputy U.S. marshal, he was elected sheriff of a Kansas hellhole. From there, he went on to serve as city marshal of Abilene, the roughest cowtown on the plains. Abilene, where he'd killed two men, was his last assignment, ended less than a month ago. He was the scourge of outlaws, reputed to have dropped nine men in gunfights.

Dime novels, the craze of Eastern readers, immortalized him forever in the minds of the public. General George Armstrong Custer, penning an article for *Galaxy Magazine*, labeled him the perfect specimen of physical manhood, unerring with rifle or pistol, a deadly adversary. Henry M. Stanley, better known for locating Dr. David Livingstone in darkest Africa, also wrote an article for *Harper's*. He portrayed Hickok in herculean terms, a plainsman and peace officer who had never killed a man without good cause. Wild Bill Hickok was enshrined into the pantheon of American folklore.

Cody, by contrast, had never killed a white man. His path to glory began in 1860, when at the age of fourteen he rode into history for the Pony Express. That same year, he met Hickok, who became his friend and mentor in the days ahead. When the Civil War erupted, he served with the Kansas Volunteer Cavalry, operating as a scout for the Union forces. Following the war, he sometimes worked with Hickok as a deputy U.S. marshal, and later found fame as Buffalo Bill with the Kansas Pacific Railroad. Later still, Hickok obtained a position for him as a scout with Custer's Seventh Cavalry.

From there, after gaining the attention of General Sheridan, Cody was assigned to the Fifth Cavalry.

Over time, he was promoted to Chief of Scouts, operating out of Fort McPherson, deep in Sioux country. His three years of service resulted in a record unequaled by any scout on the frontier. He engaged in nine expeditions against the Sioux, and fought in eleven pitched battles. At twenty-six, he was a seasoned veteran, having killed ten warriors in personal combat. His courage in the field brought a commendation for valor by direct order of the Secretary of War.

Cody, like Hickok, attracted Eastern journalists. In 1869, Ned Buntline traveled West to Fort McPherson, under contract for a series of stories in the *New York Weekly*. His first installment, entitled *Buffalo Bill, the King of the Border Men*, catapulted Cody into national fame. He depicted Cody as an intrepid scout and fearless Indian fighter, and generally sensationalized every aspect of Cody's life. Following the series, he churned out four dime novels in two years, each more heroic than the last. To an entranced public, Cody became the Galahad of the Plains, a knight in buckskin.

"Now, you must indulge me," Alexis said, as intoxicated by the men as the wine. "What were your grandest adventures?"

Cody wagged his head. "I don't know as I'd call 'em grand."

"Don't be coy," Sheridan admonished from the other end of the table. "Tell him about the Battle of Summit Springs."

"Well—" Cody tugged at the small goatee on his chin. "You reckon he wants to hear that old chesnut?"

"Of course!" Alexis thundered. "I insist."

Cody launched into a windy tale of blood on the plains. A band of Cheyenne led by Tall Bull had taken two white women captive and fled north toward the Powder River country. The Fifth Cavalry gave chase, and several days into the pursuit Cody located the hostile camp. The cavalry charged, overrunning the village, killing fifty-two warriors and recapturing one of the women captives. The other was clubbed to death during the battle, and Cody in turn shot Tall Bull in a pitched fight. The death of their chief put the Cheyenne to flight.

Alexis was round-eyed. "And you scalped him? *Da*?"

"Shore did." Cody pulled a thatch of dried hair from inside his jacket and tossed it on the table. "Peeled the bugger's top knot clean off."

There was absolute silence at the table. Cody kept a hunk of beaver pelt handy to palm off on pilgrims and complete the joke. Everyone watched Alexis as he stared at what he believed to be a Cheyenne scalp, taken in the heat of battle. Custer was on the verge of a braying laugh when Sheridan shut him down with a cold look. Before anyone could spoil the joke, Sheridan glanced over at Hickok.

"Wild Bill, it's your turn," he said quickly. "Tell the Grand Duke about that fracas in Springfield. The time you shot Dave Tutt."

"Not much to tell," Hickok said, knuckling his sweeping mustache. "Maybe he'd sooner inspect Cody's scalp."

"No! No!" Alexis commanded, averting his gaze from the beaver pelt. "I want to hear of this shooting, Wild Bill. You must tell me."

Hickok spun a wry tale of love and death. In 1865, shortly after the Civil War, he'd drifted into Springfield, Missouri. A classic love triangle developed, with he and a gambler named Dave Tutt vying for the attentions of the same woman. Finally, over a poker table one night, he and Tutt exchanged insults of the worst kind. The next morning, on the Town Square, Tutt accosted him and fired the first shot. Hickok, deliberate even in a fight, drilled him through the heart. There, on the Springfield square, he'd coined the term that speed's fine, but accuracy is final.

"You left out a salient detail," Sheridan prompted. "What was the range when you fired?"

Hickok smiled. "A measured seventy-five paces."

"Astounding," Alexis exclaimed. "Why did he fire on you at such a distance?"

"Well, Your Highness, he'd never seen me shoot before. I reckon you could say he was a mite surprised."

"Champagne!" Alexis roared. "We make a toast to Wild Bill and Buffalo Bill. We get drunk!"

Hickok and Cody exchanged a look. They'd told the tales so often that by now it was like a vaudeville act. Cody reclaimed his Cheyenne scalp as the waiters popped the corks. Hickok smiled at the fun of it all.

Alexis, Grand Duke of all the Russias, hoisted his glass with a booming laugh.

CHAPTER 3

THE LAND was stark and flat. Cornfields stood struck dead by winter, their slender stalks gone tawny with frost. The train sped westward under a dingy sky.

Katherine stared out at the bleak landscape. Thick clouds of black smoke from the engine swirled past the window. Augustus was asleep beside her on the seat, huddled within his coat against the chill of the passenger coach. She watched the fleeting cornfields with a forlorn expression.

There were six coaches on the train. Five were for orphans, and the sixth, the last in the string, was for fare-paying passengers. On each of the orphan coaches there were two attendants, a man and a woman, to look after the children. Their duties seemed more that of wardens than guardians.

Over the past week the train had followed the Union Pacific tracks westward. Slowly, with stops at every hamlet along the line, the train had made its way through Ohio, Indiana, Illinois, and finally into Iowa. The landscape became flatter and bleaker with every mile, somehow desolate. A sense of abandonment hung over the orphan coaches.

Katherine felt dazed, curiously hollow inside. The day the train left New York, she and Augustus had fought and kicked and screeched until they were forcibly carried onto the coach. They continued to protest they were not orphans, until finally Mr. Crocker, the agent for the Children's Aid Society, had threatened to bind and gag them in their seats. Their rebellion, stilled by the threat, turned to sullen apathy.

The helplessness of their situation was over-whelming. Katherine was ten, Augustus a year younger, and they'd never before been separated from their parents. At first, reduced to whispers, they wondered why they had been taken from their home in the dark of night. Even more, they were distressed that their parents had not intervened, somehow prevented their abduction. There seemed no good answers, only hard questions.

Yet, ever so slowly, they pieced together fragments of their ordeal. Katherine vaguely remembered a face, the face of a man, caught in the light of the lamp from the hallway, who had clamped a bitter-smelling rag over her face. Augustus recalled a huge man, unbelievably strong and quilted with muscle, holding him tight until he succumbed to a stinky rag. The men were shadowy figures, dim specters but nonetheless real.

Their terror the next morning was all too vivid. They found themselves at the mercy of workers at what was called the Juvenile Asylum. A man everyone addressed as Mr. Barton supervised their being dressed in clothing that was threadbare and tattered, obviously used. Then, after being manhandled onto an enclosed freight wagon, they were carted off to Grand Central Station. All their protests, like those of other children on the platform, went unheeded. They were dragged onto the train.

By the end of the first day, their spirits were at a low ebb. From talk among children in the coach, they learned they were aboard what was called the Orphan Train. There were five coaches, each packed with a hundred children, all destined to be adopted somewhere out West. For a brief moment, Katherine and

Augustus were appalled by the thought that their parents had forsaken them, put them up for adoption. All their lives they had known love and affection, and their hearts broke to think their mother and father were involved. But then, flooded with memories of their rough abduction, they knew it wasn't true. They had been stolen from their parents.

"What are you looking at?"

Katherine turned to find Augustus rubbing sleep from his eyes. He was a sturdy youngster, with the square jawline and pleasant features of their father. She shook her head with a woebegone expression.

"Nothing, really," she said, studying the dismal countryside. "Everything seems so much the same."

Augustus yawned. "Where are we?"

"I think this is still Iowa. I don't really know."

"Doesn't make any difference, does it?"

"No," Katherine said sadly. "Not unless they turn the train around."

"How far is Iowa from New York?"

"Very, very far. Why do you ask?"

"Oh, you know." Augustus shrugged, his features downcast. "I was thinking about Mother and Father. They must be looking for us."

"Not in Iowa," Katherine said. "I'm sure they're worried sick. But who would ever dream of Iowa?"

"Maybe we ought to try to escape. Next time they stop and put us out on the platform for the farmers, we could just run. Hide somewhere until the train leaves."

"Yes, I suppose we could try. Although, where would we go? How would we ever get back to New York?"

"We could find a policeman," Augustus offered.

"All he'd have to do is telegraph Mother and Father. We'd be on our way home in no time."

"You two got bats in your belfry. Go ahead, holler cop and see what it gets you."

In the seat opposite them were two young boys. One was asleep, but the other was watching them with open mockery. Over the past week they had learned that he was twelve, a tough little Irish scrapper from the Hell's Kitchen section of New York. His name was Jimmy Callaghan.

"What do you mean?" Katherine asked. "Why wouldn't a policeman help us?"

"Wake up for chrissake," Jimmy said with a wise-acre sneer. "You think a cop's gonna believe all that crap about your dear ol' mom and dad? You got another think comin'."

Augustus bridled. "Don't talk to my sister that way. Watch your language."

"And you watch your mouth, boyo, or I'll box your ears."

"Stop it!" Katherine said haughtily. "We are not orphans, and I think Augustus is right. A policeman would too help."

"Whatta laugh," Jimmy chided her. "You're on the Orphan Train and a copper wouldn't buy a word of it. He'd turn you over to Crocker quick as a wink."

"Quiet down," Augustus said, darting his eyes up the aisle. "Here he comes."

Thadius Crocker was a large, portly man with a perpetual scowl. "Breakfast time, boys and girls," he called out in a bogus jolly voice. "Let's rise and shine to a glorious new day."

The attendants followed him along the aisle. One passed out sandwiches while the other ladled milk into battered tin cups from a canister. The sandwiches were jelly and bread, served for breakfast, lunch, and supper. The milk was, as always, lukewarm.

"Look alive," Crocker said cheerily, moving away. "We're stopping in Council Bluffs this morning. Today's your day to find a home."

Augustus opened his sandwich. "Aww, wouldn't you know, it's jelly. I can't eat this again."

"Hand it over then," Jimmy said eagerly. "Anything's better'n nothin'."

"Jimmy's right," Katherine ordered. "You eat that now, Augustus. And drink your milk, too."

Jimmy Callaghan was right about many things. He was crude and foul-mouthed, a product of the impoverished Irish who inhabited Hell's Kitchen. But he had lived on the streets for almost half his life, and he was wise beyond his years. He'd told her all there was to know about the Orphan Train.

The Reverend Charles Loring Brace was the moving force behind the adoption program. A Methodist minister, he believed that vagabond children placed in Christian homes would turn out to be respectable citizens. The solution was to ship them off to the hinterlands, which also removed thousands of urchins from the streets of New York. The Truancy Law gave him the authority and wealthy do-gooders supported the plan with generous donations. He established the Children's Aid Society.

Printed circulars were sent to religious organizations from Ohio to Wyoming. In church meetings, ministers throughout the Midwest and across the Western Plains urged their parishioners to adopt displaced children. The Orphan Train quickly became a rolling adoption agency, the weekly schedule posted in churches and railroad stations at every stop along the way. There were no legal documents involved with a child's placement, but rather a simple verbal agreement by the new parents to provide a good home. Some twenty thousand children were shipped west every year.

Over the past week almost all the children on the train had been adopted. Some went along reluctantly, but others, resigned to their fate, played to the prospective parents and tried to find decent homes. Katherine noticed that boys were more acceptable than girls, and she quickly concocted a plan with Augustus. At every stop, they acted quarrelsome and unruly, passing themselves off as troublemakers. So far, their plan had worked, and they were among the less than fifty children left on the train. No one seemed partial to adopting them.

Shortly before noon, the train chugged into Council Bluffs. The engineer set the brakes, and the train ground to a halt before the depot. A crowd of farmers and townspeople were gathered outside the stationhouse, there to inspect the orphans. Some of the farmers had traveled twenty miles or more by wagon, looking for stout young boys to perform chores and work the fields. Whether moved by Christian charity, or merely drawn by the prospect of cheap labor, they edged forward as the train rolled to a stop. Everyone wanted first chance at the pick of the litter.

Thadius Crocker and his attendants ushered their charges off the coaches. The children were herded onto the depot platform, where they were formed into irregular ranks. Katherine, who was still weighing the possibility of escape, nudged Augustus and warned him off with a look. There were now ten attendants for fewer than fifty children, and the attendants were posted on the outer ranks of the group. Any thought of escape, at least in Council Bluffs, was clearly out of the question. They would be run down before they reached the end of the platform.

"Brothers and sisters!" Crocker addressed the crowd in a sonorous voice. "Allow me to welcome you on behalf of the Children's Aid Society. We invite you to provide a Christian upbringing for these poor tykes."

The invitation drew blank stares. The crowd was uncertain as to how they should proceed with inspecting the children. "Let me introduce some of the little darlings," Crocker said, like a carnival barker working a midway show. "Here's a bright lad with a head on his shoulders. Tommy Noonan, step forward for these good people."

By now, many of the children were anxious to be adopted. The farther west the train went, the land became increasingly bleak and inhospitable. Iowa was worse than Illinois, and no one doubted that Nebraska would be even more barren. There was talk as well that wild Indians still roamed the plains of Nebraska. Today seemed a good day to find a family.

Tommy Noonan was a freckle-faced red-head with a winning smile. He marched to the front of the group and recited the Gettysburg Address word for word. One of the farmers, figuring anyone who could quote Abe Lincoln was a bargain, quickly latched onto the boy. Crocker took them aside to settle the arrangements.

A girl stepped forward. She looked to be about thirteen, with small, budding breasts, and golden hair that gave her an angelic appearance. She gulped a deep breath and sang a stirring rendition of "Onward Christian Soldiers" in a quavering soprano. Some of the crowd thought she had been coached, but they were nonetheless impressed. She was adopted by a childless couple who operated the local hardware store.

Katherine and Augustus stood toward the rear of the group. A farmer and his wife approached, apparently uninterested in singers or aspiring scholars of Abe Lincoln. They studied the children with a critical gaze, as though sizing up livestock at an auction. They scarcely glanced at Katherine, who was obviously too delicate for farm work. But they thought Augustus looked promising, and the farmer moved a step closer. He took hold of Augustus, prodding with thorny fingers for shoulder muscle and strength. Katherine jumped between them.

"Leave him alone!" she shrieked, her eyes blazing. "He's not for sale!"

"Out of the way, girlie," the farmer growled. "I'm lookin' at this here boy."

"You keep your filthy hands off my brother!"

One of the attendants, an older man with spectacles, swiftly intervened. "You'll have to excuse her, sir," he said to the farmer. "They're brother and sister, and they prefer not to be separated. She's really a very nice girl."

"Don't want no girl," the farmer grumped. "Got my mind set on a boy."

The farmer selected Jimmy Callaghan instead. Walking away, the Irish youngster looked back over his shoulder at Katherine and Augustus. He gave them a sly grin and a slow wink, as if to say the farmer had made the mistake of his life. They disappeared into the crowd.

Within the hour, eleven children had been adopted. The farmers and townspeople gradually drifted away, leading the new additions to their families. Crocker and his staff herded the remaining chilren back aboard the train. The engineer tooted his whistle and the stationmaster signaled from the end of the platform. The locomotive lurched forward with a belch of steam.

Otto Richter was standing at the rear of the train. He swung aboard the last passenger coach just as the conductor was about to shut the door. He moved through the vestibule and into the coach, and found Turk Johnson eating a bag of peanuts. He slumped wearily into the seat.

Johnson cracked a peanut shell. "Any luck, boss?"

"No," Richter said stiffly. "They pulled their usual brother-and-sister act. That girl's enough to scare anyone off."

"What if nobody adopts 'em?"

"We have our orders, Turk."

"Be a shame," Johnson said, munching absently on a peanut. "You know, after we've brought 'em all this way."

Richter nodded. "Let's hope it doesn't come to that."

The Orphan Train crossed the line into Nebraska.

CHAPTER 4

THE LAST day of the royal hunt was an extravaganza of bloodsport. The Grand Duke Alexis was sated with killing, having downed thirty-three buffalo in five days. Cody arranged entertainment of a different sort.

The Indians rode into camp late that morning. Spotted Tail, chief of the Brule Sioux, led a hundred warriors mounted on fleet buffalo ponies. His band was currently at peace with the government, but he trusted no white man beyond certain limits. His warriors pitched camp on the opposite side of Red Willow Creek.

Phil Sheridan was of a like mind. He ordered Custer to turn out the troops, and two companies were kept on alert at all times. Custer's reputation was that of a man who could start a war simply for his own amusement. Yet the Sioux respected his ability as a field commander, and even more, his physical courage. The Grand Duke was safe with Custer in the role of watchdog.

Cody thought the vigilance unwarranted. Late yesterday, with the day's hunt ended, he'd sensed that Alexis was bored with killing buffalo. He talked it over with Hickok, and together, they'd convinced Sheridan to make the last day a memorable day. Cody knew that Spotted Tail's band was camped on the Republican River, some thirty miles to the west. After dark, he had made the ride aboard Buckskin Joe and counseled with the Brule chief. The upshot was a hundred Sioux braves gathered opposite the army compound.

Spotted Tail was intrigued by the idea of a great chief from a distant land. He had some vague notion of a vast water to the east, what the whites called the Atlantic Ocean. Cody impressed on him that Alexis was somewhat like the Great White Father in Washington. Though Spotted Tail was mystified about the faraway place known as Russia, he nonetheless grasped that the Grand Duke was the ruler of a powerful tribe. Still, it was Cody's skill at bartering, rather than Spotted Tail's curiosity, that brought the Sioux to Red Willow Creek. He had promised the Brule leader a hundred pounds of tobacco.

Sheridan considered it extortion. "For God's sake!" he fumed. "How am I going to justify a wagonload of tobacco?"

"All in a good cause," Cody said. "President Grant wanted the Grand Duke looked after. Today'll be the icing on the cake."

"Well, it's expensive icing, Mr. Cody."

"No more so than turnin' out the regiment for escort duty. Besides, Spotted Tail and his boys wouldn't have come otherwise. I'd say we got ourselves a bargain."

"Damn the bargain," Custer interrupted waspishly. "We should have ordered him in and had done with it. He could hardly refuse."

"Don't bet on it," Hickok countered. "I wouldn't exactly call the Brule tame Injuns."

Custer, like Hickok and Cody, wore his hair shoulder-length. He was the most flamboyant general in the army, not to mention the youngest, and overly proud of his reputation as an Indian fighter. He cocked his head with a haughty smirk.

"Hostile or tame, who cares?" he said derisively. "Give me a regiment and I'll ride through the Sioux nation. Brule, Hunkpapa, Oglala, the whole lot!"

"Gen'ral, you might be surprised," Hickok said. "They're a pretty scrappy bunch."

"Wild Bill, I'm disappointed in you. I thought you enjoyed a good fight."

Sheridan silenced them with a look. "Gentlemen, I suggest we defer that discussion for another day. Our mission at the moment is to entertain the Grand Duke." He glanced at Cody. "How do you propose to go about this?"

"Let's have a powwow," Cody said lightly. "The Grand Duke's never met a real live redskin. We'll let him palaver with Spotted Tail for a while. That'll make a story when he gets back to Russia."

"No doubt," Sheridan said dryly. "And after their . . . powwow?"

"Got it all fixed. Spotted Tail and his boys will show him how the Sioux hunt buffalo. Ought to be a regular lollapaloosa."

"All right, Mr. Cody, bring on the vaunted leader of the Brule. Tell him I expect him to earn all that tobacco."

"Yessir."

Cody swung into the saddle. He forded the creek atop Buckskin Joe and returned some ten minutes later with the Brule chief. Spotted Tail was in his early fifties, with flat, dark features, and an eagle feather affixed to his coal-black hair. He rode a magnificent chocolate-spotted pinto.

Alexis, along with Hickok and the generals, waited by an open fire in the center of the compound. Cody, acting as interpreter, introduced the Grand Duke and the Brule chief with great fanfare. Once they were seated on the ground, a camp orderly served everyone coffee in galvanized mugs. Spotted Tail laced his coffee with four heaping spoons of sugar.

"Perhaps he would prefer vodka," Alexis suggested. "I think he does not like our coffee."

"Not that, Your Highness," Cody said. "Injuns have just got a powerful sweet tooth, that's all. Liquor wouldn't be a good idea, anyhow."

"Oh, why not?"

"Well, no tellin' what a drunk Injun might do. Tends to make 'em a little loco."

Spotted Tail drained his mug. He smacked his lips with satisfaction and rattled off a guttural question to Cody. The scout turned to Alexis.

"I told him last night where you're from. He wants to know if you have red men in Russia."

"None quite like him," Alexis observed thoughtfully. "The Tatars from the east overran Mother Russia in ancient times. My ancestors drove them back perhaps three centuries ago. Some still live in the province we call Siberia."

Spotted Tail listened to the translation with great interest, nodding sagely. Then he spoke at length, gesturing off to the east, and Cody repeated his words. "He says his country has also been overrun from where the sun rises. Only in his case, it was white men who took the land. He says the whites are as leaves on the trees—too many to fight."

"Is he not a warrior chief?"

"One of the worst there ever was. 'Course, now he's what's called a 'peace chief.' "

"I do not understand this . . . peace chief?"

Cody briefly explained. Spotted Tail was a famed war chief who had fought the encroachment of white men on Sioux lands from 1854 to 1868. But finally,

convinced it was a fight that could not be won, he
signed a peace treaty and led the Brules onto a reservation in southern Dakota Territory. He had kept
the peace for almost four years.

The Brules, Cody went on, were allowed to leave
the reservation and hunt buffalo along the Republican
River. Among army men, Spotted Tail was considered the wisest of the old war chiefs, for the people
of his band would survive the deadly conflict on the
Western Plains. Yet, despite having yielded to the
whites, he remained exalted as a warrior among all
the Sioux, even with tribal leaders who continued the
struggle. One of those was his nephew, the young war
chief of the Oglala band, Crazy Horse.

"What a strange name," Alexis remarked. "Why is
he called Crazy Horse?"

"I don't rightly know. Maybe it's because he's always on the prod. He does like a fight."

"Would Spotted Tail ever join his nephew in battle?"

Cody smiled. "Well, sir, I just suspect not. You
see, he's crazy like a fox."

Spotted Tail, who understood more English than
he pretended, nodded wisely. The Grand Duke caught
the sly look, and the two men exchanged a quick
glance. Then Spotted Tail held out his mug for more
coffee.

Alexis thought the Brule leader was indeed crazy
as a fox. Old and crafty, a man who fought no fight
he could not win. And in doing so, won.

The hunting party forded Red Willow Creek early that
afternoon. Spotted Tail and the Grand Duke, flanked
by Hickok and Cody, rode out front. Sheridan and the
generals were a short distance behind.

To the rear, perhaps a hundred yards off to the west, were the Brule warriors. They rode in a loose phalanx, their lances and carbines glinting in the afternoon sun. Off to the east, two troops of cavalry rode parallel with the Indians. Their orders were to provide a protective escort for the Grand Duke.

Some while later the party topped a low hogback ridge. Spread out before them was a wide plain bordered on the south by a broad, steep-walled arroyo. A herd of a thousand or more buffalo dotted the prairie, grazing on winter grass the color of coarse straw. The arroyo appeared to be a mile or so beyond the herd.

The purpose of today's outing was to present a spectacle few white men had ever seen. The Grand Duke Alexis was to witness the manner in which the Plains Tribes traditionally hunted buffalo. Even more, he was to observe the skill with which ancient weapons were used to down the shaggy beasts. The Brule Sioux prided themselves on being great hunters.

"Watch close now, Your Highness," Cody said, pointing off to the band of warriors. "See that short, stumpy feller on the chestnut stallion? His name's Running Dog and he's a holy terror with a bow and arrow. Keep your eye on him."

Spotted Tail waved his coup stick overhead, then motioned forward. The warriors urged their ponies off the ridge and rode out onto the grassy plain. They split into two columns, kicking their mounts into a steady trot. One column fanned east of the herd and the other angled off to the west They gigged their horses into a gallop.

The herd wheeled away from the headlong charge of yipping horsemen. Running Dog rode in the vanguard of the western column, maneuvering his pony with the pressure of his knees. As he pulled alongside a large cow, he drew his heavy ashwood bow to full curve and released a steel-tipped arrow. The arrow sliced into the cow behind her right shoulder and drove clean though, exiting below her left leg. The cow faltered in mid-stride, wobbling to a stop. She collapsed onto the ground.

"Amazing!" Alexis bellowed, standing in his stirrups. "The arrow passed all the way through."

"Told you he was a terror," Cody said, grinning. "Now keep your eye peeled for a tall feller on a bay gelding. Goes by the name of Black Elk. He's hell with a lance."

The herd swerved west as the lead buffalo neared the arroyo. The warriors yipped louder, still hugging the flanks at a gallop, and drove the herd back toward the ridge. Black Elk kneed his gelding into position, singling out a huge bull. His lance was ten feet long, with a steel head honed to a daggerlike point. He leaned forward, adding the momentum of a charging horse to the weight of the lance, and thrust the point into the bull's heart. He reined aside, leaving the lance planted to the hilt as the bull slowed to a walk. Then, already dead on its feet, the bull crashed to the earth in a thick puff of dust.

"Stuck him good," Hickok said with some admiration. "Never saw it done better."

Alexis looked astounded. "There is a majesty in such a feat. To kill . . . savagely."

"Sight to behold," Cody agreed. "Not one I'd want to try. Takes some powerful doing."

The balance of the afternoon was spent watching warriors attempt to outdo one another. Their horseback skills were a thing of wonder, almost magical, and not one in five missed with the bow or lance. Yet none of them were able to match the hunting powers of either Running Dog or Black Elk. They downed forty-nine buffalo, and unlike white men, who killed for sport, nothing would be wasted. The winter robes and freshly butchered meat would be hauled back to their village on the Republican River.

By sundown the evening meal had been served to the royal party in the dining tent. Troopers stacked logs on the firepit in the center of the compound, and presently a blazing bonfire lit the camp. Orderlies rushed to arrange a row of chairs outside the dining tent, with a commanding view of the area around the fire. The evening's entertainment was to be an authentic scalp dance, performed by Spotted Tail and his Brule Sioux. Alexis was given the place of honor.

"You're in for a treat," Cody said, leaning closer to the Grand Duke. "The Sioux set some store by the scalp dance. Pretty near a holy thing."

"This ritual?' Alexis asked. "Do I understand they perform it to celebrate killing their enemies?"

"Yessir, that's a good part of it," Cody replied. " 'Course, there's times they'll honor the bravery of the poor devils that got their scalps took. Ought to be quite a show."

Sheridan laughed. "You can credit what he's saying, Your Highness. Cody knows the show business."

"Show business?" Alexis said doubtfully. "I am not familiar with the term, General."

"Stage show," Sheridan explained. "Something like an opera without the music. Our Mr. Cody is a bit of an actor."

"How interesting," Alexis said, turning to Cody. "I see you are a man of many parts. Where do you perform these stage shows?"

"New York City, mostly," Cody informed him.

"The hostiles hole up during the winter and scouting gets a little slow. I generally go back East a couple months."

Ned Buntline, the dime novel writer, also penned plays based on Cody's frontier exploits. Last year, for the first time, Cody had gone East to appear in a stage production. He was a scout by profession, but he enjoyed what he thought of as a dalliance with the stage. He liked the money as well.

Alexis glanced over at Hickok. "Are you also a showman, Wild Bill?"

"No, sir, it ain't my callin'," Hickok said with a sardonic smile. "I leave all the playacting to Cody. He's the Shakespeare of the bunch."

Cody groaned. "You'll have to excuse him, Your Highness. He's just a mite jealous."

Before Alexis could reply, Spotted Tail and his Brule Sioux appeared at the edge of the compound. Their faces were streaked with war paint, and they were armed with tomahawks and stone-headed war clubs. Drums throbbed ominously in the distance and several of the warriors loosened blood-curdling howls. They began stomping around the fire to the beat of the drums.

Alexis idly wondered if Buffalo Bill had orchestrated the performance.

CHAPTER 5

A HAWK floated past on smothered wings, briefly silhouetted against a bright forenoon sun. The weather was crisp, creeks rimed with patches of ice, a brisk wind out of the north. The rolling plains swept onward like a saffron ocean of grass.

Cody held the reins of four spirited cavalry horses. The open carriage was double-seated, with the heavy springs designed for cross-country travel. Hickok shared the driver's seat, and like Cody, wore a high-collared mackinaw. Sheridan and the Grand Duke were in the back seat, bundled in greatcoats and woolen scarves. A buffalo robe was thrown across their legs.

Alexis was still nursing a hangover. Two nights ago, to celebrate the end of the hunt, he'd overindulged himself on champagne. To the delight of everyone in camp, he had joined Spotted Tail and the Brule Sioux in their scalp dance. He proved to be agile, despite his size, and he'd introduced some Cossack leaps and whirls that fascinated the warriors. Spotted Tail pronounced him a great chief.

The next morning, the army broke camp. North Platte, a town some fifty miles to the north, was the nearest railhead. A private train awaited Alexis, and the trip to the depot would consume the better part of two days. From North Platte, he would travel to New York City, where wealthy socialites planned a formal ball in his honor. The Russian battle fleet, which had escorted him to America, was anchored off Manhattan

Island. He was to sail for his homeland in a week's time.

Today, their second day on the trail, Alexis seemed somewhat improved. Last night, when they camped thirty miles north of Red Willow Creek, he had switched from champagne to vodka. All morning he'd been sipping from a flask, and the stronger spirits worked a curative effect. Champagne, he explained without irony, was an insidious drink, whereas vodka restored fire to a man's soul. His rosy cheeks seemed to prove the point.

"Unusual weather," Sheridan said, trying to make conversation. "We've had only one snowfall of any significance this winter. Not typical of the plains."

"Come with me to Moscow," Alexis said with wry good humor. "I daresay there is several feet of snow on the ground. We Russians pride ourselves on the harshness of our winters."

"We could certainly use some of that here. A hard snow would drive the hostiles into winter camp. They'll continue to raid as long as the weather holds."

Phil Sheridan was a soldier who believed in taking the fight to the enemy. During the Civil War, his cavalry had laid waste to the Shenandoah Valley, routing Confederate forces in a brilliant campaign. He was frustrated by the will-o'-the-wisp tactics of the Sioux and the Northern Cheyenne. Hit-and-run was not his idea of a war.

"These hostiles," Alexis said, as though testing the word. "What do they hope to accomplish by raiding farmers and transport lines? How can they defeat your army unless they force a battle?"

Sheridan barked a harsh laugh. "Your Highness, you've put your thumb on the problem. Indians will avoid a full-scale battle at all costs. They harass us instead with these damnedable raids."

"The general's right," Cody said from the front seat. "Not their way to stand and fight, even when you track 'em down. They're skirmishers, strictly hit-and-run."

"Tough buggers, all the same," Hickok added. "I recollect somebody called 'em the finest light cavalry in the world. Wasn't them your words, Gen'ral?"

"Yes, that's correct," Sheridan said curtly. "But the Grand Duke made the salient point a moment ago. Light cavalry will never win a war unless they come to battle."

Hickok shrugged. "Well, maybe they don't figure to win. Maybe they're just tryin' to hold their own."

Sheridan fell silent. He turned in the seat, looking back at Custer and the other generals, their horses held to a walk behind the carriage. Beyond them, the companies of the Fifth Regiment were strung out in a long column. Not once, in all his years on the plains, had he been able to engage the Indians in battle with a full regiment. Hickok, he told himself, saw the problem with a certain finite clarity. The hostiles were fighting a holding action.

Sometimes he slept poorly, his dreams a stew of misgiving. He admired the Indians in many ways, and indeed, he believed them to be the finest light cavalry ever seen by man. All too often he felt personally sullied by the government's record of broken treaties, lies piled upon lies. But history was a litany of one people conquering another, frequently for spoils and inevitably to claim the land. However much he admired the Indians, he was a soldier no less than the Roman generals of ancient times. The Western Plains were his Egypt.

Alexis was also impressed by Hickok's insightful remark about the hostiles. He leaned forward in his seat. "I have been meaning to ask, Wild Bill. What are your plans now that our hunt has concluded?"

"Likely back to Kansas," Hickok said, twisting around. "There's a cowtown I just suspect will be needin' a marshal. Place called Ellsworth."

"Yes, of course," Alexis said, intrigued by the thought. "I have read a good deal of your Texas cowboys. Are they as ferocious as reported?"

Hickok chuckled. "I don't know as I'd call 'em ferocious. Texans ain't got sense enough to come in out of the rain. That and liquor puts 'em crosswise of the law."

"So, then, you will return to marshaling. *Da?*"

"Well, cattle season don't start till June. I doubt Ellsworth will be hirin' much before May."

Alexis considered a moment. "Would you be offended if I asked you a personal question?"

"No, I reckon not," Hickok said. "Go ahead, ask away."

"Have you ever found it necessary to kill a cowboy?"

"I shot a Texan last summer in Abilene. Gamblin' man by the name of Phil Coe. But to answer your question—no cowboys."

"I see," Alexis said. "May I ask why?"

"Not worth the trouble," Hickok observed. "I generally just toss 'em in the hoosgow. They sober up by mornin'."

"We're there," Cody broke in. "North Platte just ahead."

The carriage crested a small hill. Though it was the county seat, North Platte was a community of less than two thousand people. The town was largely an extension of the railroad tracks, a center of trade for farmers and ranchers. The Union Pacific depot was south of the tracks, with fewer than a dozen buildings scattered at random nearby. The business district was north of the tracks, surrounded by a grid of streets dotted with houses. A train, chuffing smoke, stood on a siding by the depot.

"How about it, General?" Cody called out. "Want to deliver the Grand Duke in style?"

Sheridan appeared uncertain. "What do you have in mind?"

"Let's take 'em by storm!"

Cody popped the reins with a sharp snap. The horses jumped in the traces and took off at a pounding lope. The carriage jounced and swayed as they careened down the hillside, the wheels striking the ground every ten feet or so. Custer pumped his arm overhead, signaling the troop commanders at the rear. The cavalry broke into a gallop.

They roared into North Platte at a full charge.

The private coach was elegance on wheels. The interior was paneled in rosewood, with plush armchairs and a massive leather sofa. A Persian carpet covered the floor, and to the rear was a private bedroom and lavatory. Directly forward was a single passenger coach, and beyond that a dining car. The kitchen was ruled by a French chef.

James Gordon Bennett, publisher of the *New York Herald*, owned the private coach. Bennett was a man of immense wealth and power, and he had provided the train for the Grand Duke's hunting trip. Hickok was nonplussed by the lavish accommodations, but Cody took it all in stride. A year ago he'd served as guide on a buffalo hunt for Bennett and several of

New York's more prominent businessmen. He recalled only too well that the rich liked to travel in
style.

The train was ready to roll. Sheridan and Custer
and the other generals were to accompany the Grand
Duke as far as St. Louis. Headquarters for the Division of the Missouri, Sheriden's command, was located there, and the generals would return to duty.
Alexis, now playing the role of host, turned his attention from the officers to Cody and Hickok. His Cossack manservant appeared with wrapped boxes and
he presented each of them with gifts. For Cody there
was a bag of gold coins and jeweled cufflinks. Hickok
opened his box to find a diamond stickpin.

"Well, now," Cody said, hefting the bag of gold.
"That's mighty generous, Your Highness. I'm plumb
obliged."

"Same goes here," Hickok said, clearly surprised.
"Didn't expect nothin' like this."

Alexis beamed. "Consider it a token of my appre-
ciation. You have given me a hunt I will never forget.
I return to Russia with many fond memories."

The Grand Duke walked them to the rear of the
coach. He embraced each of them with a backslap-
ping bear hug and shook their hands in farewell. As
they started down the steps, a westbound train ground
to a halt outside the depot. The royal train got underway, waiting for a switchman to throw the bar on
the siding, and pulled onto the main tracks. Alexis
waved to them from the door of the private coach.

"Fine feller," Hickok noted as the train gathered
speed. "Never once put on any airs, did he?"

Cody nodded. "Not all that bad a shot, either. Got
the hang of it pretty quick."

"You came away like a Mexican bandit. How much you got in that bag of gold?"

"Looks to be five hundred or so. I'm buyin' the drinks."

"Let's find ourselves a saloon."

The troopers of the Fifth Cavalry were ordered to mount their horses. Fort McPherson was some fifteen miles southeast of town, and the major in charge of the detail wanted to arrive there by nightfall. Cody spoke with him briefly, indicating that he planned to stay over in North Platte a couple of nights. A trooper was assigned to drive the carriage at the end of the column.

Cody and Hickok started across the tracks, leading their horses. As they rounded the locomotive of the westbound train, they saw a group of farmers on the platform outside the depot. Their attention was drawn to six bedraggled children, lined up and standing apart, as though on display. A large portly man was addressing the farmers in a mellifluous voice.

"Brothers and sisters!" Thadius Crocker said to the farmers. "Welcome on behalf of the Children's Aid Society. These poor little orphans"—he paused, gesturing to the children—"are here looking for good homes. We ask you to open your hearts in Christian charity."

Their curiosity whetted, Cody and Hickok stopped to watch. They had heard of the Orphan Train, but they'd never seen one until today. The children appeared to them somehow pitiful, dirty and plainly disheartened, dressed in tattered clothing. Hickok noticed a girl and boy standing slightly apart from the other children. He thought they looked like wild young colts ready to bolt.

Augustus was no less aware of the two plainsmen.

His eyes darted over their buckskin outfits, their shiny pistols, and their broad-brimmed hats. Then, his gaze drawn to their shoulder-length hair, something snapped in his mind. He studied their faces, one with a mustache and the other with a mustache and goatee, and suddenly he knew. He'd seen those faces many times before, in pen-and-ink drawings. On the covers of dime novels!

"Look," he hissed to Katherine, barely able to contain himself. "It's Wild Bill Hickok and Buffalo Bill Cody. The Heroes of the Plains!"

Katherine glanced at him with no great interest. "How on earth could you know that? You're imagining things."

"No, I'm not either. It's them."

"All right, then, it's them. Who cares?"

Katherine was beside herself with fear. For the past two days the Orphan Train had steamed westward through Nebraska. With each stop at some barren depot, more and more of the children had been adopted. There were only six left, herself and Augustus included, and she had no idea how far they were from New York. She felt lost and deserted, and ached desperately for the sight of her parents. She bit her tongue not to burst out in tears.

There were more farmers than children on the platform. The moment Crocker stopped talking, the farmers surged forward, intent on leaving with a child. One of them, a rawboned man with beady eyes and hard features, roughly elbowed the others aside and strode directly to Augustus and Katherine. He clapped a hand squarely on the boy's shoulder.

"I'll take this one," he said, motioning to Crocker. "Make him into a farmer in no time. Give him a good home, too."

"You will not!" Katherine screeched in a shrill voice. "You leave him alone!"

Thadius Crocker rushed to intervene. "You'll have to excuse the outburst. May I ask your name, sir?"

"Homer Ledbetter."

"Well, you see, they're brother and sister, Mr. Ledbetter. Perhaps you would consider taking both. I assure you they are hard workers."

"I dunno—" Ledbetter stared at Katherine a moment, then bobbed his head. "Yeah, sure, I'll take 'em off your hands. My missus needs a girl in the kitchen, anyways."

"You won't regret it," Crocker said, pleased to be rid of the obstreperous girl and her brother. "All I require is your solemn vow that you will give them a Christian upbringing and never mistreat them. Do you so swear?"

"We are not orphans!" Katherine squalled. "Why won't you believe me?"

"Feisty, ain't she?" Ledbetter with a sour smile. "Well, don't make no nevermind. My missus'll straighten her out."

"Bless you, brother," Crocker said hurriedly. "You've done the Lord's work here today."

The farmer took hold of Augustus. When he reached for Katherine, she resisted and he grabbed her by the wrist. He dragged her kicking to the end of the platform and lifted her unceremoniously into a wagon. Then he hefted Augustus aboard and climbed into the driver's seat, clucking to his team as he gathered the reins. The boy stared back at Hickok and Cody as the wagon disappeared around the side of the depot.

"Damn shame," Hickok said, his eyes cold. "That

sorry bastard will work 'em into the ground. He come here to find cheap labor."

"No Christian charity there," Cody agreed. "Don't think I'd want to be an orphan."

"You can say that again."

"Well, let's get ourselves a drink. I'm still buyin'."

"Lead the way, ol' scout."

They walked off toward the center of North Platte.

CHAPTER 6

HICKOK AND Cody emerged from the Cedar House shortly after sundown. The hotel was located at the intersection of First and Locust, a block north of the train station. Directly across the street was the town's only livery stable.

The plainsmen had taken a room at the hotel earlier that afternoon. Fortified by several rounds of rye whiskey, they felt the need to refurbish themselves. A scalding bath removed the trail dust, and a shave at the tonsorial parlor left them smelling of bay rum. They were prepared for a night on the town.

Their first stop was the Bon Ton Café. Hickok lived by the maxim that a full stomach offset the deleterious effects of John Barleycorn. Years ago, he'd taught Cody that a balance of solid food and snake-head whiskey was the secret to steady nerves. They ordered blood-red beefsteak with fried potatoes, canned tomatoes, and sourdough biscuits. A toothpick finished off the meal.

Outside again, they stood surveying their options. Locust Street was the main thoroughfare, crowded with shops and stores, and at the north end, was the county courthouse. The nightlife revolved around three saloons, one of which they'd sampled that afternoon, and a smaller dive devoted solely to the town's drunks. The third establishment was a gaming den and watering hole with hurdy-gurdy girls. They turned upstreet.

The Tivoli occupied the northeast corner of Locust

and Fourth. The strains of a banjo and a rinky-dink piano were mixed with the squealing laughter of women. Opposite a mahogany bar were faro layouts, dice, roulette, and three tables reserved for poker. Flanking the backbar mirror were the ubiquitous paintings of nude voluptuaries romping through pastoral fields. A small dance floor at the rear was crowded with couples who stomped about in time to the music.

Cody was a regular patron of the Tivoli. Everyone in town was aware of the royal hunt for the Grand Duke Alexis, which had been widely reported in the local newspaper. They were aware as well that Wild Bill Hickok, the deadliest pistol shot in the West, had been a member of the hunting party. Several men at the bar greeted Cody by name, and after ordering drinks, he introduced them to Hickok. The men shook hands as though a lion tamer had suddenly dropped into their midst.

Three girls joined them at the bar. The women wore peekaboo gowns, cut short on the bottom and their breasts spilling out of the top. Cody, who was handsomer than Hickok, and a better talker, invariably attracted women. He possessed all the social graces and casually presented himself as an educated man. In truth, his education had been gleaned from reading Chaucer and everything written by Charles Dickens. He'd learned how to spin a tale by studying the masters.

Hickok, by contrast, seemed almost coarse. He was taciturn, with a saturnine wit, and given to pungent language. Certain women were attracted to him in the way a cobra uncoils from a basket, drawn by the danger. But he begrudged his younger friend nothing, and even took amusement in watching the byplay. Cody was married, though he seldom advertised the fact, and boyishly faithful to his wife. For all his appeal to the ladies, it never went beyond talk. He was simply a born showoff.

"You've never seen anything like it," he said, the girls hanging on his every word. "The Grand Duke of all the Russias and a whole passel of Sioux. What a sight!"

"Tell us," a buxom brunette trilled. "Were the Indians on the warpath?"

Cody, an audience at hand, plunged into a wild tale of derring-do. Hickok figured the story would hold the crowd spellbound for a good part of the evening. He lit a cheroot, puffing a thick cloud of smoke, and wandered across to the poker tables. His own education ran more to the pasteboards than to books, and he freely admitted he'd never read Charles Dickens. Yet where cards were concerned, he considered himself something of a scholar. He knew all the tricks of the trade.

One of the first tenets was that every game was assumed to be crooked. A poker table served as a lure to cardsharps, ever on the lookout for an easy score. One of their favorite dodges was to introduce a marked deck into a game, "readers" with secret symbols on the backs of the cards. Another trick was shaved cards, trimmed along the sides, or cards with slightly rounded corners, employed by those with the dexterity to deal from the bottom. A tinhorn, no less than a magician, relied on sleight of hand.

Hickok stopped at one of the tables. There was an empty chair and he nodded to the other players. "You gents mind fresh money?"

The men exchanged glances, and one of them grinned around a cigar wedged in the corner of his mouth. "We're honored to have you in the game, Mr. Hickok. Pull up a chair."

The rules were dealer's choice, restricted to five-card stud and five-card draw. Ante was five dollars, with a twenty-dollar limit and three raises. Check and raise was permitted, which made it cutthroat poker and a game perfectly suited to Hickok's style. He prided himself that other men seldom knew what he held.

"Everybody ante," the man with the cigar said. "Draw poker, jacks or better to open."

Hickok, inscrutable as a sphinx, caught three queens on the deal.

The night was clear and bitterly cold, a bone-white crescent moon floating on the horizon. Augustus paused in the shadows, where the rutted wagon road merged with the street in front of the train station. He slowly scanned the depot for any sign of life.

A single lamp burned in the window of the office. He saw a man slouched in a chair, chin on his chest, fast asleep. Somewhere in the distance a dog barked, setting off a chorus of howls on the west side of town. He waited, listening, until the commotion died down.

"All right," he said. "Let's go on."

Katherine stepped from the shadows. She was shivering, the wind cutting through her threadbare coat. "Are you sure it's safe?"

"I got you this far, didn't I?"

She couldn't argue the point. Augustus seemed to have some sixth sense for direction, even in the dark of night. The faint moonglow afforded little light, and yet he had found the crossroads some miles to the east, and instinctively turned west. He'd brought them again to North Platte.

Their escape was no less the work of Augustus. Late that afternoon, upon arriving at Homer Ledbetter's farm, they'd discovered that he lived in a sod house. Neither of them had ever heard of a house constructed from grassy chunks of soil cut from the earth. Nor were they prepared for what they found inside the house.

Ledbetter's wife was a crone with a sharp tongue and a nasty disposition. She had immediately put Katherine to tending a cookstove in the windowless, one-room sod house. Katherine just as quickly became queasy from the stench of unwashed bodies in a confined space. Her mind reeled when she realized she was standing on a *dirt* floor.

The Ledbetter's only child, a son, was a chunky twelve-year-old with a mean streak. He took charge of Augustus and put him to work unharnessing the team of horses. Afterward, he supervised as Augustus carried firewood from the wood pile to the house, all the while bullying him in a hectoring voice. By suppertime, Augustus was ready to crown the boy with a stick of firewood.

Homer Ledbetter proved to be a petty tyrant. He sat at the head of the table, and his wife dutifully served his plate before anyone else. The boy acted cowed in his father's presence, as though he expected a beating if he opened his mouth. Supper was a tasteless stew, thick with grease, and a platter of fried cornmeal dodgers. Katherine and Augustus wished again for the jelly sandwiches on the Orphan Train. They picked at their food.

All during the meal Ledbetter lectured them on their new duties. Augustus would muck out the barn, split and haul firewood, and take care of general chores. Katherine would tend to the henhouse, work in the kitchen, and keep the house itself in order. Their duties were those of servants, and Ledbetter was a man who tolerated nothing less than obedience. His mouth stuffed with food, he pointed to a leather razor strop hanging on the wall. The penalty for disobedience was a proper hiding.

There was too little room in the house for Katherine and Augustus. After supper, Ledbetter showed them their sleeping quarters, a storage shed near the barn. They were given moldy quilts and told to be ready to start work at daylight. Almost as an afterthought, Ledbetter motioned to a rickety privy behind the house, and explained that dried corn shucks were a farmer's toilet paper. He seemed amused by the expression on their faces, and left them to arrange their bedding. Katherine promised herself she would burst before she went near the privy.

The lamps were extinguished in the house shortly after a sickle moon rose in the sky. Augustus, who was wrapped in one of the quilts, watched through a crack between the boards of the shed. His voice shaky with bravado, he informed Katherine that he wouldn't be held in slavery; he was determined to escape. She was frightened, fearful they would be caught and punished, even more fearful of the life awaiting them if they didn't run. They waited only long enough to ensure that the homesteader and his family were asleep. Then they took off.

The track leading from the house eventually connected with a crossroads several miles to the south. Augustus, following some inner compass, confidently turned onto the road to the west. They had no idea how far they'd walked, or for that matter, where they were. They were cold, exhausted by their ordeal, but driven by the urge to escape. Some hours later, almost miraculously, they saw the light of the lamp in the North Platte depot. Their relief was momentary, for their journey was not yet over.

"I'm so cold," Katherine said wearily. "Couldn't we stop and get warm in the train station?"

Augustus squared his shoulders. "We have to find Buffalo Bill and Wild Bill. They'll know what to do."

"But how on earth will we find them? They might be anywhere."

"We just have to look and keep on looking, that's all."

The town was dark, forbiddingly still. The only lights visible were those from a few buildings along the main street. Augustus took Katherine's hand and they walked north toward the lights. There was nowhere else to turn.

Faintly, off in the distance, they heard the strains of a piano.

Cody was in his glory. The crowd around the bar listened raptly as he regaled them with yet another whopper. The hour was approaching midnight, and he'd held them mesmerized throughout the evening. They kept him supplied with whiskey and he spun tales, real and imagined, from his days on the plains. He thought he could talk forever.

Hickok was on a streak. A mound of double eagles and assorted gold coins was piled before him on the table. All night he'd drawn unbeatable hands, edging out players who themselves held strong cards. On those occasions when he bluffed, the other players were so snake-bit that they folded, convinced he had the goods. He calculated he was ahead by at least three hundred.

The piano player suddenly trailed off in the middle

of a tune. Beside him, the banjo player strummed on a moment then hit a jarring chord. The few couples left on the dance floor skittered to a halt, caught off balance as the music ended. Cody stopped talking, and Hickok paused in the midst of a bet, and the crowd at the bar abruptly drew back in surprise. Their eyes were fixed on the door.

Augustus and Katherine stepped into the saloon. For an instant, caught in the wondering stares and tomblike quiet, they stood frozen in place. Then a light of recognition flashed over the boy's features and his mouth parted in a sappy smile. He tugged Katherine forward.

"Buffalo Bill! Wild Bill!" he shouted vigorously. "We thought we'd never find you!"

Hickok and Cody exchanged a bewildered look. After a moment, Hickok rose from the poker table and moved to the bar. He stopped beside Cody.

"Well, young feller," he said softly. "What brings you and the little lady out on a cold night? Why're you lookin' for us?"

"We saw you at the train station," Augustus said in a fit of agitation. "This morning, when that farmer took us off in his wagon. Don't you remember, Wild Bill?"

"By golly, that's right," Cody chimed in, staring down at the boy. "You're the brother and sister that got off the Orphan Train."

"We are *not* orphans," Katherine said stridently. "You have to believe us."

Cody knelt down, on eye level with her. "What's your name, little missy?"

"I am Katherine Stanley. And this is my brother, Augustus. We are from New York City."

"So how'd you come to be on the Orphan Train?

I mean, if it's like you say, that you're not orphans."

"We were abducted from our parents."

"Abducted?" Hickok said, watching her closely. "You was stole from your folks?"

"We were!" Augustus yelped. "I swear we were!"

Katherine suddenly became aware of the saloon girls. Her eyes went round as she stared at their exposed bosoms and their legs revealed by the short skirts. Cody failed to notice, his gaze still fixed on the boy. He leaned closer.

"Would you swear it on a stack of Bibles, young feller?"

"Yes, sir," Augustus said solemnly. "You know I wouldn't lie to you, Buffalo Bill."

"How would I know that?"

"Because you and Wild Bill are the Heroes of the Plains. Cross my heart and hope to die before I'd lie to you."

Cody flushed with pride. He stood, glancing at Hickok. "I think they're tellin' the truth."

"Yep," Hickok grunted. "So do I."

"What do we do now?"

"I reckon this here's a matter for the law. We'll let these tads tell their story to the proper authorities."

"Try the courthouse," the bartender suggested. "Two of Sheriff Walker's deputies are down with the grippe. He's tending the jail himself tonight."

Hickok nodded. "Sounds like he's our man. That suit you, young Mr. Stanley?"

"Yes, sir, Wild Bill," Augustus said quickly. "You and Buffalo Bill know what's best."

"How about you, little Miss Stanley? You willin' to have a talk with the sheriff?"

Katherine tore her eyes away from the breasts of a tall brunette. Her features went crimson and she shyly looked down at the floor. "Oh, yes, thank you so much, Wild Bill."

Hickok glanced at the bartender. "Collect my stake off that poker table. I'll be back directly."

"I'll look after it, Mr. Hickok."

"Obliged," Hickok said, turning to Cody. "C'mon, Hero of the Plains, let's go do our duty."

Cody grinned. "What the boy said was 'Heroes.' You're rowin' the same boat."

"Don't remind me."

They led Augustus and Katherine from the saloon.

CHAPTER 7

SHERIFF JACK Walker stared at the two men seated before his desk. His office was in the basement of the courthouse, with a holding pen for drunks and four jail cells down the hall. The clock on the wall opposite his desk moved steadily toward midnight.

The purpose of the late-night call was as yet unclear. But the man named Otto Richter was well dressed and well spoken, and obviously the one in charge. The other man, introduced simply as Mr. Johnson, was just as plainly a toughnut, the muscle rather than the brains. Which made the sheriff wonder why Richter needed a bodyguard.

"What can I do for you?" Walker asked. "We don't get many visitors from back East. Especially this late at night."

Richter smiled. "You're quite observant, Sheriff. I assume my accent gave me away."

"Yeah, I've known a few Easterners in my time. You don't talk like folks out here."

"We've come on a matter of business. I hoped we might speak in confidence."

"Depends on whether or not it's official business. What's on your mind?"

Earlier that day Richter had watched from inside the depot as the children were unloaded from the Orphan Train. A casual conversation with one of the attendants revealed that Katherine and Augustus had been adopted by a farmer named Homer Ledbetter. Their new home was some miles northeast of town.

Richter and Turk Johnson had then engaged rooms in the Platte City Hotel. The balance of the afternoon was devoted to discreet inquiries about the county's chief law enforcement officer, Sheriff Jack Walker. Richter discovered that the sheriff was popular with voters, but nonetheless a man of questionable character. He routinely took payoffs from the bawdy houses on the south side of town.

The call on Sheriff Walker was purposely late. Richter wanted the conversation conducted in private, and equally important, the courthouse would be deserted well before midnight. The secrecy of his mission was uppermost, and the proposition he planned to offer might be refused. In that event, the only alternative was for Johnson to kill the sheriff. The late hour ensured there would be no witnesses.

"What I have in mind," Richter said now, "might be termed a personal business arrangement. A rather generous fee for your services."

Walker looked interested. "What sort of services?"

"You're familiar with the Orphan Train?"

"I know it stops here pretty regular."

"Today, two young orphans were adopted by a farmer named Homer Ledbetter. Do you recognize the name?"

"Mr. Richter, I know everybody in Lincoln County. Ledbetter homesteaded a quarter-section about five miles outside town. What's your interest in him and these orphans?"

"I'm an attorney," Richter lied smoothly. "I've been retained to oversee the adoption of these children, a boy and a girl. My client wants periodic reports as to their well-being—and their treatment."

"That a fact?" Walker said skeptically. "Why's your client so keen on two particular kids?"

"I'm afraid that is privileged information. Let's just say the fee would make it worth your while."

"How much?"

"A thousand now and a hundred a month for the next year."

Walker's salary as sheriff was a hundred and fifty dollars a month. He thought there was something decidedly fishy about Otto Richter and the story about the orphans. Still, short of murder, there was little he wouldn't do for a thousand in cash. Not to mention the extra hundred a month.

"Mr. Richter, you've got yourself a deal. I'll keep a sharp eye on Ledbetter and those kids."

Turk Johnson pulled out a leather pouch and spilled fifty double eagles onto the desk. Richter waved his hand with idle largess. "I know Westerners prefer gold to greenbacks. I believe you'll find the count correct."

"Looks right to me," Walker said, scooping up a handful of double eagles. "I like a man who pays on the spot."

"One other thing."

"What's that?"

"When I buy a man, I expect him to stay bought. As the saying goes, come hell or high water, you're mine."

"You care to spell that out?"

"Certainly," Richter said. "Your absolute silence and loyalty are part of our bargain. Anything less is not acceptable."

Walker frowned. "You threatenin' an officer of the law?"

"A word to the wise should be sufficient."

There was a moment of profound quiet. Then Walker opened the center drawer of his desk and raked the coins in with a sweep of his arm. He looked up with a shifty grin.

"I just suspect you're some kind of crook, Mr. Richter. But what the hell, I'm no angel myself."

"I think we'll work well together, Sheriff."

"So where do you want those reports sent?"

"General delivery," Richter said without expression. "New York City."

Walker chuckled as he wrote it down in a laborious scrawl.

"You kids say you're from New York City?"

"Yes, sir, Wild Bill," Augustus replied. "We live in a house on Gramercy Park."

"Never heard of it," Hickok said. "Wasn't your folks in the house when you got carried off?"

"Well, yes, sir . . . they were."

"Then how come they didn't stop it?"

"We don't know," Augustus said in a wistful voice. "Katherine and I talked about it lots on the train. We just don't know."

Cody shook his head. "I thought Injuns was the only ones that carried kids off. Never figured New York for a dangerous place."

"Oh, it is, Buffalo Bill," Katherine assured him earnestly. "How else could we have been abducted?"

"Guess that's the question beggin' an answer."

Hickok led the way, Augustus at his side, as they crossed the intersection of Sixth and Locust. The courthouse was straight ahead, a two-story frame building that occupied half a city block. In the faint moonlight, Hickok spotted a sign for the sheriff's department above a flight of stairs leading to the basement. He turned in that direction.

A moment later they came through the door of the

sheriff's office. Hickok saw a man seated behind the
desk with a badge pinned on his shirt. There were
two other men, on their feet as though preparing to
leave, standing in front of the desk. Their manner of
dress indicated to Hickok that they were probably city
folk, and he wondered what business they had with
the law at midnight. He nodded to the man with the
badge.

"I reckon you'd be Sheriff Walker."

"That's me," Walker said, rising from his chair. "I
heard you were in town, Mr. Hickok. 'Course, everybody knows Bill Cody."

"Evenin', Sheriff," Cody said. "You busy with
these gentlemen?"

"No, we're all done," Walker announced. "Mr.
Richter and Mr. Johnson were just leaving."

Hickok noticed that the two men appeared stunned.
They were staring at the children, and though they
tried to hide it, their shock was evident. A visceral
sense of danger came over Hickok, and he'd learned
never to ignore the feeling. He survived on instinct
and quick reflexes.

Cody stepped aside as the two men edged toward
the doorway. He nodded to them, then looked back
at the sheriff. "Figured you ought to talk with these
children. Appears they were abducted from New York
City and put on the Orphan Train."

Walker's mouth dropped open. "I—" he faltered,
struggling to regain his composure. "You say they're
orphans?"

"Not exactly," Cody said. "Way it sounds, somebody tried to pass 'em off as orphans."

Katherine was watching the two men with a
strange expression. As they sidled toward the door,
Richter's features were caught in the shadowy light

from the lamp on the sheriff's desk. She suddenly gasped, clutching desperately at Cody's arm. Her eyes were wide with terror.

"Oh, nooo—" Her voice quavered, barely audible. "He's the man . . ."

"How's that?" Cody glanced down at her with bemused surprise. "What man?"

"He . . . he's the one."

"The one what?"

"He's the one who took me from my bedroom! I remember his face from the hallway light."

"That's absurd," Richter protested loudly. "I've never seen this girl in my life."

"Katherine's right!" Augustus blurted, pointing an accusing finger at Johnson. "The man who got me was big, great big strong hands. That's him!"

Hickok seemed to move not at all. The Colt Navy revolvers appeared in his hands and he earred back the hammers. He trained one on Richter and the other on Johnson. His eyes were like stone.

"Don't move," he ordered, "Stand real still."

"How dare you!" Richter said in an offended tone. "Whatever's going on here, we know nothing about these children. The sheriff will vouch for us, won't you, Sheriff?"

Walker quickly assessed the situation. He knew Richter would expose him unless he went along. The thousand dollars in his desk drawer was a dead giveaway. He opted for the lie.

"Holster your guns," he said harshly, glaring at Hickok. "Mr. Richter and Mr. Johnson are respectable businessmen. You're out of line, Hickok."

Hickok ignored the outburst. "Tell me something, Richter," he said evenly. "Whereabouts you boys from?"

Richter stiffened. "What does that have to do with anything?"

"Lemme guess," Hickok said. "You're New York born and bred—ain't you?"

"Where I'm from is no concern of yours."

"See there, you just answered my question."

"Hold on now." Walker started around his desk. "You put those guns away or I'll place you under arrest."

Cody pulled his Colt Army. "Just stay where you are, Sheriff. You're not arresting anybody."

"Goddamn you, Cody!" Walker bridled. "I'll report you to Colonel Reynolds. He'll have you up on charges."

"Likely the other way 'round," Cody said. "You're in cahoots with a couple of child abductors. I doubt you'll be wearin' that badge much longer."

"Time to make tracks," Hickok said in a commanding voice. "Bill, you go ahead and get the kids outside. I'll keep these gents covered."

Cody ushered the children through the door. Katherine darted a last hateful glance at Richter as she stepped into the night. Hickok wagged the snout of first one pistol and then the other at the three men. His mouth was set in a hard line.

"Any of you jokers follow me out, I'll stop your ticker."

No one moved as he backed through the door.

The night clerk at the Cedar House was nodding off. The bell over the door jarred him awake, and he looked up to see Hickok and Cody with two small children. His brow furrowed in a question mark.

"Don't ask," Hickok said, as they crossed the lobby. "Pretend you dreamt the whole thing."

"Yessir, Mr. Hickok, I didn't see nothin'."

"That's the spirit, bub."

Upstairs, Cody unlocked the door to their room. The children followed him inside, trailed by Hickok, and he quickly locked the door. He tossed his hat on the bed with a troubled look.

"Some kettle of fish," he said. "Got a dangblasted crook for a sheriff."

Hickok snorted. "I'd wager we've seen the last of him. He ain't got the stomach for a fight."

"Think I'll pay a call on the county judge. High time somebody heard the truth."

"Whole courthouse might be full of polecats. Let's chew on that awhile."

"So what's our next move?"

Katherine and Augustus were seated on the edge of the bed They appeared spent, their shoulders slumped with exhaustion. Hickok crossed the room and sat down next to them. He looked at Katherine.

"Need you to think real hard," he said. "Are you plumb certain about that feller they called Richter? No mistakes?"

"I couldn't forget his face." Her eyes puddled with tears, her features bunched tight. "How will we ever get back to mother and father now?"

Hickok put an arm around her shoulders. She leaned into him, snuffling tears, and he gently stroked her hair. "Don't fret yourself," he said. "We'll figure something out."

"Wild Bill won't let us down." Augustus sniffed, wiping his nose, and took his sister's hand. "Didn't you see the way he pulled his guns? I mean wow, fast as lightning! Just like it says in the dime novels."

Hickok seemed acutely embarrassed. Cody smothered a smile and looked at him with a deadpan expression. "Well, you heard the youngster, Wild Bill. Where do we go from here?"

"You know the U.S. Marshal for Nebraska?"

"Yeah, his name's Omar Drake. Headquartered at the state capitol."

"That's our play," Hickok said firmly. "We'll telegraph him first thing in the mornin'. A federal lawman will have these sprouts home in no time."

"Durn right he will!" Cody marveled. "Why didn't I think of that?"

Hickok smiled. " 'Cause there's only one Wild Bill."

The children were given the bed. They were sound asleep in seconds, feeling safe for the first time since their abduction. Hickok and Cody stretched out on the floor, saddlebags beneath their heads, their mackinaws for covers. Cody was asleep when he closed his eyes, but Hickok lay awake staring into the dark. A worrisome thought kept surfacing in the back of his mind.

He wondered why children with parents had ended up on the Orphan Train. It was a question he intended to put to the one named Richter. Tomorrow.

Just as soon as the kids were off his hands.

CHAPTER 8

A GENTLE wind chased puffy clouds around an azure sky. The sun crested the tops of buildings and stood lodged like a brass ball on the eastern horizon. All throughout town the smell of woodsmoke eddied on the breeze.

Shops and stores opened for business at eight o'clock. By then Locust Street was already jammed with freight wagons and the lighter wagons of farmers. The boardwalks were crowded with early shoppers about their errands and teamsters unloading all manner of goods. North Platte hurried to greet another day.

Hickok and Cody, followed by the children, came out of a café next door to the hotel. Katherine and Augustus were stuffed, having been treated to their first decent meal since boarding the Orphan Train. The plainsmen, hearty eaters themselves, had ordered steak and eggs, with a platter of flapjacks on the side. The children consumed an entire pitcher of milk.

From the café, they walked upstreet to Zimmerman's Mercantile. Hickok and Cody, talking about it over breakfast, decided the children were in desperate need of new outfits. Their threadbare clothing was by now soiled and unkempt from their journey west on the train. Nathan Zimmerman, elated to have Buffalo Bill Cody and Wild Bill Hickok in his store, personally waited on the children. He brought out his best stock.

Augustus was outfitted with corduroy trousers and

a blue flannel shirt, sturdy boots and a pint-sized mackinaw, and a black slouch hat. Katherine, with Zimmerman's coaxing, selected a ruffled calico dress, a woolen mantle coat, a chambray bonnet, and high-topped calfskin shoes. They changed in the fitting room, leaving their old clothing to be thrown out. Their appearance as well as their spirits were measurably improved. They felt decently attired for the first time since their abduction.

When they emerged from the store, Augustus seemed particularly proud of his Western duds. He imagined himself a courageous scout or a bold lawman, and put a swagger into his step. Katherine was simply thrilled to be clean and presentable, no longer a wretched little ragamuffin. She shyly planted a kiss on Cody's cheek and then kissed Hickok as well. Her eyes were bright with happiness.

"Thank you, thank you," she said gaily. "You're both so wonderfully kind."

Augustus stuck out his chest. "Boy, I wish Mother and Father could see us now. Wouldn't that be something!"

"That reminds me," Hickok said. "What's your pa's name?"

"Henry," Katherine said. "Henry Morton Stanley."

"And I recollect you live on a park?"

"Yes, Number 24 Gramercy Park."

"We'll telegraph your pa when we wire the U.S. Marshal. Let him know you're safe and sound."

"Oh, thank you, Wild Bill." Katherine took his hand with sudden affection. "Mother and Father must be frantic with worry."

"There you rascals are!"

Homer Ledbetter reined his team to a halt. He hopped down from the wagon and strode toward them with an angry scowl. He stopped on the boardwalk.

"You little scutters!" he said hotly. "Thought you'd run off, did you?"

"No need to shout," Cody said, stepping forward. "I remember you from yesterday, at the train depot."

"Outta my way," Ledbetter growled. "I adopted them brats fair and square. I'm here to collect 'em."

"Well, way it turns out, they're not orphans. So your adoption don't hold."

"Mister, you ain't foolin' nobody. You're not gonna make off with kids I done took in."

"You've got the wrong idea," Cody told him. "We're fixin' to send 'em back home. That's the God's honest truth."

"Don't gimme none of your gawddamn horseshit. Stand aside!"

"No, I don't think so."

Ledbetter launched a looping haymaker. Cody slipped the blow and hit him with a splintering left-right combination. The farmer staggered off the boardwalk and Cody hammered him with a solid right to the jaw. He went down with a thud, out cold.

"Wow." Augustus's eyes were round as saucers. "What a punch!"

"Yessir," Hickok said wryly. "Buffalo Bill is one fine pugilist."

Cody sucked on a skinned knuckle. "Sorry half-wit wouldn't listen to reason. What was I supposed to do?"

"Why, just what you done. What else?"

They left Ledbetter sprawled in the dust. A block downstreet they paused outside the hotel. Hickok motioned off toward the railroad tracks.

"You go on to the depot and send them wires. I'll take the kids up to the room."

Cody nodded. "What was that New York address again?"

"Henry Morton Stanley. Number 24 Gramercy Park."

The drumming sound of hoofbeats brought them around. A cavalry trooper skidded his horse to a halt and swung down out of the saddle. The horse was caked with sweat and the trooper was breathing hard. He hurried toward them.

"Mr. Cody!" he said stoutly. "The colonel wants you double-quick. There's been an Injun raid."

"Damn," Cody cursed. "Whereabouts?"

"Farnum relay station. Hostiles made off with the horses and killed both the handlers. Burned the station to the ground."

"Has the colonel put a unit in the field?"

"Cap'n Meinhold's company," the trooper said. "They're trackin' the Injuns somewheres off to the northeast. Colonel says you'll find'em up around the Loup River."

Cody turned toward the hotel. He saw the desk clerk watching them from the doorway. Then, abruptly, he turned back to Hickok.

"I've got no choice but to skedaddle. Can you manage the kids?"

Hickok considered a moment. "Don't care much for the odds. Richter and his bully-boy might come at me with the sheriff and a bunch of deputies. I doubt I could hold 'em off without you and your army connections."

"So what are you sayin'?"

"I haven't had a scrap with the Injuns in a spell. Let's take the kids along."

"You serious?"

"They'd be a damnsight safer on a patrol than here

in town. If I was to get arrested, we'd never see 'em again."

"You're sure?"

"You got a better idea?"

"Soldier!" Cody barked. "Hightail it over to the livery and get our horses saddled. Tell 'em we'll be rentin' their two best horses."

The trooper took off running. Cody swapped a look with Hickok, then glanced at the children. He shook his head with a dubious frown.

"Hope you kids can stay on a horse."

Augustus gave him a nutcracker grin. "We are trained equestrians, Buffalo Bill."

"Equestrians?" Hickok said. "What the devil's that?"

"Why, how to stay on a horse, Wild Bill."

Ten minutes later they rode north out of town.

The Platte City Hotel was a half block north of the Cedar House. All morning Richter and Johnson had posted themselves at the plate-glass window fronting the lobby. From there, they had a clear view of the street.

Richter as yet had no concrete plan. A confrontation was out of the question, for he and Johnson was no match against Hickok and Cody. But he had to resolve the matter of the children, and soon. Things were starting to spiral out of control.

From the lobby, Richter had watched as the children were taken to breakfast and then to Zimmerman's Mercantile. He'd seen the dispute with Homer Ledbetter, and the conference between Cody and Hickok following the arrival of the cavalry trooper. And now, thoroughly baffled, he watched as the plainsmen rode off with the children.

Some minutes later Richter and Johnson entered
the Cedar House. The desk clerk was properly intim-
idated by Johnson's scowl, and even more persuaded
by a hundred dollars in gold. He told Richter everything he'd overheard in the cavalry trooper's report,
and the conversation between Hickok and Cody. He
was then sworn to an oath of silence, which was not
taken lightly. Turk Johnson was clearly the penalty
for a breach of trust.

The news was better than Richter had hoped. A
plan crystallized as he emerged from the hotel and
turned uptown. To a large extent, the success of the
scheme was dependent on the cooperation of the sheriff. But Richter was reasonably confident that Walker
could be made to see the light. Any man whose livelihood was decided at the ballot box jealously guarded
his good name. All the more so if he was a crook.

At the courthouse, Richter and Johnson caught the
sheriff as he was leaving his office. One of his deputies had recovered sufficiently from the grippe to re-
lieve him, and he was headed home. His features
knotted, for he devoutly wished he'd seen the last of
the two men. Some inner voice told him the situation
had gone from bad to worse.

"We have a problem," Richter said without pre-
amble. "Hickok and Cody just rode out of town with
the children."

"Not my problem," Walker countered. "Our agreement was for reports on a couple of orphans. Turns
out those kids aren't orphans."

"Whatever their status, you're still at some personal jeopardy."

"How do you figure that?"

"Consider the consequences," Richter said impassively. "You took a bribe, which in itself is a felony.

Cody will inevitably raise the issue with army officials and someone will report it to the newspapers.
Voters tend to believe what they read, and corruption
is a dirty word." He paused for emphasis. "You
wouldn't stand a chance in the next election."

Walker felt like a man who had dipped a toe in
quicksand only to have his leg entrapped. To extricate
himself he somehow had to ensure that Richter pre-
vailed in the matter of the so-called orphans. Only
then would Richter catch a train back to New York.

"All right," he said at length. "What do you want
from me?"

"An introduction," Richter informed him. "Every
town has its rougher element, and someone who's
cock-'o-the-walk. Who would that be in North
Platte?"

"Axel Bohannon," Walker said. "Him and his men
are hide hunters part of the time and general hell-
raisers all the time. Why do you ask?"

"Would you consider Bohannon a mercenary? Will
he take pay to commit violence?"

"Hell, he might do it for free. He's kissin' kin to
a mad dog. What is it you're plannin'?"

"Do you really want to know?"

"Now that you mention it . . . forget I asked."

"Where might I find Mr. Bohannon?"

"Him and his boys have got a cabin south of the
tracks. The one with a corral out back."

"I'll tell him you send your regards."

Some while later Richter knocked on the door. The
man who answered it wore filthy longjohns and a sullen expression. "What d'you want?"

"Axel Bohannon," Richter said. "I'm here on a
matter of business."

The inside of the cabin smelled like a wolf's den.

There were three double-bunk beds, with worn clothing, saddles and camp gear strewn about the room. Four men were still in bed and a fifth sat at a table by the stove. He spilled tobacco into a rolling paper, waiting for the one who answered the door to move aside. He popped a match on his thumbnail.

"Who're you?" he said, lighting his cigarette. "How'd you get my name?"

Bohannon was lean and muscular, with brutish features. Richter left Johnson to guard his back and walked to the table. He took a chair.

"Otto Richter," he said simply. "How I came by your name isn't important. I understand your services are for hire."

"Do you?" Bohannon exhaled a wad of smoke. "What sorta services you lookin' for?"

"Wild Bill Hickok and Buffalo Bill Cody have something that belongs to me. In point of fact, two children."

"And?"

"I want you to get them back."

"Hickok and Cody," Bohannon said, flicking an ash with his little finger. "Nobody to mess with even when you're sober. Tell me why I'd do a thing like that?"

"A thousand dollars," Richter said. "Half now and half when the job is finished."

"Do you want 'em dead?"

"Only if it comes to that."

Bohannon stared at him. "What're these kids to you?"

"Does it matter?" Richter said equably. "We're talking about Hickok and Cody—and a thousand dollars."

"You cut right to the bone, don't you? Awright, let's say I'm interested. What's next?"

Richter briefly explained the problem. Cody and Hickok were riding even now to join a company of the Fifth Cavalry. Their destination, according to his information, was somewhere along the Loup River. The children were with the plainsmen.

"I'll be go-to-hell," Bohannon said, mildly amused. "Took kids off huntin' hostiles. That's what you're sayin'?"

"I'm afraid so."

"Well, now it ain't just Hickok and Cody no more. You're tellin' me a troop of cavalry and Christ knows how many hostiles. A thousand ain't enough."

"How much?"

"Double oughta get it."

"Very well," Richter agreed. "Two thousand."

"Done." Bohannon puffed his cigarette. "How you want this handled?"

"I have no interest in either the cavalry or the Indians. Once we find them, your job is to trail them without being seen. I want to catch Hickok and Cody alone—with the children."

"You're comin' with us?"

"That's correct."

"Sounds like a barrel of laughs." Bohannon motioned across the room. "You and your strongarm boy horsemen, are you?"

Johnson held his gaze with a stoic expression. "Horsemen or not," Richter said, "we're along for the ride. That's part of the deal."

Bohannon grinned. "Well, like they say, money talks."

Richter began counting out double eagles.

CHAPTER 9

THE CAVALRY troop was camped along the South Fork of the Loup River. As the sun dipped toward the western horizon, the river was transformed into a rock-studded ribbon of gold. A sharp wind rattled through the cottonwoods lining the banks.

There were forty troopers in Company B. Veterans of the Indian wars, their bivouac was tightly contained, with their horses picketed along the river. Four pack horses carried rations and grain, and small fires for cooking warded off the chill. Sentries were posted on the perimeter of the camp.

Cody sighted the fires just as sunset gave way to dusk. The children were lined out behind him, and Hickok brought up the rear. Katherine was mounted on a gentle mare and Augustus rode a blaze-faced roan gelding. Though they were trained to English saddles, they had fallen into the rhythm of Western rigs with natural ease. The plainsmen were increasingly impressed by the spunk of the youngsters.

Augustus was beside himself with excitement. To be rescued by Hickok and Cody, the Heroes of the Plains, was beyond his wildest dreams. To be included in a scout for hostile Indians pursued by the cavalry was an adventure that fired his imagination. Katherine, by contrast, was enthralled by the chivalry and valorous manner of the two plainsmen. She dreamily imagined herself the Guinevere of a grand quest into forbidden lands, fraught with danger. She wasn't yet sure whether Hickok or Cody would be her Lancelot.

The troopers were squatted around fires, cooking salt pork and softening hard tack in the fatty juices. Cody wondered how the children would take to the spartan rations that sustained the cavalry on a chase. He thought Augustus would tough it out, and Katherine, too polite to complain, would subsist on nibbles. As he stepped out of the saddle, Captain Charles Meinhold, the company commander, hurried forward. Then, looking past him, Meinhold saw the children. His face set in a glowering frown.

"What's the meaning of this, Mr. Cody? Who are these children?"

Cody ducked his head. "Cap'n, I know it's against regulations. But we didn't have a whole lot of choice."

"Tommyrot!" Meinhold railed. "You made a choice, but it was the wrong one. The worst choice!"

"Well, sir, it's a long story."

"Give me the abbreviated version."

Cody covered the details in a rapid-fire monologue. When he finished, he raised his hands in a lame shrug. "Like I said, we didn't have any choice."

Meinhold appeared stupefied. "Let me understand this. These children were abducted in New York, rescued by you and Mr. Hickok in North Platte, and now you've brought them on a sortie against hostiles. Did I miss anything?"

"No, sir, that pretty well covers it."

Cody knew he was in hot water. Meinhold was a soldier's soldier, and operated strictly by the book. A German immigrant, Meinhold had joined the army in 1851 and advanced through the ranks to sergeant major. During the Civil War, he was commissioned and awarded two brevets for valor in battle. After the war, he was assigned to the Fifth Cavalry, with the permanent rank of captain. He was widely regarded the top field commander in the regiment.

"Consider yourself on report," he said bluntly. "When we return to post, you will answer directly to Colonel Reynolds. Do I make myself clear?"

Cody nodded. "Guess that's plain enough."

"Get those children settled and then report to me."

"Yessir."

Augustus and Katherine seemed wounded by the severity of the tongue-lashing. From the nature of the reprimand, they realized they were responsible for placing Cody at risk. He smiled, rolling his eyes, as if to say it was a matter of no consequence. With Hickok trailing along, he walked them to one of the fires, where several troopers were gathered. The corporal in charge of the packhorses agreed to look after them and get them fed. One of the troopers began slicing extra rations of salt pork.

"You should've laid it on me," Hickok said as they walked back through the camp. "Tell the cap'n I'm the one that brought the kids along."

"Don't worry about it," Cody said. "Wasn't like you twisted my arm."

"All the same, you're the one with your tit in a wringer."

"Well hell, it's not like it's the first time."

Meinhold waited by a fire. He nodded genially to Hickok, seemingly recovered from his fit of temper. "Good to have you with us, Mr. Hickok. Another scout is always welcome."

"Glad to be of service, Cap'n. How many hostiles we trailin'?"

"Difficult to say," Meinhold admitted. "They stole

twenty horses, all of which are shod. Otherwise, I doubt we could have trailed them this far."

"Still headed north?" Cody asked. "Anybody check across the river?"

"Sergeant Foley rode ahead while it was still light. He found their tracks."

"I just suspect we'll overtake 'em come mornin'."

"What makes you think so, Mr. Cody?"

"Cap'n, they pushed them horses real hard for a day and a night. I doubt they figure anybody's still on their trail."

"I see." Meinhold was thoughtful a moment. "You think they may have stopped, is that it?"

Cody nodded. "Wouldn't be surprised but what they took a breather. We'll find out come first light."

Meinhold stared off into the dark. "Do you agree, Mr. Hickok?"

"Yessir, I do," Hickok said. "You'll have your fight."

"You sound quite confident."

"Well, don't you see, Cody and me know our Injuns. We ain't all that civilized ourselves."

Captain Charles Meinhold thought the statement only partially true. The presence of the children in camp seemed to him the opposite side of the coin. Though he would never say so out loud.

He preferred his scouts on the rank side.

Cody was in charge of the scouting party. Sergeant John Foley and six troopers were placed under his direct command. Hickok went along for the ride.

The detail rode out as the sky paled with the dinge of false dawn. A cursory inspection of the tracks by Cody and Hickok revealed that there were twenty-three shod horses and eleven unshod Indian ponies.

The trail, as though on a compass heading, was dead north.

The main command was to follow at first light. Cody's orders were to locate the hostiles and send a trooper back with directions. Captain Meinhold would then advance with Company B and move into position for attack. The children, secure with the pack train, would follow the main command.

Not quite an hour later the scouting party topped a low knoll in the prairie. The sun slowly crested the horizon, and below them, a tributary creek fed eastward into the South Fork of the Loup. A tendril of smoke drifted from the embers of a fire, and blanketed forms were scattered about the campsite. The horse herd was guarded by a lone warrior.

Cody signaled the men to dismount on the reverse slope of the knoll. He wormed forward on his belly, removing his hat, flanked by Hickok and Sergeant Foley. They carefully scrutinized the camp, which was perhaps a hundred yards beyond their position. The mounted warrior sat watching the herd on a grassy flatland near the creek. Cody kept his voice to a whisper.

"I count eleven," he said. "Look to be Sioux."

"Not Cheyenne," Hickok added. "Likely some young bucks off on a raid."

"Got a hunch we ought to hit 'em now. They're liable to be on the move before we get the captain up here."

"You got my vote. Catch 'em by surprise while they're still in their blankets. Wouldn't hardly be a fight."

"Not so quick," Sergeant Foley interjected. "Captain's orders were to locate 'em and report back. Didn't say nothin' about attacking on our own."

"First rule of engagement," Cody said confidently. "Take the fight to your enemy before he has a chance to escape. Says so in the Officers Handbook."

Foley appeared skeptical. "You're the one that answers to the captain. He's gonna ream you a new asshole."

"I'll worry about that when the time comes."

Cody outlined his plan of attack. Foley slithered back down the slope and began briefing the troopers. Hickok fell in beside Cody as they walked toward their horses. He arched an eyebrow in question.

"You a student of the Officers Handbook?"

Cody grinned. "Don't recollect I ever read it."

"Meinhold's liable to wet his drawers."

"Not if we bring him them horses."

Cody led them east into the sunrise. The knoll gradually dropped off onto the flatland near the creek. His plan was to capture the horse herd and leave the Sioux warriors afoot. They rounded the end of the knoll, holding their mounts to a walk, and turned upstream. The attack would be made with the sun at their backs.

The sound of their approach was muffled by the dry grassland. They were within fifty yards before the horse guard turned, shielding his eyes with his hand, and stared into the sun. He suddenly whooped a warning cry and charged them, firing a Henry repeater on the run. Cody and Hickok were armed with Winchester '66 rifles, and the crack of their shots was almost simultaneous. The warrior tumbled over the rear of his mount.

The horse herd stampeded. Three of the troopers swung west at a gallop and circled most of the herd back to the south. Some of the Indian ponies, terrified by the smell of white men, broke away and forded the creek. Cody and Hickok, with Foley and the other three troopers, charged the encampment. Four of the warriors fought a rear guard action, while the others splashed across the creek in an effort to catch the ponies. The four who stayed behind went down under a volley from the charging horsemen.

On the opposite side of the creek, five of the six warriors managed to clamber aboard their ponies. The one left on foot turned to fight as Cody and Hickok swerved toward the creekbank. Hickok abruptly reined to a halt, the Winchester at his shoulder, and fired. The slug struck the warrior in the chest and he stumbled sideways, collapsing onto the ground. Cody spurred ahead, fording the stream, and gave chase after the fleeing Sioux. Outdistanced, he finally skidded to a stop, jumped off his horse, and fired from a kneeling position. A warrior at the rear of the pack fell arms akimbo off his pony.

Cody mounted and rode back to the campsite. Hickok rose from inspecting the trappings of one of the fallen warriors. He indicated the painted markings on an arrow. "Oglala," he said. "You reckon Crazy Horse was one of them that got away?"

"Tend to doubt it," Cody remarked. "He's the big auger of the Oglalas. Got other fish to fry."

Hickok tossed the arrow aside. "I count seven with the one you just shot. They're liable to give you a medal."

"That horse herd counts more than a bunch of dead Sioux. Folks do prize their livestock."

"Not to mention we didn't lose nobody."

None of the troopers had been wounded. Sergeant Foley got them busy hazing the herd back over the knoll. Hickok and Cody paused for a last look at the bodies of the fallen Sioux. Neither of them felt any great pride about the outcome of the fight. Nor did they feel remorse.

The Oglala lived by a code that sustained any warrior in battle. Today was a good day to die.

Axel Bohannon took a small brass telescope from his pocket. He extended the telescope to its full length and scanned the distant column. The troopers were dismounted, and he watched as Hickok and Cody talked with the cavalry commander. A detail of soldiers drove a herd of horses to the rear of the column.

"Turned out to be more'n a scoutin' party." He collapsed the telescope, nodding to himself. "Appears Cody and Hickok jumped the redsticks and took back them horses. Wonder how many they killed."

"I'm not interested in Indians," Richter said. "Are the children still with the pack train?"

"Yep, nothin's changed there."

A noonday sun stood lodged in the sky. Bohannon and Richter were hidden in a copse of trees bordering one of the many creeks that emptied into the South Fork of the Loup. Johnson and the other men waited with the horses a short ways downstream. They had trailed the cavalry column all morning.

Bohannon was a seasoned plainsman. Late yesterday, after a hard ride from North Platte, he'd found the military encampment. By skirting south, they had avoided detection and taken shelter along the wooded river. Early that morning, they had observed the scouting party ride off to the north. Richter elected to shadow the main column, rather than follow Hickok and Cody. His principle interest was in the children.

Richter was in some discomfort. He was far from an accomplished horseman, and Johnson had never been aboard a horse in his life. Their buttocks were galled from long hours in the saddle, and Richter found himself walking like a spraddle-legged duck. He watched now as the cavalry column wheeled about and turned south. He looked at Bohannon.

"Where are they headed?"

"Fort McPherson," Bohannon said. "That's where the soldier-boys are headquartered."

"The question is," Richter stared off at the column, "will Cody and Hickok go with them to the fort?"

"That'd be anybody's guess. We'll have to tag along and find out."

"How far is it?"

"Well, as the crow flies, I'd judge about thirty miles."

"Jesus Christ," Richter groaned. "It might as well be in China."

Bohannon chortled slyly. "Your backsides must be hurtin' powerful bad. Sure you're up to it?"

"I'll manage somehow, Mr. Bohannon."

"Mebbe we'll get lucky. Cody and Hickok might split off from the soldiers. Head back to North Platte."

"That would certainly simplify things."

"Wouldn't it?" Bohannon said, waving his arms. "There's a half-dozen places between here and there where I could bushwhack 'em easy as pie. Everybody'd figger the Injuns done it."

Richter exhaled heavily. "I haven't said anything about killing them . . . yet."

"No, not just yet, but you will."

"What makes you think so?"

"You got no choice," Bohannon said pointedly. "Only one way you're gonna get them kids away from Hickok and Cody. You gotta kill 'em."

A strange look came over Richter's face. He was silent a moment, as though weighing some quandary known only to himself. Then he seemed to gather himself with grudging effort. He nodded to Bohannon.

"I regret to say we'd best get mounted."

"You're a brute for punishment, ain't you? Bet you wish you'd never seen a horse."

"All in a good cause, Mr. Bohannon."

"Tell me that after another twenty miles."

They walked off downstream under the dappled shade of the trees.

CHAPTER 10

FORT MCPHERSON was located on a broad plain of rolling grassland. Cottonwood Creek snaked out of the north and curled around the southern perimeter of the post. On the far side of the creek steep bluffs guarded a range of broken hills.

Company B rode into the fort shortly before ten o'clock the next morning. As the column passed through the main gate, the regimental trumpeter sounded Boots and Saddles. The troopers of the Fifth Regiment hurried into formation on the parade ground for drill call. Guidons of the assembled companies fluttered on a crisp northerly breeze.

Hickok was always impressed by the size of the garrison. One of the larger military posts on the frontier, it was spread over nearly forty acres. There were some thirty buildings, including barracks, stables, quartermaster depot, and the hospital. The regimental headquarters, a sprawling frame structure, was located on the north side of the parade ground.

Sergeant Foley and his detail drove the horse herd to a large corral at the southwest corner of the compound. Captain Meinhold brought the company on line near the flagpole in the center of the parade ground. There, he turned over command to the First Sergeant, and once the troopers were dismounted, they led their horses to the company stable. An orderly rushed to take the captain's horse.

Meinhold swatted dust off his uniform with his gloves. He waited by the flagpole while Cody and

Hickok collected the children and their horses and
walked forward. Katherine and Augustus seemed no
worse for their expedition with the cavalry, and they
gawked round-eyed as troops wheeled around the parade ground in close order drill. Meinhold adjusted
his campaign hat.

"Let's report in, Mr. Cody," he said brusquely.
"I'm sure the colonel will be interested in hearing
about these children."

Cody winced. "I'd think he'd be more interested
in the hostiles, Cap'n."

"Yes, that, too."

Meinhold marched off toward regimental headquarters. In the orderly room, Sergeant Major Daniel
O'Meara and four clerks snapped to attention. The
children were parked on a bench by a potbellied
stove, and O'Meara rapped on the door of an inner
office. He swung it open, stepping aside as Meinhold,
Cody, and Hickok filed through. His eyes touched on
Cody with a glint of amusement.

"Colonel, sir!" he barked. "Captain Meinhold, and
scouts Cody and Hickok."

Colonel John Reynolds was an austere man with
chiseled features and a neatly trimmed mustache. He
remained seated at his desk, the national flag and the
regimental flag draped from standards behind his
chair. Through the open door, his gaze settled momentarily on the children. He nodded to O'Meara.

"Thank you, Sergeant Major."

O'Meara went out, closing the door. Reynolds
stared across his desk with a curious expression.
"Gentlemen," he said amiably. "May I inquire who
those children belong to?"

"To me, sir," Cody blurted. "Me and Mr. Hickok."

"Indeed?" Reynolds said. "Would you care to explain yourself, Mr. Cody?"

Cody told him the story. As he related the odyssey of the children, Reynolds's features ran the gamut from amazement to anger. There was a moment of leaden silence when Cody finally wound down.

"You surprise me, Mr. Cody," Reynolds said curtly. "Your duty was to the mission. Those children are a civilian matter."

"Beg your pardon, Colonel," Hickok interrupted. "Cody was responsible for seven hostiles bitin' the dust and he recovered them stolen horses. Cap'n Meinhold will bear me out."

Meinhold cleared his throat. "Apart from the children, Colonel, I'd be forced to agree. Mr. Cody performed in an exemplary manner."

"What am I to do with you, Cody?" Reynolds asked in a bemused voice. "You redeem yourself even in the midst of willful disobedience."

Cody looked abashed. "I'll go along with whatever you say, Colonel."

The door swung open. Sergeant Major O'Meara stepped inside, shoulders squared. "Colonel, sir!" he boomed. "Telegraph for Mr. Cody just come over the wire."

"How providential," Reynolds said dryly. "Don't let me stop you, Mr. Cody. Go right ahead."

O'Meara handed over the telegram. Cody unfolded the form and quickly scanned the message. He read it through again.

HAVE CONTRACTED THREE-MONTH RUN OF STAGE
SHOW IN NEW YORK'S GRANDEST THEATER. YOUR
PRESENCE REQUIRED HERE POSTHASTE. TELE-
GRAPH DATE OF ARRIVAL.
                                        NED BUNTLINE

Cody looked up. "It's from my stage partner in New York. Says I've got to come right away. He's contracted a theater."

"Come now, Mr. Cody," Reynolds said. "Your leave of absence doesn't start for another week. You know that."

"Yessir, no argument there. But what's a week more or less? He wouldn't ask if it wasn't important."

Cody's arrangement with the army permitted him a leave of absence for the months February through April. The hostile tribes seldom broke winter camp before early May, and the raiding season was usually delayed for a spring hunt. By then, he would have returned to duty as Chief of Scouts.

"Perhaps you're right," Reynolds conceded. "Quite frankly, I'd rather not consider the thought of disciplinary action. We'll leave it that the success of your mission offsets the matter of the children. You have your extra week, Mr. Cody."

"I'm obliged, Colonel," Cody said gratefully. "I'll make it up to you come spring."

"Just don't return with any children."

"No, sir, I shorely won't."

There was a sense of relief all around. After a round of handshakes, Cody and Hickok collected the children from the orderly room. Outside headquarters, they walked toward the hitch rack where their horses were tied. Hickok gave Cody a sideways glance.

"I take it you're headed East."

"There's an evenin' train out of North Platte. Got plenty of time to make it."

"You're forgettin' something, ain't you?" Hickok said. "What are we gonna do with these kids?"

Cody grinned. "How'd you like to see New York City?"

*   *   *

The sun dropped steadily westward. Up ahead was a creek lined with trees, and Cody thought it a good spot to allow the horses a drink. He figured they would make North Platte with time to spare.

Earlier, before leaving Fort McPherson, he and Hickok had gathered their gear from his quarters. They were prone to travel light, and their war bags were strapped behind their saddles. Yet the matter of New York still hung between them like a gaseous shroud. Cody decided to broach it from a new angle.

"Look here now," he said. "We're dutybound to see that these kids get home. What better way than to take 'em ourselves?"

"You're wastin' your breath," Hickok said gruffly. "I ain't going to New York, and that's that."

"What've you got against New York?"

"Too damn many people to suit my style."

"You've got nothin' else to do," Cody persisted. "They won't be hiring a marshal for Ellsworth till May at the earliest. You said so yourself."

"Yeah?" Hickok grumped. "So what?"

"So what's your plans between now and then?"

"There's lots of gamblin' dives between here and Kansas. You might recollect I'm a fair-to-middlin' poker player."

"Dollar here, dollar there," Cody said dismissively. "Why not make yourself some real money?"

Hickok squinted at him. "What exactly are we talkin' about here?"

"Couple of hundred a week, steady work. That's a sight more than you make wearin' a badge."

"What kind of work?"

"There's a spot for you in my stage play. The show business pays mighty good."

"You must've popped your cork. Whatever gave you the notion I'd go on the stage?"

"You're a natural," Cody insisted. "All you have to do is stand up there and talk. Somebody else even writes the lines."

"Thanks all the same," Hickok said doggedly. "Think I'll stick to poker."

"What about the kids? You started this and you ought to see it through. Never knew you to be a quitter."

Katherine and Augustus were listening intently. From talk among the cavalry troopers, they'd heard how Cody and Hickok routed the Sioux raiders and killed seven warriors. By now they idolized the plainsmen in the way of saints or mythical dragon slayers. Augustus squirmed around in his saddle.

"Won't you please come with us, Wild Bill? Even if you never go on the stage, you'll like New York. I just know you will!"

"Yes, please do," Katherine urged. "Going home wouldn't be the same without you, Wild Bill. We so want you to meet Mother and Father."

Hickok suddenly sat straighter. The treeline bordering the creek was some three hundred yards to their direct front. His eyes narrowed.

"We got trouble," he said solemnly. "There's somebody in them trees."

"You sure?" Cody said.

"Damn right I'm sure. Somebody's fixin' to ambush us. Might be Injuns."

"We can't take any chances with the kids. We'll have to run for it."

"You kids listen to me," Hickok ordered. "When I give you the word, boot your horses and take off. Got that?"

The children nodded, their features taut with fear. Hickok barked a command and the four of them wheeled their horses west at a gallop. The distant tree-line spurted flashes of smoke, followed an instant later by the rolling crack of rifles. Katherine's saddlehorn exploded, and Augustus's hat went sailing in the air. The angry buzz of slugs whistled past Hickok and Cody. They pounded off at a dead lope.

Otto Richter watched them from the trees. On the ride south, trailing them to Fort McPherson, he'd realized that all his options had been foreclosed. Army officials were now aware of the situation, and simply killing Cody and Hickok solved nothing. There was only one solution that would end the problem. He'd instructed Bohannon to kill the children.

"Gawdammit!" Bohannon raged. "Something must've tipped them off."

"Let's get mounted," Richter told him. "We have no time to lose."

"What's your hurry?"

"I think we can assume they're headed for North Platte. Do you agree?"

"Yeah, that'd be my guess."

"I've just upped the price," Richter said. "Five thousand if those children are dead by nightfall."

"Uh-huh," Bohannon said, his eyes inquisitive. "What about Hickok and Cody?"

"I'm interested only in the children."

"And I did hear right—five thousand?"

"Precisely."

Bohannon ordered his men to get mounted.

Cody came out of the livery stable. He had returned the rented horses, and without telling Hickok, arranged to stable their horses. Hickok was waiting with the children on the boardwalk.

"We'd better eat," Cody said. "Never know what kind of vittles you'll find on a train."

"Good idea," Hickok commented. "Wouldn't want to send you off hungry."

Augustus looked at him. "Aren't you coming with us, Wild Bill?"

"I'm still thinkin' on it, sport. Haven't made up my mind."

They crossed the street to the Bon Ton Café. A waitress took their orders and a sense of gloom settled over the table. Cody finally broke the silence.

"You think it was Injuns that tried to bushwhack us?"

"Maybe," Hickok said thoughtfully. " 'Course, that'd be a helluva coincidence, wouldn't it? Tangle with one bunch yesterday and stumble across another today."

"So what are you sayin'?"

"I got to wonderin' about that Richter feller. Could be he's still after these here kids."

Cody studied on it a moment. "Way it sounded, there was at least six rifles, maybe more. Where would Richter get all them guns?"

"Don't know," Hickok admitted. "Unless he's trailin' us with the sheriff and a pack of deputies. They was in pretty thick, you'll recollect."

"I suppose stranger things have happened."

The children seemed to cringe at the mention of Richter. The waitress returned with their orders, and the men let the subject drop. When they came out of the café, dusk had fallen over North Platte. They walked toward the train station.

At the depot, Cody purchased four tickets. The

eastbound train ground to a halt as he emerged onto the platform. He handed one of the tickets to Hickok.

"You're all set."

Hickok exhaled heavily. "Haven't said I was going to New York."

"I don't think you'll let the kids down. They're dependin' on you."

"You shore know how to twist the knife."

"Oh, please, Wild Bill," Katherine pleaded, tugging at his sleeve. "Won't you please do it for us?"

"Well, little missy—"

Hickok abruptly pushed her aside. He saw a group of riders step down from their horses at the west end of the platform. In the spill of light from the depot windows, he counted eight men. One of them was Otto Richter.

"Do what I tell you," he said roughly to Cody. "Get the kids on the train. Now!"

Cody obeyed without question. He grabbed each of the children by the arm and rushed toward the center coach. They were the only ones boarding the train, and the debarking passengers were already moving through the stationhouse. As they neared the coach, the men at the end of the platform went for their pistols. The conductor ducked back onto the train.

A ragged volley of shots whistled across the platform. The slugs pinged off the side of the coach, one plucking at Augustus's coatsleeve and another nipping the hem of Katherine's skirt. Hickok pulled a Colt Navy with either hand, thumbing the hammers as the barrels came level. He opened fire in a drumming roar, the shots blending together. Two men pitched forward on their faces.

The train lurched into motion. Hickok backed across the platform, alternately firing his Colts with methodical precision. Axel Bohannon staggered, drilled through the chest, and slumped to the ground. Another man spun away, spurting blood from his throat, and collapsed in a heap. Hickok fired again, then stepped aboard as the train got under way. Cody and the children were waiting in the vestibule.

"You hit?" Cody demanded. "You all right?"

Hickok shrugged him off. "Looks like you shanghaied me after all."

The train gathered speed. As it pulled away from the depot, Richter and Turk Johnson darted from the shadows. They sprinted along the track bed and Johnson leaped onto the observation deck of the last passenger coach. He dragged Richter aboard.

The train sped through the night from North Platte.

CHAPTER 11

CODY WAS his own best press agent. He quickly befriended the conductor and set about making arrangements for their trip East. A sizable gratuity ensured they would travel in style.

The conductor hardly needed his palm greased. He was almost euphoric to have Buffalo Bill Cody and Wild Bill Hickok aboard his train. An avid reader of dime novels, he accorded them the courtesy reserved for dignitaries. They were shown to a parlor car forward of the passenger coaches.

Hickok had never heard of a parlor car. The conductor explained that it was something new, a car with four private compartments. The Union Pacific was testing the cars between New York and San Francisco, providing luxury accommodations for wealthy travelers and businessmen. Three of the four compartments were already occupied.

The plainsmen agreed that it was a godsend. With a little planning, the compartment was spacious enough for four. There was a double bunk bed, similar to the Pullman sleeping cars, and a small sitting area by the window. There was even a private lavatory, with running water and a commode. They would have no problem keeping an eye on the children.

Katherine and Augustus were still shaken by the gunfight at the train station. Yet, however great their fear, they were awed by the memory of Hickok blazing away with a pistol in either hand. The reality was far more exciting, and frightening, than anything they might have imagined from dime novels. Hickok told them to get settled in, and wisely dodged their questions about the shootout. He motioned Cody into the passageway outside the compartment.

"Need to talk," he said, waiting for Cody to close the door. "What happened back there at the depot don't make sense."

"I know," Cody said. "Where the deuce did Richter find himself an army?"

"That's not what I'm getting at. Them bastards wasn't shootin' at me, or you. They was shootin' at the kids."

"What makes you say that?"

"There wasn't a bullet come anywhere near me. Them kids was drawin' all the fire."

"You serious?"

"Hell, yes, I'm serious. You don't believe me, take a look at their clothes. Them holes is bullet holes."

"I'll be jiggered," Cody said, dumbfounded. "Why would Richter want to kill the kids?"

Hickok nodded soberly. "Told you it don't make any sense."

"We're missin' something here somewheres. Richter was the one that abducted them from New York—"

"And sent 'em West on the Orphan Train."

"—plannin' all along they'd be adopted by some farmer off in the middle of nowhere."

"So when that got bollixed, he switched tactics. Set about tryin' to kill 'em."

"Yeah, but why?"

They muddled on it a moment. "There's things we don't know," Hickok finally said. "How'd the kids get stole from their folks in the first place? Sounds like Richter pulled it off mighty easy."

Cody tugged at his goatee. "You think their folks hired Richter?"

"I reckon that'd be one answer. All we know for sure is that Richter was bound and determined they'd never return East."

"Which means there's liable to be somebody in New York that feels the same way. Somebody willin' to kill them."

Hickok grimaced. "Hate to think it's their folks, but who the hell knows? Stranger things have happened."

"You're right," Cody said gravely. "We've got to be real careful when we hit New York City. Nobody's to be trusted."

"Meanwhile, we don't say nothin' to the kids. Let'em think everything's hunky-dory."

"I'm mighty glad you're along for the ride."

"Guess there wasn't no choice when the shootin' started."

In the compartment, they found the children seated on the lower bunk. Hickok suddenly thought of something he'd overlooked. He shot Cody a quick glance.

"Hope you wasn't plannin' to stop off and see Lulu. Doubt it'd be wise to lay over in St. Louis."

Cody caught the warning in his voice. "No, we'll go straight through to New York. I'll see Lulu another time."

Augustus was overcome with curiosity. "Who is Lulu, Buffalo Bill?"

"Why, she's my wife, young feller. Her and the children live in St. Louis."

"You're married?" Katherine said, visibly shocked by the news. "You have children?"

"Shore do," Cody acknowledged. "Arta, that's my

daughter, she's just turned six. Kit, that's the boy, he's two now."

"Kit—?"

"Well, he's named after another famous scout, Kit Carson. He was a mite before your time."

"How long have you been married?"

"Going on seven years, come March. Time flies when you're not lookin'."

Hickok seated himself on an upholstered bench across from the bunks. He took a powder flask and a pouch of lead balls from his war bag and began reloading his pistols. Katherine continued to question Cody, and as he listened, he thought again that it was a strange marriage. But then, Lulu was a strange woman.

Her given name was Louisa, though everyone called her Lulu. She was originally from St. Louis, a religious girl educated in a convent. Cody married her shortly after the Civil War, and she'd followed him West on his first posting as a scout. Yet she was appalled by army life, and with the birth of their daughter, she returned to St. Louis. She tolerated an occasional visit by Cody.

Hickok was often amused by what passed for marital bliss. Lulu was content with the children and her home in St. Louis, and in their entire married life, Cody had never spent longer than a month at a time in her bed. As he reflected on it, Hickok thought his friend was home only long enough to sire children. Cody much preferred to be off with the cavalry, chasing Indians.

"Do you miss your wife?" Katherine asked. "How long has it been since you were home?"

Cody wasn't sure. "Well, near as I recollect, it was last summer sometime. June, maybe July."

"Goodness," Katherine said, surprised. "Augustus and I don't mind if you stop in St. Louis. Wouldn't it make your wife very happy?"

"Just bet it would." Cody exchanged a furtive look with Hickok. "But I've got business in New York with this stage play. I'll stop by next time through."

Katherine saw the look pass between them. Her attention turned to Hickok. "Are you married too, Wild Bill?"

Cody laughed. "Wild Bill's not the marryin' kind. Scared he'll get his wings clipped."

"I don't understand," Katherine said. "What does he mean, Wild Bill?"

"Guess it's like this . . ." Hickok paused, placing percussion caps behind the chambers on his pistol. "A feller shouldn't get married till he finds the right girl. Just any old girl won't do."

"And you've never found the right girl?"

"I can truthfully say that's a fact."

Katherine thought there was no question that Buffalo Bill was the handsomer of the two men. But she was strangely drawn to the danger that lurked behind every syllable of every word spoken by Wild Bill. All the more so since she'd now discovered that he wasn't married.

"I've been thinking . . ." she hesitated, then rushed on, certain he was the one to ask. "Why were those men shooting at us, Wild Bill?"

Hickok stuffed the loaded pistol in his belt. "Buffalo Bill and me don't rightly know. We figure to find out what's what when we get to New York."

"Mother and Father will be able to tell us. I just know they will."

"Maybe so." Hickok deftly changed the subject. "Speakin' of New York, Scout Cody, what in tarnation have you got me into with this show business?"

"Told you before," Cody said. "You get up on a stage and talk. Buntline writes the words you say. He calls it a script."

Ned Buntline advertised the production as the *Buffalo Bill Combination*. In stage terms, a combination was a theatrical troupe that presented the same play for the run of the show. A stock company, by contrast, offered a repertory of plays, often changing from night to night. The bigger difference, however, was that a stock company production was the work of professional actors. Buntline's plays relied solely on the fame of the star.

"No need to worry," Cody went on. "You'll do just fine on the stage, Jim. Just fine."

Augustus appeared startled. "Wild Bill, why did Buffalo Bill call you 'Jim'?"

"I reckon he just slips every now and then. You see, my name's really James Butler Hickok. But that sort of got lost in the shuffle."

"I think that's a nice name," Augustus said. "Why don't people call you Wild Jim?"

"That'd suit me," Hickok said, tamping powder and ball into his other pistol. "I've been tryin' to ditch Wild Bill ever since I got hung with it."

"Then why do they call you Wild Bill?"

"Well, it happened durin' the war. One of them flukes that never makes much sense."

"What is a fluke?"

"Oddball things that happen to a man."

Hickok explained that he'd been a scout during the Civil War. On one assignment, operating as a spy behind Confederate lines, he had been caught out. He fought off a swarm of Rebels in a running gun battle and finally swam his horse to safety across a river.

The Union troops on the opposite shore saw the last of the fight and his miraculous escape. Someone dubbed him Wild Bill and the name stuck.

"So that's a fluke," Hickok concluded. "Feller that tagged me with the handle didn't even know me. I ain't outrun it yet."

Augustus averted his eyes. "Will you get mad at me if I tell you something?"

" 'Course I won't get mad at you. Go ahead, speak your piece."

"Well—it's just that . . . ain't is not a word."

Hickok looked up from his pistol. "What do you mean, it ain't a word?"

Augustus gave him a shy glance. "We were taught in school that it isn't . . . a proper word."

"There's more to life than school learnin'. Take your name for example."

"My name?"

"Augustus," Hickok said slowly. "That's purely a mouthful, ain't it?"

"I guess it is."

"So wouldn't you like to have your own handle? Something easier to swallow?"

"Like what?"

Hickok grinned. "From now on, I'm gonna call you Gus. How's that sound?"

"Gus," Augustus repeated, testing the word. "I think I like it."

"Now, about your sister." Hickok nodded to him with a sly smile. "Katherine's sort of a mouthful too. Maybe we'll just call her Sis."

"You *will* not," Katherine shrieked. "I am not a— Sis!"

Hickok gave the boy a conspiratorial look. "What do you think about that, Gus?"

"Well," Augustus went along, struggling not to laugh. "When no one can hear us, I call her Katie."

"What does she call you?"

"Auggie."

"Auggie and Katie." Hickok deliberated on it a moment, abruptly smiled. "I'd sooner call you by special names. How about Gus and"—he winked drolly at the girl—"Kate."

Katherine thought she would melt. She blushed bright as a beet, certain she would love him forever. "A special name," she said in a throaty voice. "Oh, yes, thank you, Wild Bill."

"Don't mention it, Kate." Hickok stuck the second pistol in his belt. "Think I'll step out and have a smoke. Little stuffy in here for cigars."

Katherine simpered. "I love the smell of cigars."

Cody grunted a laugh. Hickok ignored him, moving through the door into the passageway. He lit a cheroot, and then, deciding to stretch his legs, walked back to the passenger coaches. The train hurtled eastward across the plains, the dark of nightfall upon the land. The coaches were dimly lighted by coal-oil lamps.

Hickok thought he might catch a breath of fresh air. There was an observation deck at the rear of the train, and he made his way to the last passenger coach. As he moved along the aisle, he suddenly squinted, hardly able to credit his eyes. Richter and his hooligan, the one named Johnson, were seated at the rear of the coach.

Richter was seated by the window. Johnson was dozing, his chin resting on his massive chest. Hickok stopped in the aisle, and Richter turned from the window, his features abruptly guarded. He poked Johnson in the ribs with his elbow.

Richter stared at him. "We're not looking for trouble, Hickok."

"Well, you done found it, you sorry sonsabitches. Why're you after them kids, anyway?"

Johnson started out of his seat. Hickok pulled one of his Colts, thumbed the hammer. He hooked the blade of the front sight in Johnson's nose.

"Sit real still," he said. "All I need's an excuse."

"Take it easy, Turk," Richter said, placing a hand on Johnson's arm. "We have as much right on this train as he does. He won't do anything."

Hickok's eyes went cold. "Here's the way it works, Richter. You or your gorilla come anywhere near them kids and I'll kill you. Take it as gospel fact."

"You don't frighten me," Richter scoffed. "I'll come and go as I please."

"You're already talkin' like a dead man."

Hickok ripped the blade of the sight out of Johnson's nostril. Johnson clutched at his nose, a jet of blood pouring over his hands. Lowering the hammer, Hickok backed away, the Colt still leveled on them. His voice was pleasantly ominous.

"Don't let me see you boys again."

Johnson watched him with a murderous glare. Hickok turned in the aisle and walked back through the train. A few minutes later he opened the door of the compartment, motioning Cody into the passageway. He waited until the door was closed.

"We've got company," he said. "Richter and Johnson are on the train."

Cody went ashen. "You talked to them?"

"After a fashion. I warned 'em off, but it won't do no good. They'll make a try for the kids."

"Judas Priest! You got any bright ideas?"

"Just one," Hickok said. "We ain't gonna let them kids out of our sight."

They decided the children would not be allowed out of the compartment. Once they were back inside, the door was locked and the sleeping arrangements were quickly settled. Katherine and Augustus shared the upper bunk, and Cody stretched out on the lower bunk. Hickok, seated on the upholstered bench, took the first watch.

Katherine smiled down at him from the top bunk. "Good night, Wild Bill."

"Get some sleep, Kate. Don't let the bedbugs bite."

She giggled. "I promise I won't."

Hickok leaned back against the bench. Cody would spell him at midnight, and until then, he had plenty to occupy his mind. Somewhere before New York, Richter and Johnson would make a play for the children. The question that wouldn't go away was *Why?*

He thought about it as the train barreled through the night.

CHAPTER 12

CHICAGO WAS the midcontinental shipping center of the nation. The city was located at the southern tip of Lake Michigan, and served as a major port on the Great Lakes. Yet it was the railroads that transformed Chicago into a metropolis. The city by the lake was in the midst of a boom.

The good times were all the more remarkable because of the fire. Three months ago, on a Sunday night in October, Mrs. O'Leary's cow became known around the world. The cow kicked over a lantern, which set the barn afire, and within hours a holocaust raged through the streets. The city's buildings, constructed of timber and slats, went up like kindling.

By the following night, the Great Chicago Fire had burned itself out. Three hundred people were dead, half the buildings in the city were destroyed, and one hundred thousand were homeless. But Chicago, like the phoenix of ancient myth, was reborn from the ashes. The city arose anew to the sound of hammers pounding nails into rip-sawed lumber.

Hickok smelled the stockyards when he stepped off the train. The longhorns trailed from Texas to the Kansas cowtowns ended up in the slaughterhouses of Chicago. By some estimates, upward of seventy thousand longhorns had been shipped north from Abilene last summer. The sweetish smell of manure permeated the railroad district.

Cody and the children joined Hickok on the depot platform. The stationhouse was immense by Western

standards, and hundreds of travelers scurried from
train to train. Hickok scanned the crowds, searching
the sea of faces for some glimpse of Richter and Johnson. His every instinct told him they were out there.
Watching. Waiting.

Chicago was the terminus for Western trains.
Hickok and Cody were forced to lay over for the
night, and catch a morning train to New York. They
were all too aware that the danger to the children
increased a hundredfold in a large city. Oddly enough,
even among the jostling throngs, they felt more exposed than on the open plains. The hustle and bustle
of the jammed railway station merely set their nerves
on edge.

A porter directed them to a nearby hotel. The sun
smoldered on the western horizon as they came out
of the depot. For a moment, they stood marveling at
the renaissance of a city virtually leveled by flame.
Just three months ago, the Great Chicago Fire had
been headlined in every newspaper in America. They
expected to see a city in ruin, and instead they saw a
forest of buildings in every direction. The transfor-
mation was startling.

The Dearborn Hotel still smelled of raw lumber.
Located a block north of the railway station, the three-
story structure had been hammered together within a
month of the fire. The hotel was unpretentious and
cheap, a stopover for travelers stranded between
trains. A lone settee positioned on a nondescript carpet provided the sole amenity in the lobby. The desk
clerk looked like a bartender in a workingman's saloon. He wore red garters on his shirtsleeves.

"Afternoon," Cody said. "We'd like to engage
rooms for the night."

The clerk scrutinized the children with an inquisitive look. "Will that be one room or two?"

"Two," Cody answered. "Adjoining rooms with a connecting door."

"We have one set of adjoining rooms on each floor. Any preference?"

"First floor," Hickok said. "Hear you're prone to fires in this town."

The clerk sniffed. "We refund in case of a fire. That will be ten dollars—in advance."

"Godalmighty," Hickok groaned. "We don't aim to buy the place."

"Do you want the rooms or not?"

Hickok bristled at the man's tone. Cody intervened before his friend could instruct the clerk in manners. Too often, he'd seen the instruction result in broken noses and missing teeth, or worse. He slapped a gold eagle on the counter and signed the register "William F. Cody." The clerk handed him two keys.

The rooms were spartan as a monk's cell. The beds were hard as planks, with dingy sheets and coarse woolen blankets. Along one wall was a washstand with a chipped basin and a faded mirror. On the opposite wall were wooden pegs for clothing and a straight-backed chair, and beneath the bed was a stained johnnypot. A lavatory at the end of the hall served the entire floor.

"Highway robbery," Hickok fumed. "Leave it to city slickers to pick your pocket."

Augustus put on a smile. "It's only for one night, Wild Bill. We'll be on our way to New York tomorrow."

"I like a man who looks on the bright side, Gus. Guess it could've been worse."

Hickok went into the adjoining room. He took the wooden chair and wedged it beneath the knob of the door leading to the hall. Katherine and Augustus watched him with puzzled expressions. She finally gave way to curiosity.

"Why did you do that, Wild Bill?"

"No harm in being careful," Hickok said. "Anybody rattles that door knob tonight, I want you to yell out real loud. You understand?"

"Do you think someone would try to come in our room?"

"Kate, it's like they say, an ounce of prevention."

Hickok glanced back at the adjoining door and Cody gave him a cryptic nod. Words were unnecessary, for they each read the other's mind. They were thinking the same thing.

Richter and Johnson were out there somewhere.

A short while later they returned to the lobby. Hickok and Cody were carrying bundles of wrinkled clothes taken from their war bags. Cody left Hickok with the children and carried both bundles to the desk. He showed the clerk a five-dollar gold piece.

"We need to get these things pressed. Think you could arrange that?"

"There's a Chinese laundry around the corner. I'll take care of it."

"Have to be back tonight."

The clerk accepted the gold piece. "How's an hour sound?"

"Just about right."

Outside the hotel, Cody and Hickok fell in on either side of the children. The streetlamps were lit and the sidewalks were crowded with people. They turned north from the hotel and went off in search of a place to have supper. Hickok kept looking over his shoulder.

Three blocks upstreet they found O'Malley's Steakhouse. The restaurant had red-checkered table-cloths and sawdust on the floor, and a small bar at the rear of the room. The waiter recommended the twelve-ounce ribeye, with mashed potatoes and gravy, and winter squash. Hickok and Cody ordered rye whiskey, and a pitcher of milk for the children. The waiter scurried off to the kitchen.

Not quite an hour later they emerged from the restaurant. Augustus and Katherine were stuffed, hardly able to finish half of their steaks. The plainsmen once again flanked them and they turned back toward the hotel. There were fewer people on the streets, and they loafed along at a leisurely pace. On the corner they passed a saloon and Hickok spotted card tables through the tall plate-glass window. He paused, drawn to a gaming den in the way metal finds a magnet, and the others stopped with him. Cody suggested it was not the night for poker.

Hickok, reluctantly, was forced to agree. He was about to turn away when a reflection in the window caught his attention. He hesitated, fishing a cheroot from inside his jacket, and struck a match on his thumbnail. The wind was out of the north, and he turned slightly, shielding the match in his cupped hands. As he puffed on the cheroot, he glanced over the flame.

Richter and Johnson were on the opposite side of the street. They were halfway up the block, standing before a haberdashery, feigning interest in the window display. He thought they were likely watching him in the shop window, and he snuffed the match, quickly looked away. All in an instant, he knew he had to end it here, tonight. He turned back to Cody.

"Everybody keep their eyes on me," he said firmly,

nodding to the children. "Don't let on what I'm about to tell you. Our friends are across the street, back a little ways."

Cody held his gaze. "Any chance we could shake them?"

"We're long past that. I'm gonna go in this saloon to play poker, and I want you to get mad as hell. Then you take the kids and go on back to the hotel. Don't argue with me, just do it."

"What am I supposed to say?"

"You're the actor, think of something."

"The devil you are!" Cody shouted, inventing dialogue to suit the role. "You're not fixin' to stick me with these kids while you play poker all night!"

"I'll do what I please," Hickok said loudly. "You're the one that signed on as nursemaid, not me. You don't like it, lump it."

"You got some brass!"

"Just leave me the hell be."

Hickok wheeled through the door of the saloon. He walked to the poker tables, which were across from the bar. Through the window, he saw Cody turn downstreet with the children. Upstreet, he saw Richter and Johnson glance at the saloon as they neared the opposite corner. He took a chair at one of the tables, certain they would follow Cody. Then, to the surprise of the other players, he pushed back out of the chair. He hurried toward the door.

Outside, he saw Richter and Johnson angling across the street. Cody and the children were approaching the next intersection, walking in the direction of the hotel. Hickok lengthened his stride, closing the distance as the two men dodged around a horse-drawn coal wagon halfway down the block. There was no one else in sight and he quickened his pace.

He caught them as they stepped onto the curb.

"Look who's here," he said tersely. "You boys don't know good advice when you hear it."

"Hickok!" Richter spun around "I thought—"

"Defend yourselves," Hickok ordered. "I mean to kill you."

"No, wait!"

"Defend yourselves."

Richter backed away, hands thrown up as if to ward off bullets. Johnson's hand snaked inside his coat and came out with a stubby bulldog revolver. Hickok was a beat faster, leveling a Colt Navy even as he cocked the hammer. He fired two shots in rapid succession, the roar reverberating off buildings. The slugs struck Johnson over the sternum, not a handspan apart, and he buckled at the knees. He toppled off the curb and into the gutter, the revolver slipping from his grasp. His eyes rolled back in his head.

A short distance downstreet, Richter ducked into an alley. Hickok rushed forward, flattened himself against a storefront, and cautiously looked around the building. The alleyway was black as a tunnel, the far end dimly illuminated by lamplights from the next street over. He saw Richter, a shadow against the fuzzy aureole of light, sprinting headlong for the opposite end. He sighted and fired, the bullet whistling harmlessly through the night. Richter disappeared around the far corner.

Hickok started to follow. Then, aware that the gunshots would draw the police, he turned away from the alley. He couldn't afford to be arrested, much less explain to a court the convoluted tale of why he'd killed a man. His overriding concern remained the safety of the children.

He hurried off toward the hotel.

* * *

The depot was mobbed with an early morning crowd. The train for New York was scheduled to depart at seven o'clock, and people waiting to board were already congregated on the platform. Cody and Hickok, with the children in tow, threaded their way through the crush. Their passage drew stares.

Hickok was attired in a handsomely tailored Prince Albert frock coat. A brocaded vest and striped trousers were set off by a colorful tie and a diamond stickpin. He wore a scarlet embroidered silk sash around his waist, with the brace of ivory-handled Colts carried crossdraw fashion. He looked somewhat like an armed peacock.

Cody was himself a dashing spectacle. His bone-white buckskin jacket was decorated with fringe and elaborate quillwork. A royal-blue shirt and gaily colored kerchief complimented the outfit, with nankeen trousers stuffed in the tops of dark oxblood boots. His Colt Army was carried in a holster at waist level.

Earlier, when they arrived at the station, Cody had again booked space on a parlor car. Their dapper attire, and the children's animated manner, attracted the conductor's eye. He personally escorted them on board, insisting a porter take their war bags, and got them settled in their compartment. The train pulled out a short time later.

All morning Hickok had kept a wary lookout for Richter. He and Cody were in agreement that they couldn't let their guard down. So long as Richter was alive, the children were still in imminent peril. Yet, for all their watchfulness, they'd seen nothing of Richter in the station or among the passengers on the platform. They were nonetheless convinced he'd somehow managed to board the train.

Last night, after the children were asleep, Hickok had related details of the fight. Cody already suspected someone was dead, for he'd heard three gunshots as he rushed Katherine and Augustus into the hotel. Upon learning that it was Johnson, he had expressed concern that their problem was far from solved. Richter was a formidable adversary, a zealot of sorts, staunch in his resolve to kill the children. His narrow escape would hardly deter him from another try.

Some miles east of Chicago, Hickok got to his feet. He commented that he needed a smoke, trading a hidden look with Cody. Outside the compartment, he moved through the passageway and proceeded to the first passenger coach. Every seat was full, and he methodically searched the faces as he walked along the aisle. There were five coaches on the train, and he went through each one like a hunter patiently stalking prey. He found Richter in the last seat of the last coach.

There was no one sharing Richter's seat. He kept his hands in plain sight, nodding to Hickok. "Won't you join me, Mr. Hickok. Perhaps it's time we had a talk."

Hickok stopped in the aisle. "What's there to talk about?"

"Let me ask you a question. Are you a wealthy man?"

"Get to the point."

"You have something I want," Richter said. "I'm willing to pay quite generously for an exchange."

"Yeah?" Hickok said without inflection. "How much?"

"Ten thousand."

"Lot of money."

"Enough to put you and Cody on easy street."

"What makes those kids worth so much? Why you after 'em anyway?"

"I'm not at liberty to say."

"Guess that's your tough luck."

"What?"

Hickok took him by the collar. Richter tried to resist and Hickok jerked him into the aisle and waltzed him to the rear door. Outside, on the observation deck, Hickok grabbed him by the collar and the seat of his pants and bodily threw him off the train. Richter hit the roadbed on his shoulder, tumbling head over heels, and rolled to a stop in a patch of weeds. He lay motionless as the train chugged eastward.

The conductor slammed open the door. "What in God's name happened?"

"Would you believe it?" Hickok said guilelessly. "That feller hadn't bought a ticket."

"How do you know that?"

"Why, he told me so himself. He was so ashamed, he just up and jumped off the train."

The conductor gawked. "Why on earth would he jump?"

"You know, it's funny, he never said. Some folks are mighty strange."

Hickok left the conductor to ponder the riddle. He walked back through the coaches and stepped into the compartment. Cody looked up with a quizzical expression.

"Enjoy your smoke, Jim?"

"There you go again, slipping up on names. You got to remember I'm the one and only Wild Bill."

Cody chuckled. "I take it you had yourself a good time?"

"That little problem we was talkin' about?" Hickok

said. "We won't be bothered with it no more."

"You handled it, did you?"

"You shore as hell got that right."

"Honestly!" Katherine admonished prettily. "Why do you curse so much, Wild Bill?"

"Well, Kate." Hickok knuckled his mustache. "I reckon it's the bad company I keep. Buffalo Bill taught me all the wrong words."

"But he almost never uses curse words."

"You just ain't been listenin' real close."

"Who cares!" Augustus laughed happily. "We're on our way to New York!"

Hickok grinned. "Gus, we'll have you there in no time."

CHAPTER 13

THE TRAIN arrived in New York on January 29.

Grand Central Station was a sprawling five-acre complex that served over a hundred trains a day. The railyard was covered by an immense overstructure of iron sheds, the most spacious enclosure on the North American continent. New Yorkers were quick to boast that it rivaled London's St. Pancras as the largest train station in the world.

Hickok and Cody stepped off the train with the children. Augustus was practically hopping with excitement, and Katherine was radiant, hardly able to contain herself. Their long ordeal on the Orphan Train, and their adventures on the Western Plains, were now at an end. Their protectors had brought them once again to Manhattan Island. They were almost home.

Ned Buntline and Texas Jack Omohundro were waiting on the platform. Buntline was a short, stout man with a game leg and a winning smile. He limped forward like a toy soldier no longer in good working order. Texas Jack was a leathery, rawboned plainsman with a soupstrainer mustache. A former scout, he was close friends with both Cody and Hickok.

"Welcome, welcome!" Buntline said with a moon-like grin. "How was your trip?"

Cody accepted his handshake. "Ned, it'd make the best dime novel you ever wrote. This here's Bill Hickok."

"Indeed?" Buntline said gleefully. "Wild Bill

Hickok in the flesh. You are just as I imagined you, Mr. Hickok."

Hickok nodded. "Glad you got what you expected, Mr. Buntline."

"Call me Ned!"

Cody and Hickok warmly shook hands with Omohundro. He ducked his chin at the children. "Who's your friends?"

"Katherine and Augustus," Cody said proudly. "These youngsters are long on grit, Jack. I'll tell you about it on the way to the hotel."

"Hotel?" Katherine echoed. "Aren't you taking us home, Buffalo Bill?"

"Well, not just yet. Wild Bill and me got a couple of things to check out first."

Her face crumpled. "But we want to go home."

"Kate, listen to me." Hickok gently touched her shoulder. "You remember the man that was after you and Gus? We've got to make sure he don't have friends waitin' for you here in New York. You understand me?"

"I think so." Her bottom lip trembled with fright. "Would they try to steal us again?"

"That's a chance we ain't gonna take. We'll have a talk with your folks and see what's what. No need to rush into things."

"Wild Bill knows best," Augustus chimed in. "Him and Buffalo Bill have brought us this far. You have to trust them, Katie."

"Oh, Augustus, you're such a ninny sometimes. I trust them with all my heart."

"Then everything will be all right. You wait and see."

Buntline and Omohundro exchanged a puzzled glance. But Cody had promised the story in good time, and they held their silence. Omohundro led the way along the platform as Buntline went into a rhapsodizing monologue about the theater he'd contracted. A few moments later they climbed the stairway from the railyard and entered the main terminal. Hickok stopped in his tracks.

Grand Central Station was the masterwork of railroad baron Cornelius Vanderbilt. The beaux-arts architecture, a mass of brick and granite, was an airy colossus completed in 1871. The central chamber rose majestically, nearly two hundred feet high, with vaulted arches above massive stained-glass windows. The marble floor stretched onward forever and the constellations of the zodiac, gold against blue on the ceiling, gave it a kaleidoscope effect. The impression was not unlike that of a vast amphitheater reaching for the stars.

"Godalmighty," Hickok breathed, looking upward. "You could put most of Kansas in here."

Omohundro chuckled. "Floored me the first time I saw it, too. These New York folks, they think big."

"Jack, it purely beats all. Damned if it don't."

"Wait'll you see the city."

Outside the terminal they emerged onto Forty Second Street. Buntline had a landau carriage waiting and they squeezed into the enclosed cab. Two blocks over they turned south onto Fifth Avenue and the traffic abruptly became chaotic. The broad thoroughfare, as far as the eye could see, was jammed with wagons and carriages of every description. All of them horse-drawn.

Even inside the cab, the air festered with the stench that was unique to New York. A ripe blend of rotting garbage, horse manure, and noxious coal smoke pouring from chimneys. Hickok wrinkled his nose, unable to hold his breath and yet overpowered by the smell. He suddenly longed for the crisp, clean winds of the plains.

"Takes getting used to," Omohundro said, noting his expression. "Couple of days, you won't even notice it."

"Jack, it'd gag a dog off a gut wagon."

"Well, mostly, it's all them horses."

Buntline, like many New Yorkers, was prone to brag on the enormity of the city in all its facets. He merrily recounted the gist of an article he'd read in the *New York Times* only yesterday. There were forty thousand horses in the city, and every day they unloaded four hundred tons of manure and twenty thousand gallons of urine. He slapped his knee with a ripsnorter of a laugh.

"You can imagine, it keeps the street-sweepers busy!"

"Jack's right," Cody remarked. "I'd forgot what it smells like here. Does take getting used to."

"Yeah, it's odoriferous," Omohundro said. "A whiff of fresh air would likely kill me now."

Texas Jack Omohundro was a Westering man who had come East. By birth a Southerner, he had served with J. E. B. Stuart's Cavalry Corps during the Civil War. Afterward, he migrated to Texas, where he'd gained his nickname and a reputation as an Indian fighter. He knew Hickok from a sojourn through Kansas, and until last year, he had worked as a scout at Fort McPherson. Cody had talked him into joining the Buffalo Bill Combination.

New York, curiously enough, agreed with Omohundro. One season on the stage seemingly turned a roughhewn plainsman into a citified dandy. All the more important, he had fallen for a beautiful Italian actress and married her in the spring of 1871. When Cody returned to duty at Fort McPherson, Omohundro had elected to remain behind with his bride. He was now a professional actor, appearing in occasional stage plays until Cody came East for the new season. These days, he acted the part of a plainsman.

Hickok thought Omohundro had taken leave of his senses. The idea of forty thousand horses in one town boggled his mind; he considered their daily droppings too great a sacrifice for the love of any woman. Yet, as he stared out the window of the carriage, he was nonetheless impressed by the sheer magnitude of the place.

They drove past buildings seven and eight stories high, so tall he had to crane his neck to see the sky. Three stories was the tallest building he'd ever seen, and now he was looking at structures that towered like mountains. He told himself he was a long way from Kansas.

Too damn far for comfort.

The Fifth Avenue Hotel was located on the southwest corner of a busy intersection. Broadway angled across Fifth Avenue directly in front of the hotel, and on the opposite side of the street was Madison Square. The landscaped seven-acre square was lined with such fashionable shops as Tiffany's and F. A. O. Schwarz.

A liveried doorman greeted the carriage. Bellmen rushed to collect the scant baggage, and Buntline led the entourage into the hotel. The lobby was a sea of pink marble, with glittery chandeliers and plush seating arrangements, and an air of decadent opulence. The hotel manager welcomed them with an obsequious smile.

Buntline had reserved a suite for Cody and Hickok.

There were two bedrooms, each with its own lavatory, and a sitting room with an onyx marble foreplace. A lush Persian carpet covered the sitting-room floor, and grouped before the fireplace were several chairs and a chesterfield divan. The view from the third-floor windows overlooked Madison Square.

Giuseppina Morlacchi, Omohundro's wife, was waiting for them in the suite. She was small and svelte, with youthful breasts, a stemlike waist, and nicely rounded hips. Her features were exquisite, somehow exotic and doll-like, with a lush, coral mouth that accentuated her high cheekbones. Her hair was the color of dark sable, and she spoke with a pronounced Italian accent.

"Beeel!" she squealed, dragging Cody into a tight embrace. "We are sooo happy to see you again!"

"Same here." Cody said with a loopy grin. "You're lookin' mighty fine, Giuseppina."

"Oh, you were always the flatterer!"

Hickok quickly learned that Morlacchi was her stage name. Buntline explained that every Western play required an Indian maiden, and Giuseppina, with her flawless olive complexion, perfectly fit the part. She graced Hickok with a dazzling smile and bold, flirtatious eyes, and he abruptly changed his mind. He thought perhaps Omohundro was wise to stay in New York.

"Pleasure, ma'am," Hickok said, offering her a courtly bow. "Texas Jack's a lucky feller."

"How gallant!" she trilled. "All of you scouting men have such a way with words."

"Well, ma'am, that's easy enough where you're concerned."

She looked at the children. "And who are these beautiful leettle darlings?"

Hickok smiled. "This here's Kate and Gus. They've been travelin' with us a spell."

"Giuseppina, my love," Buntline broke in smoothly. "We have business matters to discuss. Would you be a dear and entertain the children? We won't be long."

"But of course!" she exclaimed. "I weel tell them a story."

Hickok laughed. "You might like to hear their story. It's a real humdinger."

"Come along, then, we weel all tell stories."

Giuseppina took the children into one of the bedrooms. Augustus looked smitten by her sloe-eyed sensuality, and Katherine watched her with the alert expression of one woman studying another's worldly allure. The door to the bedroom closed with Giuseppina's spirited laughter.

On the way to the hotel, Cody had briefly explained the situation with the children. He dropped into one of the easychairs as Buntline and Omohundro seated themselves on the divan. Hickok stood staring out the widow at Madison Square.

"We got 'em here safe and sound," Cody went on where he'd left off. "But we're not just exactly sure how their folks fit into all this. You ever hear of a Henry Morton Stanley?"

"Stanley?" Buntline mused aloud. "I seem to recall there is a Stanley involved with the Guaranty Trust Bank. Old New York money and lots of it. Could be your man."

"You recollect whether he lives on Gramercy Park?"

"That would certainly be an address for a banker. Gramercy Park is old money and old New York."

Hickok turned from the window. "I ain't got the

least goddamn interest in what he does for a livin'. We don't trust nobody till we get a handle on things."

Omohundro looked at him. "You sound a mite tetchy about these kids."

"Yeah, I reckon so," Hickok said evenly. "Bill and me done planted a slew of jaybirds that was tryin' to kill Gus and Kate. Somebody wants 'em dead awful bad."

"Planted?" Buntline appraised the word. "Are you saying you killed men to protect the children?"

Hickok shrugged. "No more'n we had to."

"So what's your move?" Omohundro asked. "You mean to contact the family?"

"Think I'll handle that," Cody said quickly, glancing at Hickok. "You'd barge in like a bull in a china shop. What we need's a tactful approach. You agree?"

"Why shore," Hickok said dryly. "You always was the diplomat of the bunch. Just don't let the cat out of the bag."

"I'll drop around to Gramercy Park tomorrow mornin'. We'll keep the kids here till things come clear."

"You've no time to lose," Buntline observed. "We open in Philadelphia day after tomorrow."

"Philadelphia?" Cody said, astounded. "What happened to New York?"

"Bill, it's a new show," Buntline said defensively. "We'll play Philadelphia for a week and work out the kinks. I want it perfect when we open here in New York."

"Well, you're the boss when it comes to the show business. Guess we're headed to Philadelphia."

Buntline was indeed the maestro. His real name was Edward Zane Judson, but he had adopted the *nom de plume* Ned Buntline. A character himself, he'd had six wives and once fought a duel over a dalliance with another man's wife. Some years ago he had been jailed for instigating a theater riot against an English actor who was in competition with Edwin Forrest, America's greatest Shakespearean. He was renowned for his dime novels, and now he'd made his name as a playwright. The Buffalo Bill Combination was his entrée into the theater.

"Forgot to ask," Cody said. "What's the name of the new show?"

Buntline swelled with pride. *"The Scouts of the Plains!"*

"Yeah, that's us," Cody said, glancing around at Hickok and Omohundro. "What's the story?"

"You might say it is *The Three Musketeers* taking battle to the warlike tribes."

Cody looked blank. "Who's the three musketeers?"

"Who—" Buntline laughed deep in his belly. "Only the grandest novel ever written by Alexander Dumas. One of the immortals!"

"Never heard of him," Cody said. "Funny name for a feller that writes dime novels."

"No, no, he was a Frenchman. Dead now scarcely two years. A genius!"

"I'll take your word for it, Ned."

Hickok crossed the room. He took a firebrand from the fireplace and lit a cheroot. His gaze fixed on Cody.

"Maybe we ought to talk about Philadelphia."

"What about it?"

Hickok exhaled smoke. "Day after tomorrow's pretty damn quick. Don't give us much time to get things settled with Kate and Gus."

"Time enough," Cody said. "I'll get the lowdown from their folks in the mornin'. We'll go from there."

"What if the lowdown ain't all we need to know? What then?"

"C'mon now, don't go borrowin' trouble. Wait and see what I ferret out."

"Just so's we're clear on things," Hickok said. "Them kids are our first order of business. Not Philadelphia."

"Hold on!" Buntline protested. "We're booked into a theater. We must be there!"

Hickok pointed the cheroot at him. "I'm not talkin' to you. This here's between me and Cody."

Buntline deflated back onto the divan. Texas Jack Omohundro, who knew a warning when he heard one, stared off into space. Cody raised his hands in mock surrender.

"The kids first," he said. "That satisfy you?"

Hickok puffed a wad of smoke. "Just wanted to hear you say it."

Buntline wondered how many men they had killed over the children. Then, on second thought, he decided he didn't want to know. His one imperative was to get them to Philadelphia.

The Scouts of the Plains must go on.

CHAPTER 14

CODY LEFT the hotel at eight o'clock the next morning. The doorman whistled up a hansom cab and gave the driver the address. The cab trundled south on Broadway into the theater district, where traffic was in a state of bedlam even at the early hour. Farther downtown, the driver turned east onto Twentieth Street.

The sky was overcast, dull pewter clouds obscuring the sun. Cody sat back in the seat, staring out at brownstones that were the current architectural vogue. His thoughts raced over the surface of the last few weeks like a dragonfly skimming the still waters of a pond. He found himself incapable of penetrating the mystery of the children's abduction, and the attempts on their lives. He wondered what revelation might be provided by their parents. Or then again, perhaps none at all.

A short while later the cab rolled into Gramercy Park. Once a marshland, the area had been reclaimed by real-estate developer Samuel Ruggles in 1831. The original square was inspired by London's St. John's Park, and required the removal of a million wagonloads of earth. Ruggles built his own mansion there in 1839, and shrewdly deeded the square to buyers of the other sixty-five plots. The neighborhood quickly became the enclave of New York aristocrats.

Gramercy Park itself was enclosed by a tall wrought-iron fence with ornate filigree. The manicured landscape was filled with sundials and cozy benches, and the surrounding residents were given gold keys to the entrance gates. The mansions, expressing the taste of their owners, were an eclectic mix of Greek Revival, Italianate, and Victorian Gothic. The elite who resided there included William Steinway, of piano fame, railroad baron Samuel Tilden, and industrialist Peter Cooper. The park, even in the dead of winter, smelled of old money.

The cab stopped at 24 Gramercy Park. Cody paid the driver and climbed a short flight of steps to the mansion. He rapped the brass door-knocker and tugged the lapels of his buckskin jacket. A butler attired in black opened the door with a neutral smile. He examined Cody's outfit at a glance.

"Yes, sir," he said formally. "May I help you?"

"I'm William Cody. I'd like to see Henry Stanley."

"Who?"

"Henry Morton Stanley. I was told he lives at 24 Gramercy Park."

The butler appeared flustered. Then, stepping aside, he motioned Cody inside. "Would you wait here, sir?"

Cody removed his hat. His gaze swept the foyer and the broad, carpeted staircase. The butler walked to a set of sliding doors and disappeared inside. He returned a moment later.

"This way please, sir."

Cody entered a lushly appointed sitting room. A strikingly handsome man was seated before the fireplace in a leather wingback chair. He was in his early thirties, with dark hair and quick gray eyes. He dropped the *Wall Street Journal* on a nearby table.

"Mr. Cody?" he said tentatively. "How may I assist you? I'm Leland Stanley."

"Your man must've misunderstood. I'm lookin' for Henry Stanley."

"May I ask the purpose of your visit?"

"You might say it's personal," Cody replied. "Maybe you could tell him I'm here."

"Actually, no," Stanley said soberly. "I'm afraid my brother passed away some three weeks ago."

"I'm powerful sorry to hear that. How'd he die?"

"Well, in point of fact, he was murdered. He and my sister-in-law, murdered in their beds. What is your interest in my brother, Mr. Cody?"

Cody abruptly put it together. Three weeks ago dovetailed with the time Katherine and Augustus had been placed on the Orphan Train. His expression betrayed nothing.

"You'll pardon my askin', Mr. Stanley. Was your brother killed the night Katherine and Augustus got abducted?"

"Why, yes—" Stanley stopped, his eyes suddenly guarded. "What do you know about Katherine and Augustus?"

"I know they're alive and well. They got put on the Orphan Train to Nebraska."

"Nebraska?"

"That's where they ended up."

"They're alive?" Stanley sounded as if he were choking on a fish bone. "You've seen them?"

"Saw 'em with my own eyes."

"Where are they now?"

Cody was a clever liar when the situation demanded. Some visceral instinct warned him that the truth would better await another time. He spread his hands in all innocence.

"They're with a friend of mine. He's on his way

here now, bringing them by train. His name's Wild
Bill Hickok."

"Hickok?" Stanley stared at him. "By any chance
are you *that* Cody? Buffalo Bill Cody?"

"Some call me that," Cody acknowledged. "Do the
children have any relatives besides yourself, Mr. Stanley?"

"Their grandmother."

"That would be your mother?"

Stanley nodded. "She's still distraught over
Henry's death. She hasn't been out of her bed since
the night he died. I'm afraid grief has made her quite
ill."

"Any other relatives?"

"Not on our side of the family. Amanda, Henry's
wife, has family in Connecticut. Why do you ask?"

Cody shrugged. "Just wondered who'd look after
'em now that their folks are gone."

"I will," Stanley said. "I *am* their uncle."

"Any idea why they were abducted?"

"Until today I didn't know what to think. The police are at their wits' end."

Cody thought it rang false. Stanley should have
been rejoicing over the news of the children. Instead,
he seemed somehow on edge, oddly nervous. Lots of
questions and no smiles.

"I'll get word to you," Cody said. "Just as soon as
Hickok arrives with the children."

Stanley's eyes were alert. "Where are you staying,
Mr. Cody?"

"The Victoria Hotel."

The lie came easily. Something told Cody to be-
ware of revealing too much. On the way out, he assured Stanley he would be in touch no later than

tomorrow. The minute Hickok's train arrived in New York.

He lied all the way to the door.

Hickok and Omohundro were seated before the fireplace. They were old friends, and Omohundro felt no qualms about asking questions others would avoid. He listened as Hickok related his deadly tenure as marshal of Abilene.

The story abruptly ended. Cody barged into the suite and the look on his face brought them out of their chairs. They knew him too well not to realize that the visit to the Stanley mansion had gone awry. Hickok cocked an eyebrow.

"What was it lit your fuse?"

"Where are the kids?"

"They're changin' clothes," Hickok said. "Giuseppina figured they wasn't outfitted proper to see their folks. She went out and bought 'em some city duds."

"Their folks are dead," Cody said, lowering his voice. "Murdered the very same night the kids were abducted. Killed in their beds."

"I'll be go to hell. How'd you find out?"

"Talked with their uncle, feller name of Leland Stanley. He wasn't exactly overjoyed to hear they're alive."

"What'd he say?"

Cody recounted the gist of the conversation. He went on to note that something about Leland Stanley raised a red flag. Nothing specific but nonetheless there.

"Just a gut hunch," he concluded. "You know the feelin'."

"Damn right," Hickok said. "We're still wearin our

topknots 'cause we got good instincts. I'd trust a gut hunch any day."

"Figured it was best to keep my trap shut. None of it makes any sense."

"No, it don't, and that's a fact. Why'd Richter abduct 'em in the first place?"

"Why not kill 'em the night he killed their folks? No doubt in my mind he's the one that done it."

" 'Course he was," Hickok said. "But why'd he try to get 'em adopted? No rhyme nor reason to it."

Cody looked baffled. "All the more so since he tried to kill 'em once they got un-adopted. Somebody didn't want them kids back here in New York."

"You think their uncle's tied into it?"

"I think there's something mighty fishy there. Told me their grandma was sick with grievin' and confined to her bed. But he was plumb disappointed to learn about the kids."

"Don't sound natural, does it?"

"What about the kids?" Omohundro interrupted. "Somebody'll have to tell them about their folks."

Hickok appeared chary. He shot a glance at Cody. "You got kids of your own. You understand 'em better than me."

"God," Cody sighed. "What'll I say?"

"Guess there ain't no way around the truth."

"Ta-dah!"

Giuseppina swept into the middle of the room. Her eyes were bright with merriment and her arms were outflung in a dramatic pose. On cue, Katherine and Augustus appeared simultaneously from the two bedrooms. Katherine wore a taffeta knee-length dress and Augustus was attired in a serge suite and a foulard tie. Their faces beamed with the fun of their new outfits.

"Aren't they darling!" Giuseppina said happily. "Have you ever seen anything so precious?"

The men stared at them with stoic expressions. The children looked confused, their smiles suddenly downturned. Katherine stepped forward.

"What's wrong?" she said shyly. "Don't you like our new clothes?"

"No, it's not that," Cody said. "You look fine. Just fine."

"What is it, then, Buffalo Bill?"

"Well, honey, we have to tell you something . . . about your folks."

"Mother and Father?" she asked. "You've talked with them?"

Cody swallowed hard. "Katherine. Augustus. I want you to be brave—" He faltered, his voice choked. "Your folks have gone to heaven."

"Heaven?" Katherine watched him with the look of a wounded fawn. "You mean they—they are . . ."

"I'm afraid so. God's took them to the Promised Land. They're at peace now."

"Nooo!" Augustus screamed. *"Noooo!"*

Katherine's eyes flooded with tears. She threw herself into Hickok's arms, burying her head against his shoulder. Augustus sobbed with a low, strangling sound, tears spilling over his cheeks. Cody pulled him into a tight hug.

Giuseppina's features went rubbery with shock. Jack rose from his chair, his expression grave, and put his arm around her shoulders. The children wept and moaned, their pitiful, broken cries filling the room. Hickok gave Katherine his handkerchief, his eyes sorrowful and oddly moist. She looked up at him with sudden terror.

"Grandmama?" she murmured timorously. "Is Grandmama . . ."

"She's fine," Hickok reassured her. "Buffalo Bill says she's still mourning your folks and not feelin' all that spry. But she'll be up and about before you know it."

"I met your Uncle Leland," Cody added, alert to her reaction. "He's taking care of your grandmother and lookin' after the house. Maybe you'd like to go stay with him?"

"*No!*" Katherine wailed. "Mother hates Uncle Leland!"

Augustus blinked back tears. "Father doesn't like him, either. He always calls him the black sheep."

"Well, don't you worry," Hickok said in a soothing tone. "We'll wait till your grandma's feelin' herself again."

The softly spoken pledge opened a new floodgate of tears. Cody motioned to Giuseppina and she gently collected the children. She led them into one of the bedrooms, cooing at their wretched sobs, and closed the door. A glum silence settled over the room.

"Out of the mouths of babes," Cody finally said. "Their father didn't have no use for his own brother. Guess I was right about Uncle Leland."

Hickok grunted. "There's just one way to keep them kids safe. We're gonna take 'em with us to Philadelphia."

"We'll only be there a week. What happens when we come back to New York?"

"I reckon we'll figure something out. We've got to."

Cody thought Buntline wouldn't like it. But just as quickly he decided to hell with it. The matter was settled.

The children were going to Philadelphia.

*   *   *

Otto Richter looked like he'd walked into a buzzsaw.
His right cheekbone was skinned raw and an ugly,
purple bruise darkened his forehead. His greatcoat
was ripped at the shoulder, and his left trouser leg
hung in shreds. He was caked with filth.

The butler showed him into the sitting room. The
gaslights were lit for the evening, and Leland Stanley
was seated before the fireplace, reading the *New York
Times*. He folded the paper, placing it on a table, and
rose from his chair. He watched Richter cross the
room with thinly veiled distaste. His features were
cold.

"What happened to you?"

"Fell off a train," Richter said vaguely. "Finally
caught another one outside of Chicago. I came
straight from the station."

"I see," Stanley remarked. "Did your accident have
anything to do with Cody and Hickok?"

"How do you know about them?"

"Cody paid me a call this morning. He told me
Hickok is on the way to New York with the children."

"That's pure bunkum," Richter said. "They're both
already here and they have the children. I've been
trailing them from Nebraska."

Stanley frowned at him. "How did Hickok and
Cody become involved?"

Richter briefed him on the last three weeks. Stanley was not wholly without conscience, and he'd always preferred that no harm come to the children. He
silently commended Richter for following orders, and
waiting until there was no alternative to killing. Yet
he was infuriated by Richter's failure to complete the
assignment.

"Why didn't you telegraph me while all this was going on?"

"I had it under control," Richter said. "Things went to hell there toward the end."

"You are a master of understatement, Otto."

"I'll handle it, Mr. Stanley. They're in my territory now."

"Not for long." Stanley gestured at the newspaper. "I was just reading an article in the *Times*. You're familiar with Cody's stage show?"

Richter nodded. "I know he's involved with Ned Buntline."

"From what I read, Buntline intends to take the show on the road before bringing it to New York. They open in Philadelphia tomorrow night."

"I assume your orders haven't changed. You still want me to take care of the children?"

Stanley considered the euphemism for murder. He wished there were another way, for he really didn't want the blood of children on his hands. But there was simply too much at stake.

"How very unfortunate," he said quietly. "But the answer to your question is yes. Take care of the children."

"I'll leave for Philadelphia in the morning."

"Otto."

"Yes?"

"You musn't fail me this time."

"Consider it done, Mr. Stanley."

Richter turned toward the door. When he was gone, Stanley stared into the fireplace a moment. His expression was contemplative, curiously saddened as he reflected on the unalterable nature of events. Finally, gathering himself, he walked into the foyer and went upstairs. He knocked lightly on his mother's bedroom door.

Elizabeth Stanley was propped up on a bank of pillows. Her features were drawn, her complexion sallow in the flickering gaslight. She managed a faint smile.

"Have you come to tuck me in, Leland?"

"I wanted to say good night, Mother. How are you feeling?"

"Oh, you shouldn't worry," she said. "I believe I'm actually a little better."

"Well, then." Stanley bent down, kissed her on the cheek. "Get a good night's sleep."

"Leland."

"Yes, Mother?"

"Have you learned anything more of Katherine and Augustus?"

"I have a first-rate detective on the job. You rest now and try not to worry yourself too much. I feel confident we'll find them."

"I pray to God they're all right."

"I'm sure they are, Mother."

Stanley lowered the flame on the gaslight. He moved from the bedroom into the hall and closed the door. His face was set in a somber cast.

He thought things would be better when the children were dead.

CHAPTER 15

THE PENN Hotel was located on the corner of Sixth Street and Chestnut. Ned Buntline, ever anxious to display his expertise, noted that it was named after the founder of Pennsylvania. King Charles II of England had bestowed a large land grant on William Penn in 1682.

Hickok was deaf to the lecture. As they walked from the hotel to the theater, he was in a highly agitated state of mind. He had faced armed men and hostile Indians and survived the bloody killing ground of the Civil War. All of that he had done with equanimity but now his nerves fairly jangled along his backbone. Tonight he would face a live audience on stage.

Cody and the others were attentive to Buntline's dissertation. The children were all eyes as they passed the most hallowed ground in the nation's history, Independence Square. Buntline explained that the Continental Congress had convened there in 1775, and appointed George Washington General of the Army. A year later, on July 4, the Declaration of Independence had been adopted.

Buntline was a fount of information. He went on to note that Philadelphia was a Greek word for "brotherly love." Thus it had become known as the City of Brotherly Love, the birthplace of American freedom. The children hung on his every word, peppering him with questions about the Liberty Bell and the Constitution. Ever the ham, Buntline basked in their wide-eyed wonder, playing the scholar to eager young acolytes. His initial displeasure at having them along had long since disappeared. He found them a receptive audience.

Cody was gladdened by the children's animated manner. Yesterday, on the train from New York, they had withdrawn into despair and heartsick torment over their loss. Then, drained of tears and emotionally exhausted, they had fallen into a troubled sleep. Late last night, when the train arrived in Philadelphia, the resilience of youth had seemingly restored their spirits. They were by no means recovered, and moments of grief still shadowed their eyes. Yet they had bounded back remarkably well.

A good part of their invigorated manner had to do with the show. The play was to be staged at the Arch Street Theater, and Buntline had assembled the cast early that morning. Local actors had been hired for the roles of savage Indians, and there was a full complement of lighting men and stagehands. The entire day had been spent in rehearsal, with Buntline coaching the actors, sometimes berating them, as they struggled to memorize their lines. Buntline's frenzied energy had at last brought vitality to the production.

Katherine and Augustus were exhilarated by the sound and fury of the play. The lights and action and bloodcurdling war cries left them agog with marvel. Neither of them had ever seen a stage production, and they spent the day watching the madness of a rehearsal unfold in the theater. Buntline was seemingly everywhere at once, and they were all but mesmerized by his stage directions and his leather-lunged exhortations at the actors. By day's end they saw chaos and confusion transformed into some semblance of orderly stagecraft. They were bewitched by the wonder of it all.

The children's turnaround eased Cody's concern for their welfare. But the burden of putting on a stage play was measurably increased by his distress at Hickok's wooden performance. Hickok seemed incapable of memorizing lines, and thoroughly bewildered by the dazzling lights and Buntline's stage directions. There were times when Buntline's frustration, expressed in shrill anger, put Hickok on the verge of throttling the voluble showman. Cody intervened, warning Buntline to calm down, and counseling Hickok to simply be himself rather than act the role. Yet he worried that Hickok and Buntline were a volatile mix. One the gunpowder and the other the match.

The Arch Street Theater was emblazoned with lights. The top line on the backlit marquee proclaimed in foot-tall letters THE SCOUTS OF THE PLAINS. The lines directly below, equally bold, announced the stars of the show: BUFFALO BILL CODY, WILD BILL HICKOK, and TEXAS JACK OMOHUNDRO. Buntline whizzed past as though he were a whirligig on course with momentous events. Hickok, startled to see his name in lights, felt a chill ripple along his spine. Cody thought it a fine display, with perhaps one exception. He wondered if his name might have been bigger.

The stage door was through an alleyway beside the theater. When they came through the door, the backstage area was in a state of pandemonium. The prop man was scurrying around with tomahawks and feathered lances, and stagehands were putting the final touches on the scenery. The ten actors playing Sioux warriors were decked out in black wigs with braids and tawny costumes meant to resemble fringed buck-skin. They were applying nut-brown greasepaint to their faces and hands in an effort to counterfeit the look of redskins. Buntline waded in like an evangelist exhorting the faithful

"Godalmighty," Hickok woofed, halting just inside the door. "I've done joined the circus."

Cody laughed. "It'll all come together when the curtain goes up."

"I ain't sure I've got the gall for this, Bill."

"Jim, you're just a little nervy, that's all. The show business people call it 'opening-night jitters.' "

"I'd sooner hunt bears with a switch."

"Stop carryin' on so. You'll be fine."

"Says you."

The show was sold out. Every seat in the house was full and a lucky few got standing room at the rear of the theater. As the audience leafed through the play-bill, they saw that the show would be presented in three acts. The subtitles fairly fired the imagination.

ACT 1. THE SCOUTS AND THE RENEGADES

ACT 2. THE SCOUTS' OATH OF VENGEANCE

ACT 3. THE TRIUMPH OF THE SCOUTS

The playbill also indicated an opening number by Mlle. Giuseppina Morlacchi. Under her resume, the audience discovered that she had studied dance at La Scala, in Milan, Italy. Her debut was in Genoa, and from there she had appeared throughout Europe and England before immigrating to America in 1869. She was the toast of New York, and her legs were insured for $100,000 by Lloyds of London. The audience fully expected to see a classical ballerina.

The curtain rose at eight o'clock. The orchestra blared to life and Giuseppina exploded out of the wings in a knee-length peekaboo gown and sheer net stockings. She pranced around the stage, her eyes bright with laughter, flapping her skirts ever higher. Then, as the tempo of the music quickened, she whirled to center stage, squealing and kicking in a rousing exhibition of the French cancan. She ended the number by leaping high in the air and landing on the stage in a full-legged split. The audience broke out in cheers.

Giuseppina blew them kisses as she skipped offstage. The curtain dropped as the orchestra segued into a stirring rendition of "The Battle Hymn of the Republic." When the number was finished, the orchestra fell silent and the curtain rose on Act One of the play. The set was designed to replicate grassy plains with majestic mountains and an endless azure sky painted on the backdrops. A campfire, constructed of orange and red crepe paper, was positioned at center stage. Cody and Hickok stood warming their hands by the fire.

The audience gave them a thunderous ovation. There were shouts from all around the theater of *"Buffalo Bill!"* and *"Wild Bill!"* Cody beamed a jack-o'-lantern grin and Hickok looked everywhere but at the crowd. After a minute, Cody finally raised his arms and stilled the applause. He struck a dramatic pose and cued Hickok with the opening line.

"Glad you found my camp, Bill. What've you been up to lately?"

Hickok froze. He opened his mouth but nothing came out. His line in the script had to do with renegade Sioux warriors raiding settlers. But his mind went blank, and he was acutely aware of the audience waiting for him to speak. Cody cued him again.

"What've you been up to lately, Bill?"

Hickok nervously cleared his throat. He said the first thing that popped into his mind. "I've been out on the hunt with the Grand Duke Alexis."

Cody blinked, momentarily thrown. But the royal hunt had been widely reported by newspapers, and he figured the audience would think it was all part of the play. He quickly improvised, feeding Hickok questions about the Grand Duke and the hunt. Once they started talking, Hickok, little by little, recovered from his stage fright. Cody gradually steered their dialogue back to the script.

The story revolved around a hostile band of Sioux. Texas Jack Omohundro next appeared onstage, to complete the trio of scouts. Shortly afterward, Giuseppina made her entrance, costumed in a wig and braids and buckskin dress. She played the part of Dove Eye, a Sioux maiden in love with Cody, offering to help the scouts thwart the renegades. The audience was held rapt by the love interest.

Act One closed with Dove Eye being captured by the hostiles. Cody, with Hickok and Omohundro at his side, swore an oath of vengeance. Throughout Act Two there were a series of running skirmishes, as the scouts pursued the renegades back and forth across the plains. The actors disguised as Sioux warriors were slaughtered wholesale, only to crawl offstage and reappear in the next battle scene. At the close of Act Two, the scouts were wearied from killing but had yet to rescue Dove Eye. They stood talking at center stage.

"We go forward," Cody emoted, dramatically

thrusting an arm overhead. "I will not cease the fight until Dove Eye is safe again."

Omohundro postured. "We are with you unto the death. Isn't that right, Wild Bill?"

A calcium spotlight from high above the balcony swung onto Hickok. He shielded his eyes, suddenly blinded, and took a step aside. The spotlight trailed him, and his temper, already frayed by an hour on-stage, abruptly snapped. He shouted at the operator. "Turn the durn thing off!"

The dazzling light held him pinned in place. One of his pistols was charged with blanks, but the other was fully loaded. He cursed under his breath, jerking the loaded Colt, and fired. A shattering of glass exploded above the balcony and the spotlight went dead. He grinned at Cody.

"Guess that jaybird'll listen now."

The audience roared with laughter. The curtain fell, ending the scene, and Buntline rushed onto the stage. Hickok waved him off, ignoring his outrage, and Cody kept them separated until the curtain rose on Act Three. The story played out in a final volcanic battle, which left the ten renegade Sioux sprawled in death. Dove Eye was saved, the scouts emerged triumphant, and the packed house erupted with applause. The cast took four curtain calls.

Otto Richter was seated at the rear of the theater. He watched as Cody and Hickok came center stage for a standing ovation. The play seemed to him more farce than drama, and quickly forgotten. His thoughts turned instead to the children, how to finish the job. A plan would evolve once he trailed them from the theater, located the hotel where they were staying. All he needed from there was a fix on their habits, their daily schedule.

A way to separate them from the Scouts of the
Plains.

Buntline hosted a breakfast for the cast the following
morning. The reviews were in and his pudgy cheeks
were cherry-red with excitement. He passed out cop-
ies of the *Philadelphia Journal* to everyone seated
around the table. The talk stopped as they fell to reading.

> *Last night at the Arch Street Theater was the scene
> of a most extraordinary drama. The occasion was
> Ned Buntline's new play with the very appropriate
> title of* The Scouts of the Plains. *Buffalo Bill Cody
> and Wild Bill Hickok, noted Western characters of
> national fame, were presented in a hair-raising
> tale of blood on the plains. They played their own
> original selves with considerable élan.*

"Élan?" Hickok said dubiously. "What the devil's
that mean?"

Buntline chortled. "You gentlemen have been
highly complimented. It means spirited and with great
self-assurance."

"Well now," Cody said with a broad smile. "I like
the sound of that."

"Keep reading," Buntline said. "There's more!"

> *Texas Jack Omohundro, a frontier figure in his
> own right, played a stalwart scout with dash and
> skill. Mlle. Giuseppina Morlacchi, the Italian dan-
> seuse, essayed the part of a beautiful Indian
> maiden with a weakness for scouts. She sustained
> the dramatic interest from first to last, captivating
> the audience.*

"You are beautiful!" Katherine bubbled. "I loved watching you, Giuseppina."

Giuseppina blushed. "You are a leetle dear to be so kind."

Augustus jiggled in his chair. "Don't forget Buffalo Bill and Wild Bill, and Texas Jack, too. They were all wonderful."

"We have a hit!" Buntline announced grandly. "We'll take New York by storm!"

"Thanks to you," Cody said. "You wrote another corker, Ned."

"Casting modesty to the winds"—Buntline preened—"I have to say I outdid myself."

"So then," Cody said, holding his gaze. "How'd we do at the box office?"

Buntline briskly rubbed his hands together. "We'll easily clear twenty-five hundred for the week. We're in the chips!"

Cody did a quick mental calculation. Buntline, the writer and producer, received the lion's share, fifty percent. Texas Jack and Giuseppina, who were worth every penny, jointly shared twenty percent of the proceeds. By rough estimate, he and Hickok would pocket close to four hundred dollars apiece for the week. He gave Hickok a sly grin.

"How do you like them apples? Told you we'd have ourselves a payday."

"No complaints," Hickok said amiably. "Long as you keep that damn spotlight out of my eyes."

Buntline's cheery manner evaporated. He pulled in his neck and puffed up like a toad. "So far as I'm concerned, we should deduct that from your share of the receipts. Do you have any idea how much calcium lights cost?"

"Who the hell cares?" Hickok said with open scorn. "That thing was so bright I couldn't see ten feet. I won't have it."

"Which raises another matter. Why were you carrying a loaded pistol? You were instructed to use blanks."

"For openers, I don't go nowhere without a loaded gun. And you don't *instruct* me to do anything. Got it?"

"Hold on now," Cody intervened. "Ned, I wanted to talk to you about that spotlight, anyway. I'm glad you brought it up."

Buntline pursed his mouth. "What about it?"

"Well, you saw for yourself, the audience went for it in a big way. I think we ought to let Wild Bill shoot out the light in every show."

"You must be joking."

"What's more important?" Cody said. "A calcium light or a nifty piece of showmanship? You stop and think about it."

Buntline thought about it. His forehead squinched with concentration and he seemed to drift off. He finally looked up. "By golly, you're right," he conceded. "The show's the thing and showmanship's the game. Wild Bill can shoot out the light."

"Figured you wouldn't let a good idea slip by."

"Of course, we'll have to have an extra spotlight. Dramatic effect is vital to the show."

"I reckon so," Cody agreed. "Just don't put the spare on Wild Bill."

"Why not?"

Hickok smiled. " 'Cause then I'd shoot out two a night."

Everyone laughed except Buntline. The humor of

it escaped him, for the show business was serious business. Nothing to be ridiculed.

He thought the Prince of Pistoleers was going to be a handful.

CHAPTER 16

TWO DAYS later Hickok stepped off the train at Grand Central Station. He walked through the terminal, again dazzled by the zodiac painted on the ceiling. He wondered how the hell painters worked that high in the air.

Outside the terminal, he flagged a hansom cab. The driver was a gnome of a man, with a dented derby hat and the apple-red nose of a drinker. He stared down at Hickok's Western garb with watery, bloodshot eyes.

"Where to?"

"The police station."

"Which one?"

"How many you got?"

"Last count there was seven, maybe eight."

"Try the one for Gramercy Park."

"That'd be the Twenty Ninth Precinct."

Hickok climbed into the cab. He settled back in the seat, wishing he'd slept more on the overnight train from Philadelphia. Yesterday, when he announced he was going to New York, Buntline had been livid. He'd told the fat man to stuff it.

The purpose of the trip was Katherine and Augustus. They were still in the dark about the children's family, and the show was scheduled to open in New York in five days. Cody agreed that it was prudent to investigate the family before returning with the children. Particularly their uncle, Leland Stanley.

The show was the least of Hickok's concerns. After two performances of *The Scouts of the Plains*, he'd never felt more the fool. Strutting about the stage, spouting ridiculous lines, seemed to him far too much humiliation for a grown man. His attention turned instead to the safety of the children, and who wanted them dead. He planned to start with the police.

The precinct house was located off Broadway on Twenty Second Street. Hickok began with the desk sergeant, insisting that he would talk only with the precinct commander. He was directed to the office of Captain Alexander Williams, located on the second floor. Williams was a square-jawed man with dark salt-and-pepper hair and the powerful build of a dockworker. His gaze fixed on Hickok's pistols.

"I see you're armed, Mr. Hickok. We have an ordinance against carrying firearms."

"Most towns do," Hickok said, taking a chair before the captain's desk. "Don't you make an exception for fellow lawmen?"

"From your dress, I take it you're a Westerner."

"Last job was marshal of Abilene, Kansas. I work off and on as a deputy U.S. marshal."

"Hickok?" Williams said in a quizzical tone. "I think I've read about you in the *Police Gazette*. Wild Bill Hickok?"

Hickok rocked his hand. "Don't believe everything you read."

"Well, it's an honor to have you in New York, Mr. Hickok. Anybody asks you about those pistols, you tell them to come see me."

"I'm obliged, Cap'n."

"Don't mention it."

Captain Alexander "Clubber" Williams was an institution in New York. As a patrolman, he had averaged a fight a day for four years, clubbing street hoodlums cold with his nightstick. In the Twenty Ninth Precinct, he formed a squad devoted to bashing neighborhood thugs senseless, with or without provocation. Newspapers quoted him as saying, "There is more law in a policeman's nightstick then in a decision of the Supreme Court." Hickok was his kind of lawman.

"Well now, what can I do for you, Mr. Hickok?"

"I'm lookin' into a matter," Hickok said. "Has to do with the murder of a New York man. Henry Morton Stanley."

Williams gave him a measured stare. "Stanley and his wife were murdered in their home, smothered to death. What's your interest in the case?"

"You done answered the first question. That's a tough way to get killed."

"We haven't got the first lead in their murders. Do you know something I don't?"

"I know their children were abducted. That's why I'm here."

"What about the children?"

Hickok told him the story. He ended with his concern about returning them to New York. Someone, he observed, meant to see them dead.

"I'd say you're right," Williams ventured carefully. "What makes you suspect their uncle?"

"Well, like I said, he wasn't exactly tickled to hear they're alive. That makes a man wonder."

"The family could force you to return the children, Mr. Hickok. That's the law."

"Yeah," Hickok conceded. " 'Course, they'd have to find 'em first. I don't aim to let that happen."

"So what do you want from me?"

"Anything you can tell me about this Leland Stanley."

Williams debated a moment. Tammany Hall, the ruling force in politics for decades, had been brought down in the 1871 elections. William "Boss" Tweed, the leader of Tammany Hall, had been exposed by the *New York Times* and indicted on charges of corruption. The reform party was now in control of the city, and wealthy businessmen were at the forefront of the movement. The Stanleys were one of the most prominent families in New York.

"I've got kids of my own," Williams said. "I'd like to help you, but it would be political suicide. I'd be kicked off the force before you could blink."

Hickok frowned. "You're sayin' the family's got political muscle?"

"They own the Guaranty Trust Bank. In this town, money talks."

"I was dependin' on the police to lend a hand. Hell, Cap'n, we're talkin about murder."

"Here's a name." Williams jotted something on a scrap of paper. "If you turn up anything solid, I'll back your play. Otherwise, we never met."

Hickok studied the name. "Who's Charlie Phelan?"

"The best private investigator in New York."

CHARLES M. PHELAN
INVESTIGATIONS

The lettering on the door was faded and chipped. The office building was located on Sixteenth Street, a block east of Union Square. Hickok rapped on the door.

"It's open!"

The voice carried the wisp of a brogue. Hickok stepped through the door and found himself in a cubbyhole of an office. There was a battered desk, a single chair for visitors, and a row of filing cabinets along one wall. A grimy widow overlooked the street.

"What can I do for you?"

Charlie Phelan rose from behind the desk. He was a broad-shouldered Irishman of considerable girth and blunt edges. His eyes were a crackling blue and he had the flattened nose of a pugilist. He extended a meaty hand.

"I'm Charlie Phelan."

"Hickok," Hickok said, accepting his handshake. "I got your name from Cap'n Williams, over at the police station."

"Did you now?" Phelan said. "You must have a delicate problem indeed, Mr. Hickok. Clubber doesn't often send business my way."

"Clubber?"

"That's his moniker. Clubber Williams, the toughest cop in the city."

"How'd he get the name?"

Phelan warmed to the subject of crime in New York. The underworld operated in three principle districts of the city. Satan's Circus, where theaters and fine restaurants were mixed with bordellos and gambling dens, was between Fifth Avenue and Eighth Avenue. Hell's Kitchen, controlled largely by the Irish, was west of Satan's Circus and dealt in every vice known to man. The Bowery, with its saloons, dance halls, and brothels, was on the Lower East Side. The gangs extorted tribute from merchants, pulled daring robberies, and performed mayhem for a price. Murder for hire was a specialty among the Bowery toughs.

"Clubber gives 'em rough justice," Phelan concluded. "They avoid him like the devil dodges Holy Water."

Hickok nodded. "Never thought of New York as a

dangerous place. Sounds worse than Kansas."

"Kansas?" Phelan studied him intently. "By the Christ, I thought you looked familiar. I've seen your picture on dime novels."

"Yeah, guess you have."

"You're Wild Bill Hickok!"

"Guilty."

Phelan laughed. "I'm proud to have you in my office, Mr. Hickok. Why'd Clubber send you to see me?"

"Murder and child abduction."

Hickok again recounted the story. He added the gist of his conversation with the police captain. When he finished, he appeared puzzled. "What's Tammany Hall, anyway?"

"Just a building," Phelan said. "Headquarters for Boss Tweed and his political cronies. In New York, Tammany Hall and dirty politics are spoken in the same breath."

"Never saw politics that wasn't dirty. Cap'n Williams acted plumb spooked about these new reformers."

"Indeed, you're talking about one of the oldest families in the city. Any investigation of the Stanleys might well put you at loggerheads with the reformers."

"Don't bother me," Hickok said. "You willin' to take the case?"

"I'm expensive," Phelan replied. "Twenty dollars a day plus expenses."

"Consider yourself hired. I want everything you can turn up on this Leland Stanley."

"And the children's grandmother? I happen to know her name is Elizabeth Stanley. She's one of the grand dames of New York society."

Hickok shrugged. "Might as well check her out, too."

"Anyone else?"

"From what Cody learned, the uncle and the grandma are the only family. I reckon that's it."

"Hmmm." Phelan steepled his fingers, thoughtful. "That raises an interesting point, Mr. Hickok."

"Like what?"

"The family fortune must be in the millions. The mother and father were murdered, which made the children the natural heirs. Sound right so far?"

"Yeah," Hickok said. "So what's your point?"

"A little known law," Phelan said. "In New York, once a person has been missing for seven years, he's declared legally dead. Maybe that's why the children were abducted, put out for adoption. To make them disappear."

"The uncle and the grandma inherit everything after seven years. That the idea?"

"There's motive enough with so much money involved."

Hickok reflected a moment. "Guess that'd explain why Richter tried to kill 'em after the adoption fell through. Except for one thing."

"Which is?" Phelan asked."

"Why not kill 'em the night their folks was murdered? Why wait seven years?"

"Killing the parents *and* the children might have tipped the police. So they were shipped off on the Orphan Train instead."

"I suppose it's possible."

"Something else to consider," Phelan added. "Maybe the grandmother—or the uncle—didn't have the heart to kill them. Not until the adoption fell through."

"Too many 'maybes,' " Hickok said. "Wish now I hadn't thrown Richter off that train. A dead man don't make much of a witness."

"Well, as they say, water under the bridge. How would you like me to handle the investigation?"

"Trail this Leland Stanley night and day. One way or another, we've got to get the goods on him."

"I'll do my best," Phelan said. "But I have to tell you, it won't be easy. So far he's kept his hands clean."

"That's the whole idea," Hickok informed him. "Way it looks, Stanley ain't much for doing his own killin'. He'll need somebody to replace Richter."

"By all the saints, you're right! A hired killer."

"Get me a name and I'll do the rest."

"What do you mean—the rest?"

Hickok smiled. "I won't throw this one off a train."

Union Square was a madhouse. The sidewalks were lined with men, and north and south on Broadway, the street was mobbed with women carrying placards. The women marched ten abreast, forcing traffic to the curbs by sheer weight of numbers. Their voices rang out in a strident chant.

"We want the vote! We want the vote now!"

Hickok heard the roar as he approached the corner. The men on the sidewalks jeered back with catcalls and ribald shouts. The women waved their placards, drowning out the men with the shrill vibrato of their chant. Union Square pulsated with the riotous clamor.

Policemen were stationed all along the street. On the near corner, Hickok saw Captain Clubber Williams watching the crowds with a jaundiced eye. He bulled his way through knots of men bellowing to make themselves heard over the women. He stopped beside Williams at curbside.

"Howdy, Cap'n," he said, gesturing at the women. "What the hell's all this?"

"A suffragette parade," Williams said dryly. "The ladies think they're entitled to the vote."

"I never heard of such a thing." Hickok seemed shocked. "Women and politics ain't . . . natural."

"You don't have suffragettes out West?"

"None I've ever seen."

"Well, I estimate you're looking at three thousand or more today. There's their leader. Victoria Woodhull."

Hickok saw a woman in a skirt and mannish jacket, wearing a floppy tie. "I'll be jiggered," he said in amazement. "Looks like she's tryn' to be one of the boys."

Williams snorted. "Well she should, Mr. Hickok. She's running for president."

"You're joshing me."

"No, sir, it's no joshing matter."

Williams went on to explain. The National Women's Suffrage Association and its sister organization, the American Woman Suffrage Association, advocated the right of women to vote. Victoria Woodhull, the radical of the movement, agitated for legalized prostitution, birth control, and the ballot. Her crusade for the enfranchisement of women led to an open challenge against Democrats and Republicans. She was the presidential candidate of the new People's Party.

"Think about it," Williams said. "How'd you like to have her in the White House?"

"Plumb scary," Hickok grumped. "A president in bloomers ain't no way to run a country."

"Not to worry yourself, Mr. Hickok. Hell will freeze over before women get the vote."

"Yeah, I suspect you're right, Cap'n."

Williams lowered his voice. "Did you have that talk with Charlie Phelan?"

"Shore did," Hickok said. "I've just come from there. He's on the case."

"Where will he start his investigation?"

"Told him to stick to Leland Stanley like a tick on a dog."

"Charlie knows his business. If there's anything shady, he'll get to the bottom of it. You're in good hands."

"I'm obliged for the introduction."

"Afraid I have to move on, Mr. Hickok. Let me know how things work out."

Williams walked off as the suffragettes marched north on Broadway. Hickok waited until the crowds thinned out and street traffic was restored to normal. He flagged a cab and told the driver to take him to Grand Central Station. He planned to be back in Philadelphia by morning.

On the ride uptown Hickok fell into a reflective mood. He couldn't shake the thought of three thousand women parading in their crusade for the vote. Nor could he fathom a woman candidate for president.

New York, he told himself, was a strange place. Damn near another country, and a world apart.

He longed yet again for the Western Plains.

CHAPTER 17

OTTO RICHTER took three days to formulate a plan. He worked on the premise that Hickok and Cody were immune to offers of money, however great the amount. Nor would they surrender the children when confronted by violence and violent men. He needed something to offer in exchange.

A trade.

The first step was to organize a gang. He'd wired Billy McGlory, the underworld boss of New York's Bowery district. McGlory was the undisputed czar of vice and criminal enterprise on the Lower East Side. Theft, robbery, even murder for hire fell under his domain. His word was law.

Their friendship went back to childhood. Richter was the son of German immigrants, and McGlory was third-generation Irish-American. Despite their cultural differences, they were drawn together in youthful paroxysms of muggery and violence. They grew to manhood by ruling the streets.

McGlory, with Machiavellian ruthlessness, became the kingpin of the Lower East Side. He bought corrupt politicians and bribed cops, and operated with impunity from the law. Richter, with an aptitude for intrigue and violence, became the enforcer. His trademark was murder for hire.

Within hours after his wire to New York, Richter had a reply, and a name. McGlory's counterpart in Philadelphia was Teddy Ryan, overlord of crime in the City of Brotherly Love. A meeting with Ryan re-

sulted in the loan of four hooligans for whatever purpose Richter saw fit. The men were seasoned thugs,
adept with knife or gun.

Richter put them to work the same day. He
couldn't afford to be seen, for both Hickok and Cody
knew him on sight. So he established an around-the-
clock surveillance, employing the four thugs as his
eyes and ears. From morning till night, the men shadowed the movements of everyone in the stage troupe.
No one went anywhere without being followed.

The first two days, the problem became apparent.
The children were constantly accompanied by Hickok
and Cody, either at the hotel or the theater. A direct
confrontation would have resulted in a gunfight, and
Richter was wary of violence in a strange town. Even
more, he was wary of Hickok and Cody. He'd seen
them in action.

Then, after the second performance of the show,
Hickok had boarded the night train for New York.
The move caught Richter by surprise, and he was at
a loss as to the purpose of the trip. But Hickok's
departure improved the odds, and he thought he'd at
last gained the edge. The notion was quickly dis-
pelled.

Texas Jack Omohundro stepped in to fill the void.
He assumed Hickok's role as bodyguard, and along
with Cody, escorted the children to and from the theater. Omohundro carried a Colt six-gun strapped to
his hip, and there was small doubt he would use it if
the occasion demanded. His reputation as an Indian
fighter was second only to Cody.

Richter felt stymied at every turn. Time was dwin-
dling away, for he had to complete the job before the
end of the week. The show was scheduled to open in
New York next week, and he'd given his word to

Leland Stanley. He was a godless man, unburdened by conscience or scruple; but he prided himself on always keeping his word. He would somehow ensure that the children never returned to New York.

The four thugs routinely kept him abreast of their surveillance. Last night, sifting through all he'd learned, he suddenly came up with the masterstroke. Texas Jack Omohundro, his tastes refined by city life, was apparently fond of brioche for breakfast. Yet he clearly couldn't be bothered to run his own errands. He sent his wife instead.

Giuseppina, though a star of the stage, was nonetheless a dutiful spouse. Every morning she walked to a French bakery on Seventh Street, to fetch a bag of the buttery, freshly baked rolls for her husband. One of the thugs had followed her three days running, and her errand never varied by more than a few minutes. She was there when the brioche came out of the oven.

Early that morning a closed carriage parked at the corner of Seventh and Walnut. One of the thugs occupied the driver's seat and the other three were inside the cab. Marcel's French Bakery was a half block north of their position, on the west side of Seventh. The sky was bright and clear, and they watched as Giuseppina hurried along the street. She ducked into the bakery.

The driver snapped the reins. The matched set of bays leaned into the traces and the carriage slowly rolled north along Seventh. A moment later Giuseppina emerged from the bakery, carrying a bag of piping-hot brioche. The carriage swerved across the street, the driver timing it perfectly, and skidded to a halt before the bakery. The three thugs jumped from the cab.

Giuseppina screamed as they grabbed her. But she was overpowered, lifted off her feet, one of the men clamping a hand over her mouth. They quickly wrestled her into the cab, forcing her onto the floorboard, and slammed the door. Several passersby watched helplessly, frozen by the swift and brutal efficiency of the attack. The carriage rounded the corner onto Sansom Street.

Some ten minutes later the carriage rolled through the doors of a warehouse on the Delaware River. One of the thugs closed and barred the doors, and Giuseppina was unloaded from inside the cab. Richter walked forward as she shook free, straightening her coat, and looked at him with a terrified expression. His mouth crooked in an evil grin.

He had his hostage.

Hickok entered the hotel shortly before eleven o'clock that morning. Upstairs, he proceeded to the suite that he shared with Cody and the children. He unlocked the door and stopped dead in the entryway. His eyes swept the room.

Cody stood at the window, staring out over the city. Buntline was seated on the sofa, his gaze fixed on the crackling flames in the fireplace. Omohundro was hunched forward in a chair, head in his hands, his eyes hollow. They looked like three men at a wake.

Hickok closed the door. "What's going on here?"

"Jim!" Cody turned from the window, rushed forward. "God, I'm glad you're back."

"That makes two of us. Why the long faces?"

"They've got Giuseppina!"

"Who's got Giuseppina?"

"We don't know." Cody snatched a sheet of paper off the table by the sofa. "Here, read this."

We have Mrs. Omohundro. She is safe for now, but dead unless you follow orders. Bring the children to Penn's Landing at midnight, the park by the river. We will exchange Mrs. Omohundro for the children. Try anything smart and she dies.

Hickok looked up. "Where'd you get this?"

"A bellman delivered it," Cody replied. "He said a man walked in and gave him a dollar to bring it up. He couldn't tell us much about the man."

"Let's hear it, anyway."

"Stoutly built, medium height, rough-looking. Wearing a cheap suit."

"You called in the police?"

"We talked it over and decided it's not a good move. Jack's afraid it'd hurt Giuseppina's chances."

"How do we know somebody's actually got her? You're sure she's missing?"

Cody explained about Giuseppina's morning trip to the bakery. When she failed to return, Omohundro went looking for her and discovered that she'd been abducted off the street. The note had arrived shortly after his return to the hotel.

"No question they've got her," Cody said at length. "The question is who's 'they'?"

"Probably the kids' uncle," Hickok said. "If we're right, he's the one that Richter feller was workin' for. Like as not, he hired somebody to replace Richter."

Omohundro rose from his chair. His features were a mask of tightly constrained fury. "Whoever the hell it is, I'd like to get my hands on him. What sort of slimy bastard steals women and kids?"

"Don't worry, Jack," Cody said, trying to calm his fear. "We'll get Giuseppina back."

"Damn sure will," Hickok said, nodding agreement. "Where are the kids, anyway?"

"In their bedroom," Cody said. "They're pretty upset about Giuseppina. Got it in their heads it's their fault."

Omohundro grimaced. "I tried to tell 'em it wasn't so. Guess they're too young to understand."

"Not anybody's fault," Hickok said tersely. "We're dealin' with the sorriest sonsabitches I ever run across."

Cody pulled at his goatee. "You find out anything in New York?"

"Hired us a private investigator."

Hickok related how he'd come to retain Charlie Phelan. The political situation, he noted, made it difficult, for the Stanleys were one of the most influential families in New York. He was nonetheless confident.

"Got a good feelin' about this Charlie Phelan. Whatever's to be found, he'll root it out."

A knock sounded at the door. Buntline scooted off the sofa and hurried across the room. When he opened the door, two midgets stood in the hallway. He greeted them effusively.

The midgets were in their late thirties. They were dressed in pint-sized business suits, and appeared to be somewhere around three feet tall. Buntline ushered them into the suite.

"Gentlemen," he said, turning to the others. "This is Orville Beatty and Noah Foster. They're headliners over at the Orphieum Vaudeville Theater."

Hickok looked baffled. Cody laughed and slapped him on the shoulder. "Orville and Noah have agreed

to help us rescue Giuseppina. They're gonna imper-
sonate Katherine and Augustus."

"Yeah?" Hickok said hesitantly. "How you figure
to pull that off?"

"We're actors," Beatty said in a piping voice.
"Noah will wear a dress and I'll wear boy's clothes.
We'll look—and *act*—the part of children."

Cody nodded. "Nobody'll be able to tell the difference in the dark. We'll fool 'em pretty as you
please."

"Might just work," Hickok said, studying the
midgets more closely. "Whose idea was it?"

"Ned come up with it," Cody said, grinning.
"Leave it to a showman when you need a little
magic."

Hickok thought he might revise his opinion of
Buntline. His gaze shifted to the midgets. "What is it
you gents do in vaudeville?"

"Song and dance men." Noah Foster straightened
to his full height. "We're the best in the business."

"Well, I have to hand it to you, you've got guts.
There's liable to be some fireworks tonight."

Foster proudly cocked his chin. "Giuseppina Morlacchi is a fellow actor. How could we not help her?"

"Exactly!" Beatty chimed in. "One for all and all
for one in the show business. It's a matter of honor."

Hickok thought the midgets were taller than they
looked.

A brisk wind whipped in off the river. The indigo sky
glittered with stars, flooding the park grounds in a
spectral light. The eerie moan of the wind echoed
through the trees.

Penn's Landing fronted the shoreline of the Delaware River. There, in 1682, William Penn first

stepped ashore to claim his land grant. The park, named in his honor, comprised nearly forty acres of trees, with a broad meadow in the center. From north to south, the park stretched almost a half mile.

Not long before midnight a carriage halted along Delaware Avenue. The wide thoroughfare bordered Penn's Landing on the west, and the carriage stopped almost midpoint with the park. The door opened and Hickok stepped out, the brace of ivory-handled Colts wedged in his sash. Cody was next, followed by Omohundro and Buntline, and the two midgets. They stood scanning the expanse of trees.

Cody and Omohundro wore gun belts with holstered pistols. Buntline, game for a fight and armed with a bulldog revolver, tried to keep his hands from shaking. Orville Beatty was attired in a knee-length coat and a slouch hat, which obscured his features. Noah Foster was tricked out in a dress and shawl, and a long, black wig taken from the theater. In the dark, without close inspection, they would pass for the children.

North of Penn's Landing, the masts of ships moored at wharves were framed against the sky. The men waited a moment longer, wary of trickery, alert to any movement in the trees. Earlier that evening Cody, Hickok and Omohundro had managed a stilted performance in *The Scouts of the Plains*. Beatty and Foster, their minds elsewhere, had mechanically plodded through their act at the vaudeville theater. But now, waiting by the carriage, their focus was on the show ahead. They were about to give the performance of their lives.

Hickok led the way. He walked along a pathway through the trees, followed by Cody and the costumed midgets. Omohundro and Buntline, their guns drawn and leery of every shadow, brought up the rear. The pathway ended at the edge of the treeline, opening onto a grassy meadow dimly lighted by the stars. The men paused on the verge of the meadow, where Hickok, Omohundro, and Buntline melted into the trees. Cody stepped forward.

"This is Bill Cody!" he shouted. "Anybody out there?"

"We're here," a voice called back. "Do you have the kids?"

"Look for yourself." Cody put his arms around the midgets. "Do you have Mrs. Omohundro?"

"Here she is." A man stepped from the trees across the way, holding Giuseppina's arm. "We'll meet in the middle and make the trade."

"I warn you, don't try any dumb stunts. I have men covering me with guns."

"That goes both ways, Cody. My boys have got you in their sights right now."

"Then we've got ourselves a standoff. Let's get this business done."

Cody walked forward with the midgets. On the opposite treeline, the man moved out, still holding Giuseppina by the arm. They were on a direct line, and some moments later, they came together in the center of the meadow. Giuseppina looked terrified, and Cody, peering closer, was astounded by what he saw. The man before him was a man he'd thought dead—Richter!

Richter squinted in the pale starlight. He looked from one midget to the other, visibly startled. "What the hell—"

Their plan went off like clockwork. Cody tackled Giuseppina, throwing her down, and the midgets dropped to the ground. Hickok opened fire from the trees, followed an instant later by Omohundro and Buntline. The air sizzled with the whine of slugs.

Richter took off running. The opposite treeline blossomed with flame as the roar of four pistols split the night. Hickok sighted on a muzzle flash and lightly feathered the trigger. A man screamed, stumbling from the trees, and pitched to the ground. Omohundro, aiming at a streak of muzzle blast, wounded another man. Richter disappeared into the trees.

Cody opened fire. Hickok, along with Omohundro and Buntline, sprayed the opposite treeline with lead. Orville Beatty and Noah Foster pulled Giuseppina to her feet and scuttled back across the meadow. Cody retreated, firing as he moved, covered by a rattling volley from Hickok and the other men. He made it into the trees unscathed.

The meadow went silent. Giuseppina fell into Omohundro's arms, and Hickok stood vigilant as the gunfire abruptly ceased from the opposite treeline. Omohundro led his wife back through the darkened pathway, trailed closely by Buntline and the midgets. Cody and Hickok acted as rearguard.

Cody huffed. "You're not gonna believe it when I tell you."

"Tell me what?"

"That jasper back in the meadow—it was Richter."

"Richter!" Hickok parroted. "You know damn well I threw him off that train. I killed the bastard."

"Well, Jim, he's done riz from the dead."

"Sonovabitch!"

CHAPTER 18

HICKOK HURRIED through Grand Central Station. His mind was focused on other matters, and he scarcely glanced at the colorful zodiac on the ceiling. He hopped into a cab on Forty Second Street.

The buildings of New York's skyline rose stark against overcast clouds. Hickok had caught the milk-run train from Philadelphia, departing at three that morning. He was tired and still confounded by Cody, who had argued against his leaving. He decided he'd taught Cody more about scouting than about trailing desperadoes. He knew he was right about Richter.

The cab dropped him at Union Square. He hadn't eaten since last night, and he stepped into a café, where he wolfed down a quick order of hash and eggs. Outside again, he felt somewhat restored, and took a moment to light a cheroot. He checked his pocket watch and saw that it was approaching two o'clock. He crossed the square to Sixteenth Street.

Charlie Phelan was seated at his desk. He looked up as Hickok came through the door. "You're a regular gadabout, Mr. Hickok. I hadn't expected to see you so soon."

"Have to stay on the move," Hickok said, taking a chair. "Things are happening fast."

"Are you talking about Philadelphia?"

"You recollect me mentioning a feller named Richter?"

"Why sure, the one we thought was working for Stanley."

"Appears he's come back from the grave."

"He's alive?"

" 'Fraid so."

Hickok briefed him on the abduction and rescue of Giuseppina. Phelan appeared dumbstruck as he listened to the role played by the midgets, and openly impressed by the outcome of the shootout. He wagged his head.

"I see why they call you Wild Bill," he said humorously. "That's the damnedest story I ever heard."

Hickok waved it off. "Thing is, I think Richter's headed back to New York. Maybe he's already here."

"What leads you to believe that?"

"Well, he made his play in Philadelphia and he lost. I've got a hunch his next try will be on home ground. Just figures he'd know the show opens here in two days."

"Let me understand," Phelan said. "He botched the job there, and two days gives him time to hatch a plan for New York. Is that the idea?"

"Yep." Hickok puffed his cheroot, sent eddies of smoke curling toward the ceiling. "Way I've got him pegged, he don't do nothin' on the spur of the moment. He plans it out first."

"Sounds reasonable to me."

"On top of that, he'd likely want to check in with Stanley. We might just catch 'em with their pants down."

Phelan smiled. "Wouldn't that make our case!"

"Damn tootin'," Hickok said, almost jovial. "How're you doing with your investigation?"

"Not to brag, but I've uncovered enough dirt to plant a garden."

Phelan recounted the details. Leland Stanley was a wastrel and a spendthrift, heavily in debt to many of

New York's classier casinos. His livelihood was derived from a trust fund established by his long-deceased father, and the principle was badly depleted. Until his brother's death, he had been living in a modest flat, and to all appearances, practically broke. To top it off, he reputation was that of a dissolute libertine.

"Never worked a day in his life," Phelan said sardonically. "He's what New Yorker's call a playboy."

"Playboy?" Hickok repeated. "What's that mean?"

"A term coined by the social crowd. Someone who spends his time chasing after showgirls. Our Mr. Stanley is out on the town every night."

"You work fast. How'd you find out all this?"

"Last night I tailed Stanley to John Morrissey's casino. I've done Morrissey a favor here and there over the years. He gave me the lowdown on Stanley."

"What about the bank?" Hickok asked. "Stanley spend any time there?"

"Not much," Phelan said. "When his brother died, he took over as president of Guaranty Trust. But the rumor's about that he's little more than a figurehead. His work day is usually eleven to three."

"So he'll be leavin' pretty quick, won't he?"

"You can set your watch he's out the door at three sharp."

"Let's go." Hickok got to his feet. "We'll just tag along and see what happens. We might get lucky."

"How long do you plan to tail him?"

"Till he leads us to Richter."

Twenty minutes later they were posted at the lower end of Fifth Avenue. A block south of their position was the tall marble archway that opened onto Washington Square. Directly across the street was the granite façade of the Guaranty Trust Bank. Everything about the building reeked of old money.

Leland Stanley emerged from the bank at two-fifty-nine. He was nattily attired in a chesterfield topcoat with a velvet collar and a silk stovepipe hat. A carriage waited at curbside, and the driver jumped down to open the door. Stanley tipped his hat to a lady as he crossed the sidewalk.

"Handsome devil, ain't he?" Hickok joked. "Bet he's hell with the women."

"God loves a sinner," Phelan joked. "First time you've see him?"

"Yeah, but it won't be the last time. We're gonna stick to him like a burr under a saddle."

"I take it that's fairly tight."

"Charlie, it don't get no tighter."

Phelan flagged a hackney cab. He held the door for Hickok, then ordered the driver to follow the carriage. As he stepped inside, he smiled to himself, struck by the vagaries of a detective's life. He was actually on the chase with Wild Bill Hickok.

He wondered if he would earn his spurs tonight.

Gaslights flickered like fireflies around Gramercy Park. The overcast sky made the night dark as pitch, and there was a sharp bite to the air. Hickok and Phelan sat huddled in a hackney cab.

Their vigil was now into its fourth hour. After following Stanley from the bank, they had parked just off the corner of Twentieth Street and Irving Place. Their stomachs groaned with hunger and the collars of their coats were turned up against the chill of the night. They watched the mansion through the foggy cab window.

"Wish we'd got supper," Hickok said, staring at the mansion. "You sure he'll come out again?"

"Quite sure," Phelan said with conviction. "Our Mr. Stanley is a night owl. He always goes out."

"Guess a man in your line of work gets used to waitin'. How long you been a detective?"

"I worked with the Pinkertons during the war and a year or so after the peace. I finally decided to go on my own."

The Pinkerton Detective Agency, operating out of Chicago, was the largest investigative agency in the world. Under the direction of founder Allan Pinkerton, the agency had organized a spy network for the Union during the Civil War. The Pinkertons were currently involved in tracking the Missouri bandit leader, Jesse James.

"I done a little spy work myself," Hickok said. " 'Course, out West, we wasn't as organized as the Pinkertons."

"I remember reading about it," Phelan said. "Your adventures have been well-documented in the dime novels."

"Half that stuff is pure beeswax. Damn writers invent—"

Hickok stopped. A carriage rolled to a halt outside the mansion. The front door opened and Stanley came down the steps. He was dressed in white tie and tails and a long evening cape. He crossed the walkway to the carriage.

"Look at that outfit," Hickok said. "He's a regular dandy, ain't he?"

Phelan laughed. "A man about town has to look the part. The showgirls expect it."

"Does he have a special girl?"

"Our Mr. Stanley likes to spread his charms around. A different girl every night."

They followed the carriage to the Strand Theater

on Broadway. The feature attraction was the Lydia Thompson Burlesque Company, fresh from England. The company consisted of eight buxom blondes who sang wicked ballads and performed high-stepping dance routines. Their act flaunted conventional morality with gleeful satire.

The advent of showgirls in burlesque theaters gave rise to the playboy. Wealthy businessmen, the majority of them married, vied for the attentions of tartish singers and dancers. The men lavished jewelry and flowers on the girls, and openly squired them around to New York's after-hours nightspots. The girls, accustomed to bartering their wares, offered love for sale.

Leland Stanley was considered a prize. Unlike most playboys, he was a wealthy bachelor, and perhaps susceptible to marriage. Late that evening, he left the burlesque theater with the star of the show, Lydia Thompson. She was voluptuous, with an hourglass figure, and seemingly entranced by his urbane wit. He took her to a concert saloon on the west side of Union Square.

A theatrical variety hall, the concert saloon was a New York institution. The nightspots presented comedians, half-nude chorus lines, and singers who belted out raunchy tales to the accompaniment of a small orchestra. There were tables and chairs on the main floor, and private booths on the balcony overlooked the stage. The waitresses wore high tasseled red boots and dresses that covered hardly anything.

Stanley and his British showgirl were escorted to a booth on the balcony. Hickok and Phelan took a table downstairs, which afforded a direct view of the booth. The room was packed with a boisterous crowd laughing and cheering at the rowdy antics of the performers. The orchestra segued into a high-stepping number and a bevy of chorus girls pranced out of the wings. The audience greeted them with giddy applause.

Hickok ordered a whiskey and Phelan a beer. The chorus line was still jiggling around the stage when the waitress returned with their drinks. Hickok sipped his whiskey, then suddenly tensed, lowering his glass to the table. He nodded at the balcony.

"Take a peek," he said. "There's our boy."

Phelan glanced at the booth. "That's Richter?"

"In the flesh."

Richter tapped Stanley on the shoulder. Stanley turned, acknowledging him with a curt look, then said something to the British showgirl. She smiled engagingly, and Stanley rose from his chair, joining Richter at the rear of the booth. Their conversation appeared heated, with Richter subjected to a sharp grilling. Stanley's features were flushed with anger.

"No doubts now," Hickok said. "Stanley was behind it the whole time."

Phelan nodded. "Doesn't look too happy, does he?"

"I'd just guess he expected better news from Philadelphia."

Stanley abruptly ended the conversation with a jerky wave. Richter turned away, his mouth clamped tight, and disappeared through a curtain at the back of the booth. Hickok dropped a double eagle on the table. "Let's go."

"You mean to follow Richter?"

"I aim to capture the bastard. He don't know it but he's gonna give us Stanley."

They rose from their table. As they started forward, they were blocked by a crush of people watching the show from the rear of the room. Hickok cleaved a path through the crowd and spotted Richter hurrying out the entrance. He cursed, roughly shoving people aside.

On the street, they saw Richter step into a hansom cab. Phelan whistled another cab to a stop and jerked open the door. Hickok clambered aboard beside the driver, ordering him to move out. Phelan jumped inside.

They trailed Richter's cab down Broadway.

The Bowery glittered with clusters of varicolored glass globes lighted by gas. The streets were alive with working-class theaters presenting flea circuses, equestrian acts, and blackface minstrel shows. One marquee boasted the risqué attraction of *Fifty Nice Girls in Naughty Sketches.*

Billy McGlory's Armory Hall was located on Hester Street. Headquarters for McGlory and his gang of hooligans, Armory Hall was infamous throughout the Bowery. The establishment was a saloon and dance hall, with the dance floor occasionally converted to an arena for prizefights. No one went there expecting light entertainment. Richter's cab let him off in front of Armory Hall. As he pushed through the door, Hickok ordered his driver to stop at the corner. He gave the driver a gold eagle and hopped down to the curb. Phelan stepped out of the cab.

"Let's not rush into anything," he said, as the cab pulled away. "You're probably not familiar with Billy McGlory."

Hickok looked at him. "Who's Billy McGlory?"

"The boss of all that's unholy on the Lower East Side. He's nobody to mess with."

"You think Richter's tied in with him?"

"I do now," Phelan said. "He leaves Stanley and comes straight to McGlory's dive. I'd say there's a connection."

"One way to find out," Hickok observed. "I'm going in there and get Richter. You coming along?"

"Well never get out of there alive."

"You armed?"

"Yes."

"Just follow my lead."

Hickok walked directly to Armory Hall. As he went through the door, Phelan fell in at his side. A long mahogany bar was at the front of the room, with tables and chairs along the opposite wall. The dance floor was at the rear, with a piano, a fiddle player, and a trumpeter. The place was jammed with a late-night crowd.

Richter was seated at a table toward the rear. He was talking to a beefy, thick-shouldered man with the face of a cherub and the eyes of a stone-cold killer. He glanced up and saw Hickok by the door and his face went chalky. He spoke to the man, who gave Hickok a look that could have cracked a rock. Then he pushed back his chair and hurried across the dance floor. He disappeared through a door at the rear of the room.

Hickok started forward, Phelan a pace behind. Billy McGlory stood, circling the table, and walked to the end of the bar. He motioned to four men ganged around the counter and they quickly formed a phalanx behind him. He moved to block Hickok's path.

"Far enough," he said, hooking his thumbs in his vest. "You and your friend get while the getting's good."

Hickok stared at him. "Hand over Richter and we won't have any trouble."

"Otto's out the back door and well gone by now. You've come up short this night."

"I'll just have a look in that back room."

"I think not," McGlory said in a rumbling voice. "I'm told you're none other than Wild Bill Hickok. Is it true?"

"You were told right," Hickok said. "You and your boys stand aside. I'm comin' through."

McGlory gestured with his head. The four hooligans started around him, three armed with blackjacks, and one with brassknuckles. Hickok pulled his Colts in a blurred motion, thumbing the hammers. His eyes went cold.

"Which one of you peckerheads wants to die first?"

The men shuffled to a stop. A muscle ticced at McGlory's jawline and his features went flat. Phelan edged closer to Hickok.

"Time to leave," he said. "There's a bunch of his men behind us. Not the best of odds."

"Cover my back."

Hickok waited for the detective to draw his revolver and turn to face the crowd. Then he nodded to McGlory. "Tell Richter he's dead the next time I see him."

McGlory laughed. "You're out of your league, Hickok. Don't come back to the Bowery."

"You got it bassackwards, bub. Don't make me come back."

Phelan cleared a path through the crowd. Hickok slowly backed away, one Colt still trained on McGlory as they went out the door. On the street, they turned north toward Union Square.

"Whew!" Phelan let out a gusty breath. "There for a minute, I almost wet my drawers."

Hickok wasn't amused. "That goddamn Richter's got more lives than a cat."

"You think he'll show up again?"

"I shorely do hope so, Charlie."

"What do you mean?"

"Richter's the key to Leland Stanley."

"You don't quit, do you?"

"Not while I can fog a mirror."

They walked off into the night.

CHAPTER 19

THE BUFFALO Bill Combination arrived in New York the morning of February 7. The show was scheduled to open that night, and everyone in the troupe was in high spirits. The Philadelphia engagement had played to sold-out houses.

Hickok met them at the platform. He was accompanied by Charlie Phelan, who was now retained as a full-time bodyguard for the children. Their dustup in the Bowery had convinced him the detective was reliable in a tight situation, and willing to use a gun. He thought the children would be safe in Phelan's care.

Katherine ran ahead of the others. "Oh, Wild Bill!" she squealed, throwing herself into his arms. "I've missed you so!"

"Missed you, too," Hickok said, holding her with one arm as he reached for Augustus with the other. "How's tricks with you, Gus?"

"I'm fine, Wild Bill." Augustus hugged him tightly. "Why didn't you come back to Philadelphia?"

"Well, I had business that needed tendin' here. Figured I'd just wait till Buffalo Bill brought you along."

Cody gave him a look. "Got that business tended to, did you?"

"Tell you about it later," Hickok said. "Shake hands with Charlie Phelan."

"Glad to," Cody said, clasping the detective's hand. "Heard good things about you, Charlie."

Hickok exchanged handshakes with Buntline and

Omohundro, and Giuseppina gave him a big kiss. Three porters appeared with large steamer trunks loaded onto carts. The trunks were packed with the show's costumes and assorted paraphernalia. Buntline told them he'd wired ahead for a delivery wagon.

"I have to run," he said, fidgeting with excitement. "I'll arrange everything at the theater for this afternoon's rehearsal. Remember, one o'clock sharp!"

"We'll be there," Cody assured him. "I just suspect Wild Bill needs a little rehearsal."

"Yes, I daresay he does!"

Buntline dashed off after the porters. The children clung to Hickok as the party mounted the stairs to Grand Central Station. Phelan fell in behind the children, his eyes searching the throngs of passengers as they walked through the main terminal. They emerged onto Forty Second Street.

A horse hooked to a cab relieved itself as they crossed the sidewalk. "How's your nose holding out?" Omohundro inquired of Hickok. "You got used to all these horses yet?"

"Tell you what, Jack," Hickok said, deadpan. "Day I do, that's the day to move on. I'll know my sniffer's ruint for good."

Giuseppina giggled. "I must say I love it anyway. It is so—New York!"

"Yeah," Hickok agreed. "Ain't roses, that's for shore."

Some while later they were again settled into the suite at the Fifth Avenue Hotel. Giuseppina took the children into their bedroom to unpack, and closed the door. Hickok dropped into a chair by the fireplace and the other men got themselves seated. He looked across at Cody.

"How's Gus and Kate holdin' up?"

"Pretty fair," Cody said. "They get weepy now and then, but that's to be expected. It's only been a week."

"Seems more like a month," Hickok allowed. "Fightin' Injuns ain't nothin' compared to the savages hereabouts."

"Had your hands full, have you?"

"Yeah, and then some."

Hickok gave him a quick account of the past two days. He established the connection between Richter and Stanley, and went on to relate the Bowery stand-off with Billy McGlory. He ended by nodding to Phelan.

"Charlie will bear me out. There ain't no bottom to this goddamn sinkhole."

Cody shook his head. "You're sayin' this McGlory will back Richter's play?"

"No doubt about it," Hickok said firmly. "We're up against a whole passel of the bastards."

"You're the expert on cutthroats and desperadoes. How do we handle it?"

"For openers—" Hickok pointed to Phelan. "I've hired Charlie to guard the kids while we're busy with the show. He'll stick with 'em like a mustard plaster."

"Sounds like a good start. What else?"

"Jack and Giuseppina," Hickok said. "I want 'em moved into this hotel today. Jack can spell Charlie when need be, and we'll know Giuseppina's safe. I don't see no other way."

Cody turned to Omohundro. "That all right with you, Jack?"

"Bet your boots," Omohundro affirmed. "We can't have her abducted again. Once was enough."

"Buntline will pay for the room," Cody said. "He'll squeal like a pig, but the hell with it. We're through taking chances."

"Let's understand," Hickok told them. "Here in the hotel, at the theater, wherever we are—them kids ain't never left alone."

Cody considered a moment. "You got any idea a'tall how Richter will come at us?"

"Nope," Hickok admitted. "Forgot to tell you we learned his first name. He's called Otto."

"Sorry scutter," Omohundro cursed. "I'd sooner call him dead."

"Jack, you mark my word," Hickok said. "You'll get a bellyful of killin' before it's over."

Charlie Phelan thought it the words of an oracle.

The theater district was known simply as The Rialto. To New Yorkers, the term alone implied the very heart of American theater. The world's greatest actors were to be found there.

Lawrence Barrett was starring in *Julius Caesar*. Edwin Booth, brother of Lincoln's assassin and the country's foremost tragedian, was in a year-long run of *Hamlet*. Joseph Jefferson, one of the most popular actors of the day, was playing in *Rip Van Winkle*.

The Rialto was situated along Broadway. A half-mile stretch, from Union Square to Madison Square, encompassed virtually the whole of New York's legitimate theater. The term "legitimate" was commonly used to distinguish traditional theater from burlesque and vaudeville. The wealthier class considered The Rialto fashionable in any season.

The Lyceum Theater, located at Broadway and Twenty Second, was a modern showcase along The Rialto. The marquee was emblazoned with THE SCOUTS OF THE PLAINS, and the crowds began arriving shortly after seven o'clock. A long line of landau and brougham carriages deposited the city's aristocracy outside the theater.

The opening night show was sold out. Buffalo Bill Cody and Wild Bill Hickok, and to a lesser extent, Texas Jack Omohundro, were all the rage among New York's elite. The mythical wilderness of the Western Plains, where knights in buckskin rode forth to battle warlike tribes, captured the imagination of theater-goers. The Wild West was the allegorical Arthurian legend of America.

The audience might have been disabused of their romantic notions had they been allowed backstage. Buntline was in the midst of a raging tirade, shouting at prop men, stagehands, and the cast. His most scath-ing remarks were directed at the ten actors who had been hired to play the Sioux warriors. The rehearsal that afternoon had left him all but apoplectic.

"This is *not* Shakespeare!" he railed. "You are playing Indians. Indians!"

Cody and Hickok watched from the door of their dressing room. They were attired in buckskins, with broad hats and colorful shirts, and suitably armed with pistols and bowie knives. Hickok shook his head.

"Buntline would've made a good drill sergeant. He's hell on givin' orders."

"Don't fault him too much," Cody said. "It's just that he wants everything perfect. He's got a lot at stake."

"Christ, he's pullin' in a ton of money. You'd think he'd be tickled pink."

"Well, the money's not everything. Ned's lookin' to make his mark in the show business. That'll open all kinds of doors."

Hickok squinted. "Doors to what?"

"The swells," Cody said with a rueful smile. "Ned

wants a foothold into the New York social set. He aims to use the theater to get there."

"Might as well teach a pig to waltz. He ain't got the breedin' for it."

"Yeah, but it's a barrel of fun watchin' him try. Never saw a man with his spring wound so tight."

Hickok glanced back into the dressing room. Phelan was seated on a lumpy couch with Katherine and Augustus. He'd found a ball of string and held them fascinated as he fashioned a cat's cradle with his fingers. The affinity between the children and the detective was already apparent, and Hickok thought he'd made a wise choice. Phelan was a man of many talents.

"Places, everybody!" the stage manager yelled. "Five minutes till curtain!"

"Jumpin' Jesus," Hickok grouched. "Time to kill them make-believe Injuns."

Cody laughed. "We'll make an actor of you yet."

The curtain went up at eight o'clock. Giuseppina performed the opening number, a dance involving gossamer veils and balletic twirls, more suitable for sophisticated New Yorkers. The opening scene of the play, with Cody and Hickok around the campfire, had been revised to include the bit about the Grand Duke Alexis. Hickok got over his jitters with a recounting of the royal hunt.

In Act Two, Hickok shot out the spotlight. The audience thought it a delightful touch of stagecraft and roared with laughter. Hickok was so pleased with himself that he hammed it up even more in one of the skirmishes with the Sioux warriors. Instead of killing them, as called for in the play, he fired blanks at their heels. The powder burns caused a riotous departure from the script.

Taken unawares, the greasepaint Indians hopped and screeched, frantically gyrating around the stage. Hickok kept them dancing, firing with a devilish grin, until his pistol ran dry. Then, singed and furious, but actors to a man, the bewigged warriors toppled helter-skelter in feigned death. The audience broke out in hilarious applause and Hickok took a bow.

Act Three played out with a final, tumultuous battle scene. The warriors were massacred en masse, and Dove Eye, the delectable Indian maiden, was reunited with that stalwart of the plains, Buffalo Bill. The cast took five curtain calls, and Cody and Hickok were called back for a standing ovation from the crowd. Buntline was waiting in the wings when they came offstage, surrounded by the powder-burned actors. He looked like he could chew nails.

"Are you mad?" he ranted at Hickok. "How dare you fire at these men!"

"What're you yellin' about?" Hickok said with a crooked grin. "That crowd ate it up."

"Wild Bill's right," Cody interceded. "Why not add it to the show, Ned?"

"Now you've gone mad!"

"Hear me out. Wild Bill could fire at the floor instead of their legs. The boys could do all that hoppin' and wailin', and the audience wouldn't know the difference. We'd still get the laughs."

"Well—"

"You know it'd work."

"Perhaps."

"Think of all them laughs . . . and the publicity."

Buntline put it in the show.

James Gordon Bennett, publisher of the *New York Herald,* hosted an opening-night party. The affair was held at Delmonico's, the preeminent dining establishment in the city. The guest list included the luminaries of the New York aristocracy.

Among those in attendance were Commodore Cornelius Vanderbilt, William Waldorf Astor, and Jay Gould. They were the robber barons of the day, shrewd financiers who had plundered railroads, the stock exchange, and assorted industries with piratical zeal. Their combined wealth was second only to the United States Treasury.

Their excesses gave rise to what was commonly known as the Gilded Age. The era was marked by galvanized capitalism, industrial expansion, and ostentatious displays of wealth. The leisure hours of the social set were consumed by the opera, the theater, and lavish parties unrivaled by European nobility. One financier threw a party to honor his cocker spaniel, who arrived sporting a collar studded with diamonds.

The party tonight was to honor Cody and Hickok. Yet the titans of industry, no less than the masses, were captivated by plainsmen who had braved a wilderness as exotic as darkest Africa and fought the savage tribes to the death. Hickok, even more than Cody, was phantasmal, a sorcerer of armed conflict. He was death astride a pale horse, the Prince of Pistoleers.

Cornelius Vanderbilt, a heavyset man with muttonchop whiskers, cornered him while drinks were being served. "I say, Mr. Hickok," he inquired with wily curiosity. "Are these reports in the press to be taken literally?"

"Depends," Hickok said, sipping the finest whiskey he'd ever tasted. "Which reports was that?"

"Why, the allusion to you having killed a hundred

men in the war. I ask you, sir, a *hundred*?"

James Gordon Bennett and William Waldorf Astor were drawn closer by the question. Hickok quaffed his whiskey, letting them hang on his reply. "Well, don't you see," he said with a straight face, "some men, God rest their souls, was born to be killed. Just happened I was their grim reaper."

"Grim reaper, indeed!" Vanderbilt's wattled features creased with a jolly smile. "You have a droll sense of mortality, Mr. Hickok."

"What's life without a few laughs?"

Hickok was amused by the conversation. He thought the mythical stature accorded to Cody and himself was a gem of a joke. These men, citified Easterners, were never able to separate the truth from what they read in the papers or saw on the stage. So in the end, the joke was on them.

Dinner was an elaborate affair. The meal began with imported salmon, a confection of sweetbreads and pâté de foie gras, followed by a rich terrapin soup. The main course was canvasback duck, accompanied by asparagus, savory mushrooms, and artichokes. A different wine was served with every course.

Mrs. Jay Gould was seated beside Cody. Her gown was Parisian, with a breast-heaver that swelled her bosoms, and she wore a diamond necklace with an emerald pendant the size of a peahen's egg. She smiled at him over a bite of duck.

"I'm simply overcome with curiosity, Mr. Cody. Do you enjoy fighting the savages?"

"No, ma'am," Cody said without hesitation. "Fact is, I admire the Injuns. They're good fighters and fine people."

She looked confused. "Then why do you fight them?"

"Why, ma'am, we're buildin' ourselves a nation here. Some folks have to move aside so others can move on. The Injuns just got in the way."

"You sound as though you sympathize with them, Mr. Cody."

"Don't know about that, ma'am. But I shorely do respect 'em."

Cody glanced across the room, his attention drawn to Buntline. The showman was seated beside Alexander Stewart, one of the richest men in New York. Katherine and Augustus, who had been passed off as Phelan's children, were at a table with the Omohundros and several social lions. He looked back at Mrs. Gould.

"Talkin' about Injuns," he said breezily, "how'd you like the show?"

She tittered. "May I ask you a question, Mr. Cody?"

"Shore thing."

"Are all Indian maidens as ravishing as Mlle. Morlacchi?"

"Yes, ma'am, they're the fairest flowers of the plains."

"Oh, my, do tell me more."

Cody spun a titillating tale of love in the Wild West.

CHAPTER 20

THERE WERE rave reviews in the morning paper. Cody, beside himself with pride, poured over the critics' words. He read the *New York Times* aloud to Hickok.

"*The Scouts of the Plains* is an extraordinary production with more wild Indians, scalping knives, and gun powder to the square inch than any drama ever before seen on a theater stage. Buffalo Bill Cody and Wild Bill Hickok are the epitome of valiant frontiersmen."

"Epitome?" Hickok said. "What the hell's that mean?"

"Don't know," Cody said absently. "Think it's a compliment."

"They say anything about me shootin' out the lights?"

"Yeah, you wowed 'em with that one. Called you the 'finest pistol marksman extant.'"

"Extant?"

"Way it sounds, that means still livin'."

"Still livin', huh?" Hickok knuckled his mustache. "Well, I reckon they got that right."

Cody held out a copy of the *New York Herald*. "Wait'll you read this. Glory be!"

The play is beyond all precedent in the annals of stage lore. It has all the thrilling romance, treachery, love, and revenge of the richest dime novels ever written. The subject is so popular with read-

ers of border tales that the temptation to see the real actors cannot be resisted.

Hickok snorted. "Helluva way to make a livin'. I'd be a red-faced baboon if anybody out West saw me on that stage."

"They'd be pea-green with envy," Cody said. "We're in high clover and no end in sight. How many of them earns what we do?"

"That ain't the point. I'm talkin' about all the phony claptrap we spout. I feel like an impostor."

"Well, that's the show business. You mix a little fact and a little fancy, and folks are entertained. Where's the harm in that?"

"I ain't no entertainer," Hickok said dourly. "I'd sooner be an organ grinder with a monkey. Nothin' phony about that."

"Tell you what's a fact," Cody confided. "There might come a day when I'd go full-bore into the show business. I have to admit I like the stage."

"You sayin' you'd give up scoutin'?"

"I'm sayin' I like the applause. Don't matter that it's play actin' and mostly nonsense. There's worse places than standin' in the limelight."

A log crackled in the fireplace. Hickok stared out the sitting room window, as though some profound revelation were to be found in the sunny sky. He finally looked around.

"I always figured it for a joke. You know, like April Fool's."

"April Fool's?" Cody said blankly. "What're you talkin' about?"

"All this hurrah they make about you and me. We fed 'em some guff and they printed it up in them dime novels, and folks swallowed it whole. But that don't make us the Heroes of the Plains."

"Who's the heroes, then?"

"Hell's bells, I don't know," Hickok barked. "I'm just sayin' we invented most of what we told 'em. All a load of hogwash."

Cody took his fame seriously. "I don't recollect I ever bent the truth out of shape. Besides, there's nothing wrong with spinnin' a tale. Folks want to believe that stuff."

"Maybe you was made for the show business. April Fool's every night of the week."

"Well, like I said, there's worse things than the limelight. The money's not bad, either."

The door burst open. Katherine and Augustus hurried into the suite, followed by Phelan. Their faces were animated and they seemed themselves again. Whatever they were thinking about their parents, they rarely spoke it out loud. Their grief, if not diminished, was somehow suppressed.

"Have fun?" Cody asked.

"Oh, yes!" Katherine said gaily. "Giuseppina has such wonderful gowns. And her jewelry . . . !"

"A pretty lady needs fancy things. We'll buy you something nice over at Tiffany's."

"Will you—*truly*?"

The children had grown antsy cooped up in the suite. They'd spent the morning visiting Giuseppina and Omohundro, in their room down the hall. Phelan, the youngsters' constant shadow, had accompanied them.

"Who cares about Tiffany's?" Augustus scoffed. "Texas Jack showed me how his gun works. Even let me hold it!"

Hickok frowned. "Guns ain't boy's toys, Gus."

"No harm done," Phelan said. "Jack unloaded it and let me check it. He was careful."

"Pow! Pow!" Augustus shouted, his thumb and forefinger cocked like a pistol. "I bet I could shoot the lights out, too, Wild Bill."

Hickok exchanged a look with Cody. Then his gaze shifted to Phelan. "Bill and me got an invite to the racing heats this afternoon. You and Jack stick close till we get back. Don't let Gus and Kate out of here."

Phelan nodded. "We'll be on our toes."

"Well, foo!" Katherine pouted. "We have to stay here and be bored silly. It isn't fair, Wild Bill."

"Think so?" Hickok said with a teasing smile. "What if me and Buffalo Bill stop by that store, Tiffany's? How's that sound?"

"Honestly, you promise?"

"Cross my heart."

Harlem Lane was north of Central Park. The area was largely countryside, some five miles north of the theater district. The terrain was flat and open, perfect for racing horses. A few farmhouses were scattered along the broad, dirt lane.

The elite of New York adopted ducal pastimes during the Gilded Age. Every afternoon, when the weather permitted, men of prominence gathered at Harlem Lane for the racing heats. Their presence signified that they could afford to curtail their working day to the mornings. Their rivalry was yet another display of their wealth.

Dexter, a champion trotter owned by Robert Bonner, was reportedly purchased for thirty-three thousand dollars. Leonard Jerome, another racing enthusiast, quartered his horses in a stable paneled in walnut and floored with wall-to-wall carpet. Gould and Vanderbilt, even the Reverend Henry Ward Beecher, were known for their prize racing stock. Everyone who was anyone in the New York aristocracy came to Harlem Lane on a sunny afternoon.

Their ladies spent the afternoon at Central Park. No less than the men, the women of high society flaunted their wealth on a carriage promenade. Decked out in sable and gaily feathered hats, they were driven through the park in stately broughams, or an occasional barouche, the carriage favored by European nobility. The coaches were hauled by sleek steeds and piloted by liveried drivers in brass-buttoned uniforms. Pedigree, in New York, was often mirrored by pageantry.

Cody and Hickok prided themselves on their knowledge of horseflesh. On the Western Plains, where the warlike tribes bred superb mounts, a scout's horse was often the margin between life and death. Last night, during the party at Delmonico's, the robber barons had openly bragged on the bloodlines of their racing stock. Jay Gould had extended an invitation to today's heats, and Cody and Hickok had readily accepted. They were curious to see if New Yorkers knew anything about horses.

Cody, in particular, considered himself an authority on the subject. His favorite mount, Buckskin Joe, was fleet as the wind, descended from stock brought to the New World by the Conquistadors. He had raced Buckskin Joe against the prize mounts of army officers and Indian chiefs, and he'd never lost. Yet the horses paraded around Harlem Lane today were almost beyond his ken, and certainly beyond his means. He quickly revised his opinion of New Yorkers.

Dexter was a stallion imported from Kentucky. He

was a barrel-chested animal, all sinew and muscle, standing sixteen hands high and well over a thousand pounds in weight. A blood bay, with black tail and mane, his hide glistened in the sun like dark blood on a polished redwood. He whinnied a shrill blast and pawed the earth as though he spurned it and longed to fly. His nostrils flared in anticipation of the first race.

A horse named Copperdust was his opponent. Tall and powerful, the rangy chestnut looked like Dexter cast in a different color. Jay Gould, who owned Copperdust, was confident his fiery-eyed stallion could not be beat. Like all robber barons, he thought of any endeavor in terms of money, including a sporting event. He casually offered Robert Bonner, Dexter's owner, a gentleman's wager of ten thousand dollars. Bonner, as though dealing in spare change, accepted the bet with an insouciant nod. The challenge match was on.

Cody and Hickok were floored. Neither of them had ever seen ten thousand dollars, much less possessed such a princely sum. In a time when the daily wage for the average working man was two dollars or less, ten thousand was a veritable fortune. The nonchalance with which the wager had been made convinced the plainsmen that they were in rarified company, and out of their element. Except for their celebrity, they would have never been invited.

Cornelius Vanderbilt joined them as the race got under way. He was in his seventies, a mogul among moguls who had recently endowed a university, to be named in his honor. Yet, for all his years, he was still a feisty competitor, all the more so where it involved Jay Gould. Though Gould was in his middle thirties he had wrested control of the Erie Railroad from Van-

derbilt in a brutal financial struggle. Vanderbilt
blithely wagered Gould another ten thousand on the
race.

The heat was set for a mile along the country lane.
The horses were attached to sulkies, light two-
wheeled carriages with a flimsy seat for the driver.
The drivers were professionals, on salary to the owners and paid handsomely for their services. On signal,
the drivers snapped their reins, exhorting the stallions
with crisp shouts, and surged across the starting line.
Copperdust jumped to an early lead, the wheels of the
sulkies leaving a rooster-tail of dust in their wake.
Dexter quickly narrowed the lead to a single length.

A crowd of some two hundred men lined Harlem
Lane. The robber barons comprised perhaps a quarter
that number, with the rest divided between socially
prominent businessmen and hangers-on. The betting
was heavy, and their voices were raised in rollicking
cries as the stallions pounded along the road. The race
was neck and neck most of the way, and the drivers
began popping their whips as the sulkies blasted past
the three-quarter mark. At the finish line, Dexter put
on an explosive burst of speed and took it by a nose.
The crowd shouted themselves hoarse.

Gould was magnanimous in defeat. He boasted that
Copperdust would prevail next time, and amiably
congratulated Bonner and Vanderbilt on their victory.
Gentlemen never settled wagers with cash, and the
winners knew they would receive a check by mes-
senger sometime tomorrow. The hubbub died down
as grooms hurried forward to attend the sweat-
lathered stallions. Gould walked off to have a word
with his driver.

The crowd retired to their carriages to await the
next heat.

* * *

Vanderbilt invited Cody and Hickok to join him for refreshments. A manservant rushed to unfold a storage compartment at the rear of the carriage. He set out whiskey and brandy, an assortment of meats and cheese, and a basket of seasonal fruits. Cody thought he'd seen a regiment subsist on less.

"By Godfrey," Vanderbilt crowed. "It does my heart good to trim Jay Gould. A little comeuppance will do wonders for his soul."

"That was some race," Hickok said, accepting a whiskey. "You and Mr. Gould longtime rivals, are you?"

"Yes, it would be fair to say we are rivals, But understand, I have the utmost respect for Jay. He is brilliant in matters of business and finance."

Cody tried the brandy. "Never been much of a businessman myself. High finance tends to make me dizzy."

"To each his own," Vanderbilt observed. "You and Mr. Hickok are scouts and Indian fighters without peer. I seriously doubt I could survive as much as a day on the Western Plains."

"That's mighty good brandy," Cody said, holding his glass to the light. "Got a nice bite to it."

"Napoleonic Brandy, imported from France. I'll have a case sent over to you."

"Well now, I'm obliged, Mr. Vanderbilt."

"No need to stand on ceremony. All of my friends call me Commodore."

"You a navy man?"

"Hardly anything so dashing." Vanderbilt paused, accepting cheese on a wafer from his manservant. "More of an honorary title from business and charitable works. I'm quite active in civic affairs."

"Civic affairs?" Cody mused. "You talkin' about politics?"

"Actually, I'm more involved in projects to benefit the city. The new museum is our latest effort."

"What sort of museum?"

"One more ambitious than the Louvre in Paris."

Vanderbilt warmed to the subject. In league with the Astors and other members of the social hierarchy, he had set about to create the finest art museum in the world. Over the generations wealthy New York families had amassed impressive private art collections. Their goal was to establish a museum and donate their art treasures for public display. The project, in the end, would further exalt the status of New York.

The Metropolitan Museum of Art opened in 1870. The temporary quarters were on Fourteenth Street, near Union Square. But ground had been broken for a permanent home, a granite colossus to be built uptown on Fifth Avenue. Even now, a drive was underway to expand the collection with the works of Rembrandt, Van Dyck, Vermeer, and the contemporary master, Albert Bierstadt. Upon completion, the museum would be the standard for all the world.

"Imagine, if you will," Vanderbilt concluded. "A museum grander than any edifice known to man. Here in New York."

"Sounds big," Cody said, more interested in the brandy than the art. "Bet it'll cost a bundle."

"Before we're through, in the tens of millions."

Hickok was scarcely listening. He was thinking instead that Cornelius Vanderbilt had been around a long time. The financier was elderly, rich beyond reckoning, and doubtless privy to the darkest secrets of New York's social elite. On the spur of the moment, Hickok decided to take a chance. He tried to edge into it sideways.

"Talkin' about money," he said vaguely. "I was readin' in the *Police Gazette* about a wealthy family that got murdered. Think the name was Stanley."

"Dreadful thing," Vanderbilt commented gravely. "I've known the Stanleys for thirty years, perhaps more. One of the finest families in New York."

"I recollect the paper mentioned a name—Leland Stanley?"

Vanderbilt's features clouded. "Leland would be the exception. I haven't much use for him."

Hickok looked curious. "How's that?"

"To put it charitably, the man is a cad. He lived off his brother—Henry, the one who was murdered— and devoted his time to debauchery and loose women. I closed my account when he assumed control of the family bank."

"What about his mother?" Hickok asked casually. "The paper said she wasn't murdered. I forgot her name."

"Elizabeth Stanley." Vanderbilt's tone softened. "A saint of a woman, in every sense of the word. I wonder that she ever gave birth to Leland."

"Know her well, do you?"

"As I said, thirty years or more. What prompted your interest in the Stanleys?"

"Well, you know, once a lawman always a lawman. Never like to see a murder go unsolved."

Cody sensed it was time to end the conversation. He deftly diverted the financier's attention. "Are you racin' a horse today, Commodore?"

Vanderbilt went off on a fervent soliloquy about his prize trotter. The stallion's name was Midnight.

CHAPTER 21

"I TEND to buy it."

"Why's that?"

"Vanderbilt's nobody's dummy. He's known the woman for thirty years."

Cody waved a hand. "I've been married to Lulu near on seven years and I still don't know her. Women have got a way of foolin' a man."

"Not Vanderbilt," Hickok said with conviction. "He didn't get rich as Midas on bad judgment. We can forget about the grandma."

"Jim, I shorely do hope you're right. That'd mean the kids have some family that's not tryin' to kill'em."

"I think we're safe there."

"Well, just for the sake of argument, let's say it's so. We've still got Leland Stanley to worry about . . . and Richter."

"Yeah, I've been ponderin' on Richter."

A shaft of sunlight spilled through the window of the sitting room. Last night, after the show at the theater, they'd returned directly to the hotel. Hickok had been moody and thoughtful, and this morning he was still somewhat withdrawn. They were alone in the suite, seated before the fireplace. He stared into the flames.

"And?" Cody prompted. "What about Richter?"

Hickok's features were serious. "Much as I'd like to kill the bastard, that won't work. Billy McGlory would just replace him with another hired gun."

"You think Stanley's dealin' directly with Mc-Glory?"

"That'd be my guess."

"So what's our move?"

"We ain't got a helluva lot of choice. We've got to capture Richter."

Three days had passed since Hickok's encounter with Billy McGlory. Though he hadn't spotted a tail, he was confident their movements were being shadowed night and day. He sensed Richter was watching and planning, awaiting an opportune moment. The children's lives were still in peril.

"Richter's slippery," Cody said absently. "How you figure to collar him?"

"Don't know the how or where just yet. I want to talk with Phelan."

There was a rap at the door. Cody answered it and Charlie Phelan walked into the suite. He guarded the children from morning till night, leaving once they were safely returned from the theater. His bloodshot eyes indicated he wasn't getting much sleep.

"Morning," he said, doffing his hat and coat. "Hope you haven't had breakfast. I could use some coffee."

"The kids are getting dressed," Cody remarked. "Soon as they're ready, we'll go downstairs."

"Sounds good." Phelan crossed to the sofa, took a seat. "Anything special on for today?"

Hickok lit a cheroot. "We've just been talkin' about Richter. We need to track him down."

"Does that mean you're back to the original plan? Take him into custody and turn him against Stanley."

"I don't see no other way to end this mess."

"Any ideas where we start?"

"Armory Hall," Hickok said, exhaling a streamer

of smoke. "I want you to mount a watch on Mc-
Glory's place and get a line on Richter. Find out
where he lives, or when he's alone. Somewhere we
can grab him off the street."

"Easier said than done," Phelan informed him. "A
stakeout on Armory Hall wouldn't last ten minutes.
Somebody would tip McGlory."

"You sayin' it can't be done?"

"The Bowery's no place to pull a surveillance.
Everybody knows everybody else, and I'd stick out
like a sore thumb. Probably get myself killed."

Hickok's gaze became abstracted. He was in Phelan's town, and he was forced to accept the detective's word that surveillance wasn't the answer. Yet
he couldn't afford to wait for Richter to make still
another attempt on the children's lives. All along,
from Nebraska to New York, he'd been reacting to
Richter's moves, ever a step behind. It was time to
take the initiative.

"Let's go at it another way," he said. "Anybody
you know who could act as a go-between with
McGlory?"

"John Morrissey," Phelan replied. "You'll recall he
gave me the inside dope on Stanley."

"The feller that owns a casino?"

"That's the one."

"Tell me about him."

Morrissey, Phelan explained, operated the finest
casino in New York. For years, always playing the
angle, he'd been aligned with Boss Tweed and Tammany Hall. But with the shift in political winds, his
allegiance had shifted to the wealthy reformers, many
of whom patronized his casino. He was, nonetheless,
an Irishman, a product of Hell's Kitchen, and never

far from his roots. He still maintained his ties to the underworld.

"You might say he walks the fence," Phelan went on. "He hobnobs with the swells and he's pals with all the gang bosses. Nobody in this town ignores Johnny Morrissey."

"So McGlory would trust him?"

"Probably more than he'd trust the Pope. What do you have in mind?"

"Charlie, we're fixin' to run ourselves a bunco game. I want you to set up a meetin' with Morrissey."

Phelan squinted. "What reason do I give him?"

"Tell him Wild Bill Hickok aims to do a helluva favor for one of his pals."

"You're talking about McGlory?"

"None other."

"You lost me," Cody interjected. "What's this got to do with Richter?"

Hickok grinned. "We're gonna trap the son-of-a-bitch."

The Savoy Club was on Twenty Fourth Street, east of Madison Square. The location was within walking distance of the theater district, and the clientele comprised the male aristocracy of New York. Women were not allowed in the Savoy.

The main salon was heavily carpeted, with dark paneled walls and crystal chandeliers. A collection of Old World art the envy of any museum was scattered about the room. The club was divided by an aisle, one side of which was devoted to chemin de fer and roulette. On the opposite side, an equal number of tables were covered with faro layouts.

Faro was a game originated by French kings and currently all the rage from New York to San Francisco. At the far end of the salon were a dozen poker tables, covered with baize cloth and lighted by overhead Tiffany lamps. There was a small afternoon crowd, almost lost in the baronial magnificence of the room. The club was pervaded by the decorous atmosphere considered *de rigueur* among gentlemen gamblers.

The ambience of the salon was an elegance far beyond Hickok's experience. Phelan led him to a door at the rear of the room, which was guarded by a strong-arm thug in a fashionable suit. Down a hallway, they were admitted to an office lushly appointed with leather chairs and walnut furniture. John Morrissey rose from behind his desk.

"Mr. Hickok," he said pleasantly, extending a hand. "A pleasure to meet you."

"Same here." Hickok accepted his handshake. "Appreciate you takin' the time to see me."

"Not at all, not at all. Any friend of Charlie's is welcome in the Savoy."

Morrissey motioned them to chairs. He exuded a sort of patrician assurance, as though his profile might once have graced an ancient coin. He was impeccably attired, his hair flecked with gray, and he spoke in a resonant, organlike voice. Yet, despite a ready smile, his eyes were sharp and alert, filled with craftiness. He nodded across the desk with a benign look.

"I've read the reviews on your show. You and Mr. Cody are the toast of the town."

Hickok played along. "We'd like you to be our guest. I'll send around some tickets."

"That's very nice of you." Morrissey hesitated, still smiling. "Now, how can I be of service? Charlie tells me it has to do with Billy McGlory."

"I reckon McGlory and me got off on the wrong

foot. I was hopin' you might act as peacemaker."

"Yes, I heard about that unfortunate incident at Armory Hall. What would you like me to say to Billy?"

Hickok leaned forward with a conspiratorial air. "I've got something he wants. You know, that business Charlie asked you about—Leland Stanley."

"No, I don't know," Morrissey said smoothly. "And quite frankly, I don't want to know. Let's leave it that I'll try to broker a truce."

"Whichever way you want to handle it. Just tell him I'm fed up with this stage nonsense and ready to head back West. I'm willin' to strike a deal."

"When would you like to meet with him?"

"The sooner the better so far's I'm concerned."

Morrissey reflected a moment. "I could probably have Billy here in an hour or so. Are you a gambling man, Mr. Hickok?"

"I'd have to say I'm partial to poker."

"I believe there's a game going on now. You can amuse yourself while you're waiting."

"Don't mind if I do."

Morrissey led them back into the club. Five men were seated at a poker table and he made the introductions. He insisted Hickok's marker was good, ordering a houseman to bring a thousand dollars in chips. Once Hickok was settled into a chair, he nodded amiably. His gaze shifted to Phelan.

"Take good care of our friend, Charlie. I shouldn't be long."

"We'll be here," Phelan said. "Thanks again, Johnny."

"Think nothing of it."

Morrissey returned to his office. Hickok quickly discovered that poker was played differently in Eastern casinos. The traditional rules had been revised to include straights, flushes, and the most elusive of all combinations, the straight flush. The highest hand was now a royal flush, ten through ace in the same suit. The rules gave the game an added dimension.

Poker out West was still played by the original rules. The top hand was four aces, drawn by most players only once or twice in a lifetime. The other cinch was four kings with an ace, which precluded anyone holding four aces. For Hickok, the Eastern rules altered the perspective of the game, but not the game itself. His style was to read the players rather than their cards.

He bluffed them out of three pots in a row.

Billy McGlory arrived at the club shortly before four o'clock. Hickok excused himself from the game, ahead by some three hundred dollars. Morrissey, who wanted nothing to do with the meeting, ushered them into his private office. He then walked Phelan out to the bar for a drink.

McGlory tossed his hat on the desk. He seated himself in one of the chairs, his eyes narrow with suspicion. "I'm told you're after making a deal. What's on your mind?"

Hickok stared at him. "The kids for twenty thousand."

"Richter offered you ten thousand once before and you turned him down. Why the switch?"

"Cody swore I'd make my fortune in the show business. Turns out it's him and Buntline stuffing their pockets. All I've seen is peanuts."

"Horseshit." McGlory's gaze bored into him. "You and Cody have been protecting those brats like you was on a crusade. What's changed?"

"The price has changed," Hickok said impassively.

"Cody was the one all hearts-and-flowers about them kids. I was just along for the ride."

"That why you shot Turk Johnson and threw Richter off the train?"

"I was lookin' after my investment. Cody all but took a blood oath I'd get rich in the show business."

"So now you're ready to ditch Cody and hand over the kids. That it?"

"Yeah, for twenty thousand simoleons. Way I see it, money talks and bullshit walks."

"Why should I pay you a red cent? Only a matter of time till Richter gets hold of those kids."

Hickok paused like a magician reluctant to reveal his last best trick. "Why fight a war when it ain't your money? Leland Stanley's the one payin' the freight."

McGlory tugged thoughtfully at his ear. "You tried your best to kill Richter in Philly. Maybe this is just another setup."

"I ain't plannin' to harm him. I'm strictly in it for the money. You've got my word."

"I'll hold you to it. You kill him and that's egg on my face. Understand me?"

"Nothing wrong with my hearing."

"So how do we work this exchange?"

"I recollect Richter's partial to midnight. We'll meet on the pathway west of the zoo."

"Why the zoo?"

The idea was Phelan's. Late that morning, scouting for out-of-the-way locations, they had walked through Central Park. The zoo fitted Hickok's plans perfectly.

"Neutral territory," he said. "Nobody's in the park at midnight."

McGlory shrugged. "All right, the zoo it is."

"Just Richter and me," Hickok warned him. "I see anybody else and the deal's off."

"You'll have the kids there?"

"They'll be close at hand. Once Richter shows me the money, I'll deliver the kids. Won't take ten minutes."

"You have a helper, then." McGlory gave him a cagey look. "Charlie Phelan's in it with you, is he?"

Hickok smiled. "Don't ask and I won't tell you no lies."

"You remember one thing, Mr. Wild Bill Hickok."

"What's that?"

"No tricks," McGlory said with blunt vindictiveness. "Otto Richter walks out of that park alive or you'll answer to me. Got it?"

"Got it," Hickok said evenly. "Richter will leave there alive and kicking. I guarantee it."

"Then we're on for midnight."

Neither of them offered to shake hands. Hickok left him in the office and walked back into the club. He found Phelan at the bar with Morrissey.

"Well, Mr. Hickok," Morrissey said. "Everything work out to your satisfaction?"

"You might say things never looked better. I appreciate all you done."

"You're welcome at the Savoy anytime, Mr. Hickok. Drop around whenever you'd like a poker game."

"I'll do that."

Morrissey walked them to the door. On the street, Hickok and Phelan turned toward Madison Square. The detective was brimming with curiosity.

"You really pulled it off?"

"Slicker'n a whistle."

"How the Christ did you convince him?"

"Charlie, there's nobody easier to con than a con man."

Phelan appeared confused. "What's that mean?"

"McGlory thought he gaffed me," Hickok said, amused by it all. "He'll rig it for Richter to grab the kids and keep the money. Likely try to kill me, too."

"You talk like you knew it all along."

Hickok chuckled. "Tell you, these New York desperadoes give me a laugh. They think they invented the game."

"What game?"

"The one we're gonna play tonight."

CHAPTER 22

THE SHOW was standing-room-only that night. Hickok's shooting out the spotlight again brought down the house, and Giuseppina, as Dove Eye, enthralled the audience when she was reunited with Buffalo Bill. The cast took five curtain calls.

By now, the drill following the show had become routine. Katherine and Augustus, surrounded by Cody, Hickok and Phelan, were escorted out the stage door. Tonight, Giuseppina and Omohundro were accompanied by Buntline, and they trailed close behind. Two carriages, hired for the run of the show, awaited them on the street. They stepped aboard for the short ride back to the hotel.

Katherine snuggled close to Hickok as the carriage pulled away. Cody and Phelan, with Augustus between them, settled back on the opposite seat. Though the children now considered themselves troupers, their energy invariably began to flag each night when the show ended. Hickok, one arm around Katherine, checked his pocket watch with the other hand. In the light from the street, he saw that it was a few minutes after ten. He thought they had little time to spare.

A short while later they all trooped into the suite. The children went to their bedroom, to change into their night clothes. Hickok and Cody, with Phelan in the middle, took a seat on the sofa. The others, their faces solemn, found chairs by the fireplace. Phelan extracted a hand-drawn map from his inside jacket pocket, and spread it on the table before the sofa.

Earlier, during the stage show, he had rendered the sketch from memory. The map was of Central Park.

"Go ahead, Charlie," Hickok said, then glanced across at Cody. "Bill, you need to pay close attention to the layout. I got a look this mornin' when Charlie and me scouted the park."

Cody nodded. "I'm all ears. Let 'er rip."

"Here's Fifth Avenue," Phelan said, pointing with his finger. "The building closest to the street is the old Arsenal, and directly behind it is the zoo. This dotted line west of the zoo is a footpath."

"Over here?" Cody tapped the map. "What're these scratchy marks?"

"Trees," Phelan noted. "They wind around south of the zoo and thin out along the pathway. You can see they get heavier between the pathway and this road back of the zoo. That's East Drive."

The map covered a relatively small area in the southeast corner of the park. A large pond was indicated north and west of where Fifty Ninth Street, a broad thoroughfare, crossed Fifth Avenue. East Drive followed a serpentine line between the pond and the western perimeter of the zoo. The Arsenal, which fronted the zoo, was at the intersection of Fifth Avenue and Sixty Fourth Street.

"Looks clear enough," Cody said. "How do we pull it off?"

Hickok leaned over the table. "We'll drop Charlie off here." He jabbed at a spot on the map. "Once he works his way through them trees, he'll take a position to cover me on the path. You and me will drive on to the Arsenal, and you'll stay there. I'll head for the zoo to meet Richter."

Cody frowned. "You mean to leave me in the carriage?"

"Richter's got to believe you're waitin' in the carriage with the kids. I don't see no other way."

"You know good and well he's gonna jump you with a bunch of thugs. I'd feel a sight better if I was with you."

"Bill, we've got to bamboozle him into thinkin' the kids are there. Nothin' for it but that you stick with the carriage."

"I don't like it," Cody said. "You and Charlie are liable to have a fight on your hands."

Hickok ignored the objection. "You just let me worry about Richter."

The bedroom door opened. Katherine hurried across the room, having changed into a flowery nightgown. Augustus, who wore a billowy nightshirt, looked asleep on his feet. They made the rounds, hugging everyone good night, saving Hickok and Cody for last. The youngsters went from one to the other, kissing the plainsmen on the cheek, lingering a moment in their arms. Then they scampered off to the bedroom.

"So touching," Giuseppina sighed, her eyes moist. "How those leetle darlings love you both."

Cody wagged his head sadly. "Guess they figure we're all the family they've got."

"Jack. Ned." Hickok stood, again checking his pocket watch. "We're dependin' on you to look after the kids. Don't open that door for nobody."

Omohundro and Buntline were both armed. They exchanged a glance, then Omohundro nodded. "You take care of Richter," he said stoutly. "We'll hold down the fort here."

"Indeed!" Buntline added with an air of bravado. "You needn't worry yourselves. The children are in good hands."

"Do take care," Giuseppina said softly. "Come back safely."

Cody pulled a grin. "Nothin' more certain in the world, Dove Eye."

Hickok led the way out of the suite. Cody and Phelan followed him to a staircase at the end of the hall, a narrow passageway normally used by maids and servicemen. On the ground floor, they went through the kitchen and exited into a darkened alley. None of them doubted that Richter had someone watching the front of the hotel.

Outside, they walked through the alley and turned west on Twenty Fifth Street. One of the carriages retained for their nightly trips to the theater was waiting for them at the corner of Sixth Avenue. The driver was trustworthy, sworn to secrecy, and paid handsomely for tonight's venture. They clambered aboard with a last look along the street.

The carriage trundled north toward Central Park.

Some twenty minutes later the carriage stopped at the corner of Sixth Avenue and Fifty Ninth Street. They were not quite two miles north of the theater district, and directly across the street lay Central Park. The wide thoroughfare was virtually deserted so late at night.

Hickok stepped from the carriage. He stood for a moment inspecting the T-shaped intersection in all directions. Finally, satisfied they had not been followed, he motioned smartly to Phelan. The detective hopped down to the pavement and without a word hurried across the street. He disappeared into the park.

Central Park was the masterwork of Calvert Vaux, a London-born architect transplanted to New York. Five years ago, in concert with Superintendent of

Parks Frederick Olmsted, he broke ground on the
project. A vast expanse of raw countryside was re-
molded in his vision, with landscaped hills, open
meadows, and rolling copses of trees. Thousands of
laborers and stonemasons literally sculpted the earth.

Vaux's dream was a pastoral sanctuary away from
the congestion and demonic rhythm of the city. The
end result was 843 acres of meandering paths, tranquil
lakes, and sprawling meadows that stretched north
from Fifty Ninth Street to Harlem Lane. The park was
over two miles long and a half mile wide, crisscrossed
by carriage lanes, sunken transverse roads, and forty
stone bridges. There was nothing to rival it in all the
world.

Charlie Phelan paused inside the treeline. He
watched the carriage round the corner onto Fifty
Ninth Street and some moments later turn north on
Fifth Avenue. Directly ahead of him lay the Pond, a
horseshoe-shaped basin that froze over in the winter
and became a natural skating rink. The Pond was illuminated by calcium lights, and a solitary pair of
skaters, a man and a woman, glided gracefully about
the icy surface. He idly thought they were lovers, immune to time or the frosty chill.

The moon hung high and cold, diamond-hard in
the dead-of-night sky. Phelan ghosted through the
trees, skirting the Pond, and several minutes later
paused before the Inscope Arch. The ornate bridge
was constructed of pink and gray granite, with a spacious underpass to accommodate a bridal path. The
archway supporting the bridge was fourteen feet wide
and twelve feet tall, and the bridge itself was a hundred feet long. Beyond lay the westerly bend of East
Drive.

Somewhere in the distance the mournful hoot of

an owl floated eerily through the night. Phelan hesitated, surveying the terrain in all directions, and darted across East Drive. On the other side he vanished into the shelterbelt of the trees and cautiously made his way north in the dappled moonlight. He was alert to sound and movement, for he was certain that Richter and his men were even now infiltrating the park. His every instinct told him they were not far ahead.

The trees thinned out over the slope of a stunted, rock-studded hill. Phelan warily watched his footing, moving step by step, and halted in the shadow of a tall oak. His position overlooked the footpath west of the zoo, and beyond, not thirty yards away, was another stand of trees. He slowly scanned the treeline, and some inner voice told him that there were men, guarded and silent, waiting in the darkened timber. He pulled a Colt New Model Police revolver from his waistband and hooked his thumb over the hammer. His eyes continued to search the trees.

On Fifth Avenue, the carriage rolled to a halt on the east side of the street. The aristocracy of New York, ever determined to outdistance the lower classes, were moving farther and farther uptown. Several mansions were under construction across from Central Park, towering monuments to the robber barons and merchant princes of the city. Opposite the construction sites was the Arsenal, built prior to the Civil War as a storage facility for munitions. The building now housed the Museum of Natural History.

Lampposts along Fifth Avenue cast aureoles of light on the cobblestone sidewalks. Hickok opened the carriage door and subjected the Arsenal to long, careful scrutiny. All looked quiet, and his gaze shifted a block upstreet, where a lone carriage was parked by the curb bordering Central Park. Beneath the glow of a nearby lamppost, he made out the form of the driver, sitting motionless, wrapped in a heavy great-coat. He gestured to Cody.

"I'm layin' odds," he muttered sourly. "Dollar to a donut says that coach belongs to Richter. He's already here."

Cody looked out the door. "You think him and his gang are waitin' in there now?"

"Nope," Hickok said shortly. "I figure they're somewheres over by the zoo. Waitin' for me to show."

"Goddarnit, it's just like I told you before. You're gonna walk straight into a hornet's nest."

"Wouldn't be the first time."

"Damn well might be the last," Cody fumed. "I still say I ought to come with you."

"No dice," Hickok said. "You stick here and shoot anybody that comes within shoutin' distance. Only way Richter's gonna believe you've got the kids."

"You're hell on givin' orders. Who made you the general?"

"Somebody's got to brace Richter and I reckon that's me. I shoot straghter'n you, anyhow."

"Jim, I have to tell you, that's a mighty lame excuse."

"Well, it's the only one I've got. Guess it'll have to do."

"You always was a hardhead."

"Just sit tight and I'll see you directly."

Hickok stepped out of the door. One eye on the carriage upstreet, he crossed Fifth Avenue at a measured stride. The Arsenal loomed before him like an ancient monolith.

He walked into Central Park.

* * *

The zoo was dark. A flagstone walkway wound past cages that housed grizzly bears, sea lions, monkeys, and other exotic species. The cages were heavily barred, with enclosed dens at the rear for protection against the cold. The quiet was deafening.

Hickok felt his nerves shut down. A strange calm, something akin to fatalism, came over him whenever he went in harm's way. Yet he was acutely aware of his surroundings, vision inexplicably sharper and sounds magnified. His senses notched upward to a finer pitch.

A wakeful monkey chattered as he moved past a darkened cage. The pungent odor of dung and the ripe blend of animal smells hung over the zoo. In another cage, a boar grizzly, disturbed by the monkey, woofed a guttural warning. The bear's yellowed eyes glowed like embers behind the steel bars.

Hickok was not alarmed by the sounds. The element of surprise had never entered into his plans for tonight's encounter. He wanted Richter to believe that it was on the square, a straight business deal, the children in exchange for money. Even more, it was important that Richter believed he had the edge. There was weakness in overconfidence.

The pathway beyond the zoo was lighted by a silvery moon now at its zenith. Hickok resisted the impulse to look at the trees on his left, trusting that Phelan was already in position. His gaze fixed instead on a dense stand of trees to his right, obliquely north of the path. He felt certain that was the direction by which Richter had entered the park. He stopped in a patch of moonlight.

Otto Richter seemed to materialize from the treeline. One moment there was nothing, and the next moment he was moving forward at a deliberate pace. He carried a small leather satchel, and his eyes darted back toward the zoo, wary someone else might step from the shadows. He halted on the pathway.

"Hickok," he said in a guarded voice. "After Philadelphia, I have good reason not to trust you. Are you alone?"

"Are you?" Hickok countered. "Let's get down to it, Richter. You got the money?"

"Twenty thousand." Richter hefted the satchel in his left hand. "Do you have the children?"

"Charlie Phelan has them."

"Where?"

"Here in the park," Hickok said. "You show me the money and let's make sure the count's right. Then I'll take you to them."

"Yeah, you'll take me," Richter said roughly. "Not just the way you planned, though. All right, boys!"

Three men stepped out of the treeline. The glint of moonlight on metal reflected off the pistols in their hands. Hickok considered them with a level stare, then glanced back at Richter. "You sure you want it this way?"

Richter's features went cold as a stone adder. "You'd better have those kids, Hickok. Otherwise you're a dead—"

A split second was all Hickok needed. His hands moved even as Richter was still talking. The three men, caught off guard, were a beat behind. He produced the Colts, and shot one of the men in the chest. Phelan appeared from behind the tall oak and drilled another one through the stomach. The third man got off a hurried snap-shot that went wide.

Richter slammed Hickok upside the head with the satchel. Hickok stumbled, knocked off balance, and

Richter sprinted toward the zoo. The third hooligan fired again, the slug plucking at the sleeve of Hickok's coat. His attention focused on the gunman, Hickok was vaguely aware of chattering monkeys as Richter disappeared along the zoo walkway. His arm came level and the Colt bucked in the same instant Charlie Phelan fired. The thug went down as though he legs had been chopped off.

Richter dashed out of the zoo. He saw Cody hurrying across Fifth Avenue and abruptly forgot about the carriage waiting upstreet. His hand dipped inside his coat, frantically drawing a revolver, and he snapped off a shot. The slug whistled harmlessly through the night, and Cody stopped, clawing at a Colt holstered on his hip. As the pistol came to bear, Richter's nerve deserted him and he dropped the satchel. He turned back into the park.

A mounted policeman, drawn by the gunshots, clattered up from Fifty Ninth Street. He skidded to a halt, aware of one man in the middle of Fifth Avenue and another bolting headlong through the park. He glowered down at Cody.

"What the hell's going on here?"

"Officer, I don't have time to explain."

Cody jerked him off the horse. The policeman hit the pavement with a thud and Cody vaulted into the saddle. He sawed at the reins, booting the horse in the ribs, and took off at a lope. Off in the distance, the landscape bathed in moonlight, he saw Richter running south through the trees. He urged the horse into a gallop.

Richter barreled across East Drive. He ducked into the underpass beneath Inscope Arch and darted out the other side on the bridal path. He heard the drum of hoofbeats and glanced over his shoulder at the rider bearing down on him. His legs pumped as he put on a burst of speed and bore off in the direction of the Pond. Cody leaped from the saddle, collaring him around the neck, and drove him to the ground. His lungs exploded with a whoosh of air.

"Gotcha now!" Cody shouted jubilantly. "You dirty rotten bastard!"

Otto Richter collapsed in the moonlit earth of Central Park.

CHAPTER 23

HICKOK EMERGED from the trees by East Drive. Phelan was a step behind and trailed him across the roadway. They were following Cody.

On the far side of Inscope Arch, they found him at the edge of the bridal path. He was standing over Richter, whose hands were bound behind his back with his necktie. A horse was cropping brittle winter grass at the verge of the treeline.

"Where you been?" Cody said jovially. "You missed our little wrestlin' match."

"We started into the zoo," Hickok said. "Heard a shot and saw you jerk that cop off his horse. Figured you was after Richter."

"I rode him down pretty as you please. How'd he slip past you and Charlie?"

"We was busy with them pistoleros he brought along. They're back there pushin' up daisies."

"Thought as much when I heard the shootin'. Then our boy here come bustin' out of the zoo. Say hello for yourself, Richter."

"Go to hell," Richter said. "The whole lot of you."

Hickok stared down at him. "We're fixin' to find out how tough you are, sport. I want some questions answered."

"You won't get anything out of me."

"Don't bet on it."

"We can't take him to the hotel," Cody broke in. "The kids are there and that wouldn't rightly do. Not if you're thinkin' what I'm thinkin'."

"Charlie, you got any ideas?" Hickok said, glancing at Phelan. "We need somewheres that's private. Somewheres we won't be disturbed."

"Sheep Meadow." Phelan pointed off to the northwest. "One of the biggest meadows in the park. Should be deserted this time of night."

"Things are liable to get a little loud."

"No one will hear us out there."

"Good enough," Hickok said. "Bill, you'd better get rid of that cop's horse. We don't want nobody doggin' our trail."

Cody led the horse to the end of the bridge. He swatted it on the rump and the horse clattered off toward Fifth Avenue. Hickok hoisted Richter to his feet and followed Phelan deeper into the park. Cody fell in behind.

Sheep Meadow was a quarter mile or so to the northwest. Once a grazeland for sheep farmers, it was now a spacious field where families gathered for picnics in the summertime. The meadow was ringed by trees washed in the silvery glitter of the moon. There was no one in sight.

Hickok halted near the trees on the southern fringe of the meadow. He looked at Richter. "Here's the deal," he said. "You're gonna tell us about McGlory and Stanley, and there ain't no other way. Not if you aim to leave this place alive."

"You won't kill me," Richter said with a cocksure laugh. "I'm no good to you dead."

"Friend, you got it bassackwards," Hickok informed him in a hard voice. "You're no good to me alive—unless you talk."

"Let me have him," Cody snorted gleefully. "I'll make him squawk like a duck."

"What've you got in mind?"

"A little trick the Injuns taught me. Works every-time."

Cody untied Richter's hands. He slammed him up against a leafless birch and bound his hands behind the tree. Hickok seemed to get into the spirit of things, and helped Cody collect armloads of fallen branches from the woods. Phelan watched them with a be-mused look, wondering it they were serious. The stacked branches were soon piled higher than Rich-ter's knees.

Hickok provided the matches. Cody built a teepee of twigs beneath the branches and lit the fire. He fanned it with his hat and the dried wood caught with a sharp crackle. Flames licked around the tops of Richter's shoes.

"You're crazy!" Richter shouted, his expression suddenly frenzied. "You can't burn me alive!"

"Why shore we can," Cody said breezily. "I've seen the Injuns burn a man to a crisp. Stinks some-thing awful."

"For God's sake, it's not human!"

"Well, we can stop it anytime you say. All you gotta do is start talkin'."

The cuff of Richter's trousers caught fire. Flame lapped about his ankles and his mouth opened in a banshee howl of terror. Phelan looked no less terri-fied, his eyes wide with horror. He grabbed Hickok's arm.

"Jesus, call it off," he blurted anxiously. "We're not savages."

"Turns your stomach, don't it?" Hickok said. "But you know, you're right, Charlie. This ain't a fit way for any man to die."

Hickok kicked the fiery branches aside, smothering the flames on Richter's trousers. He gave Cody a rue-

ful look. "Bill, you been around them heathen redsticks too long. Damned if it ain't just a little savage."

Cody sulked. "You want him to talk, don't you?"

"Yeah, but you can tell he ain't fixin' to squeal.
The man's got brass balls."

"So what're you gonna do?"

"Just have to kill him."

Hickok pulled one of his Colts. He thumbed the
hammer and pressed the muzzle between Richter's
eyes. "You got any last prayers, get 'em said. You're
on your way."

"Wait," Richter croaked pitifully. "I'll tell you
everything, all of it. Just don't kill me."

Charlie Phelan was never sure whether it was all
an act. Later, reflecting on it, he suspected Hickok
and Cody might have staged a mock execution. But
there was no doubt they'd broken their man.

Otto Richter told them everything.

A bright morning sun flooded Gramercy Park. There
was a snap in the air and the horses snorted steamy
puffs of frost. The carriage stopped before the Stanley
mansion shortly before eight o'clock.

Inside the cab, Hickok and Cody, with Richter
wedged between them, occupied one seat. Omohundro and Phelan were crowded into the other seat with
Augustus and Katherine. The children seemed to have
lost their fear of Richter, who was singed around the
ankles, his hands bound behind his back. His eyes
were empty with defeat.

Hickok crawled out of the carriage. He assisted
Richter down and waited until Cody stepped onto the
sidewalk. Late last night they had returned to the hotel, where Richter was held under guard in the suite.
The children, upon awakening, greeted the news of

Richter's capture with a sense of deliverance. Their long ordeal was nearly at an end.

"Charlie. Jack." Hickok looked back into the carriage at Phelan and Omohundro. "You boys keep a sharp lookout till this business is finished. I doubt it'll take too long."

Omohundro bobbed his head. "Charlie and me will take care of the kids. Don't worry about a thing."

"Wild Bill," Katherine said in a plaintive voice. "Aren't you taking us with you? We want to see Grandmama."

"You and Gus sit tight," Hickok said gently. "We'll come get you directly. I promise."

Hickok and Cody walked Richter toward the mansion. During the night, they had decided to confront Lelend Stanley with Richter's confession. They were wary of contacting the police until all the loose ends had been tied together. Richter, who feared Billy McGlory more than he feared them, had refused to implicate the underworld czar. They hoped Stanley would break under pressure.

The butler answered the door. Hickok shoved past him, with Richter and Cody in tow. They proceeded along the central hall, checking rooms as they went. Halfway down the hall, they came upon the dining room. Stanley and his mother were seated at the breakfast table.

"Stanley, the jig's up," Hickok said bluntly. "You remember Otto Richter, don't you?"

All the color leeched out of Stanley's features. Elizabeth Stanley, by now recovered from her illness, appeared confused. "How dare you!" she protested. "Leland, who are these men?"

"Ma'am," Cody said, doffing his hat. "I'm Bill

Cody and this here's Bill Hickok. We've got some bad news."

"Don't get no worse," Hickok said, halting at Stanley's end of the table. "Richter spilled the beans, gave us the whole story. Ain't that right, Richter?"

"Yeah," Richter mumbled with a hangdog look. "I told them."

Stanley struggled to regain his composure. "I don't know this man and I want you out of this house. Now!"

"Won't wash," Cody said. "Richter put your neck in a noose hopin' to save himself. You're headed for the gallows."

"Unless you get smart, real fast," Hickok added. "You testify against Billy McGlory and we'll ask the judge for leniency. That's your only out."

Richter stiffened. "Don't say a—"

Hickok cuffed him upside the head. "Keep your trap shut."

"Stop that!" Elizabeth Stanley rose from her chair. "I demand to know the meaning of this. Instantly!"

Cody wished there were another way. "Ma'am, I hate to be the one to tell you," he said, moving a step closer. "You son—Henry—and your daughter-in-law?"

"Yes, what about them?"

"This feller—" Cody motioned to Richter. "Well, he's the scoundrel that done them in. And much as it's gonna hurt you, Leland hired him to do it."

"How absurd!" she said, outraged, casting a glance at Stanley. "Leland, tell them there has been some mistake."

"Mother . . ." Stanley's voice trailed off. "You musn't believe these men. I've done nothing wrong."

Elizabeth Stanley stared at him. His features were

waxen and he was unable to hold her gaze. She saw the desperate look and she suddenly gasped, a hand to her mouth. "My God," she said, collapsing into her chair. "How could you?"

"Mother, you have to believe me . . ."

"I see it in your face." Her eyes welled over with a sudden rush of tears. "The mark of Cain on my own son. Henry and Amanda and . . . the children."

"No, ma'am," Cody said hurriedly. "Augustus and Katherine are gem-dandy, just fine. We've got'em waitin' outside."

"Mr. Cody, was that your name? I'm so confused by all this. Where have they been?"

"Well, ma'am, it's sort of a long story. Why don't we let them tell you?"

A few moments later Katherine and Augustus rushed into the dining room. "Grandmama!" they squealed in unison and threw themselves into her arms. Elizabeth Stanley clutched them to her bosom, her face wet with a mixture of tears and joy. The children hugged her as though they would never let go.

"Would you look at that," Cody said, absently swiping at his nose. "Guess it was worthwhile after all."

" 'Course, it was," Hickok said vigorously. "Knew that from the very start."

"Appears they've got some catchin' up to do. Maybe we ought to get on about our business."

"Bill, I just suspect you're right. We'll see 'em another time."

Hickok jerked a thumb into the hallway. Richter obediently hobbled past, and Stanley, his eyes downcast, fell in behind. Cody and Hickok, with a last look at the children, followed them through the house.

Omohundro and Phelan were waiting in the vestibule.

"All set?" Omohundro asked.

"All set," Cody replied. "Whereabouts is the jail in this town?"

"Twenty Second Street," Hickok said. "I know the man in charge. Clubber Williams."

"How'd he get a name like that?"

"Same way you got hung with Buffalo Bill."

They marched Otto Richter and Leland Stanley out of the front door.

"I want you tell me about Billy McGlory."

Richter stared straight ahead. "There's nothing to tell."

"How about you, Mr. Stanley?"

"Captain, I'm at a loss," Stanley said uneasily. "I don't know anyone by that name."

Captain Clubber Williams glowered at them a moment. They were standing before his desk, and Hickok and Cody were seated off to one side. He wagged his head with disgust.

"Mr. Cody. Mr. Hickok," he said. "I think we're getting nowhere fast. Would you agree?"

"Yessir," Cody agreed. "They're not too talkative."

Hickok nodded. "Looks like a case of lockjaw."

"Sergeant O'Hara." Williams bellowed. "Get yourself in here."

The door slammed open. Sergeant Alvin O'Hara was built like a tree stump, wide and square without an ounce of suet. He stamped to attention in front of the desk.

"You called, Cap'n?"

"I did indeed, Sergeant," Williams said. "These gentleman are being uncooperative. Any suggestions?"

"I could take'em down to the basement, Cap'n."

"Excellent idea, Sergeant. They're all yours."

O'Hara grabbed Richter and Stanley by the scruff of the neck. He waltzed them out of the office like marionettes on jiggling strings and closed the door. Cody glanced around at Williams.

"I'd just bet nobody wants to visit the basement."

"Not with O'Hara," Williams said wryly. "Of course, whatever the outcome, you gentlemen deserve the credit. I doubt we'd ever have solved the case on our own."

"Will you have any problems?" Hickok asked. "I recollect you told me it was political suicide to take on the Stanleys."

"Thanks to you, we have Richter as a songbird. There'll be no politics involved when we charge Stanley with murder."

"Well, Cap'n, it couldn't happen to a nicer feller."

Williams studied them at length. "Did you hear we found three dead men in Central Park last night? Billy McGlory's men, they were."

Hickok looked like a sphinx. "New York's a mighty dangerous town."

"And saints preserve us, we stumbled across a satchel filled with cash. Twenty thousand, it was."

"That' a powerful lot of money."

"Yes, it's all very strange," Wiliams said. "Then one of our patrolmen had his horse stolen. Some fine figure of a man jerked him clean out of the saddle."

Cody feigned innocence. "Sounds like a big night in the park."

"Indeed, one mystery after another. I've been wondering what to do about it."

"See what you mean." Hickok knuckled his mustache as though pondering the problem. "Don't you have a widows' fund?"

"I'm proud to say we do," Williams remarked. "Every nickel goes to assist the wives of slain officers."

"Why not toss in the twenty thousand? Found money ought to go to a worthy cause."

Williams stared across the desk. He knew Hickok and Cody were behind last night's ruckus in Central Park. Yet he was equally aware that they were responsible for solving a heinous double murder. One thing balanced another on *his* scales of justice.

"I admire a lawman with a generous spirit, Mr. Hickok. The widows' fund thanks you."

There was a rap at the door. Sergeant O'Hara marched in and snapped to attention. "Cap'n, sir," he barked. "I'm sorry to report the rascals won't talk."

"Perhaps you haven't reasoned with them sufficiently."

"We beat the livin' bejesus out of them, Cap'n. They fear Billy McGlory more than they do hangin'. I suppose it's his reputation for butcherin' people."

"Yes, you're probably right," Williams said. "I'm sure you did your best, Sergeant. Thank you."

O'Hara quick-stepped out of the office. Hickok arched one eyebrow in question. "What'd he mean about 'butcherin' people'."

"McGlory's trademark," Williams explained. "Anybody who turns on him gets hacked to pieces with a meat cleaver. You can imagine it inspires loyalty—and silence."

Cody exhaled heavily. "I tend to doubt I'd talk, either."

"Well, look on the bright side," Williams said. "Our friends Richter and Stanley have a date with the hangman. Half a loaf is better than none."

"Don't forget the kids," Cody added. "What counted most was gettin' them home safe. I'll settle for half a loaf."

"You're right," Hickok said with a sly smile. "One way or another, McGlory's day will come. Ain't that so, Cap'n?"

Williams laughed. "Are you a prophet, Mr. Hickok?"

"I've been known to predict a thing or two."

"I believe you've done so again."

"How's that, Cap'n?"

"Doomsday is just around the corner."

Hickok thought Billy McGlory was as good as dead.

CHAPTER 24

DUSK SWIFTLY faded into nightfall. The lamplights along Broadway flickered to life like bright-capped sentinels routing the dark. Theater marquees glowed throughout The Rialto.

Hickok and Cody ambled along the street at a leisurely pace. The weather was brisk and invigorating, and they had decided to walk to the theater. For the first time in weeks, their time was their own. The fight was fought and won.

Neither of them felt any great sense of victory. Richter and Stanley were in jail, charged with murder, and they were satisfied justice would be served. Yet there was no feeling of triumph or jubilation. Their mood was oddly melancholy.

"Funny the way things work out," Cody said glumly. "Don't think I ever felt so low in my life."

Hickok grunted. "Maybe I'll get drunk tonight."

"You miss 'em, too, don't you?"

"Gus and Kate?"

"Who else we talkin' about?"

"Well hell, guess it's only natural. We got used to havin' them around."

"That's a fact," Cody said, thoughtful a moment. "You reckon they'll do awright with their grandma?"

"Don't see why not," Hickok allowed. "She'll give 'em what they need most. Grandmas are good at lovin' kids."

"Yeah, you're likely right. All the same, I'll still miss 'em."

"You ain't rowin' that boat by yourself."

For a time, they walked on in silence. The Rialto was stirring with the pulse of nightlife, and all along the street actors were hurrying toward theaters. They passed the Eaves Costume Company, the major supplier of wigs and beards, tights and swords for Broadway productions. A man rushed out the door with a Viking helmet, complete with horns.

A block farther down Cody stopped before the window of stage photographer Napoleon Sarony. A genius with a camera, Sarony was all the rage with the stars of Broadway shows. Over the years daguerreotype had been replaced by tintype, and Sarony was the master of a new wet plate process. In the window, handsomely framed, was a photograph of Edwin Booth.

"Look at that," Cody said. "Edwin Booth, the greatest stage actor alive. Not bad, huh?"

Hickok inspected the photograph. "Why's he holdin' that skull?"

Booth was attired in costume for *Hamlet*. He was posed in a dramatic stance, a human skull cradled in the crook of one arm. Cody studied on it a moment.

"Always heard Shakespeare writes some pretty rough stuff. Way it looks, he must've killed somebody."

"Just more of that stage tomfoolery. Wonder where they got the skull?"

"Beats me." Cody cocked his head, staring at the photograph. "Maybe I ought to let 'em take my picture. You know, buckskins and all the trappins."

Hickok glanced at him. "Why you want your picture took?"

"Told you I've got a notion about the show business. Might just turn into a regular thing."

"I still say it's not fit work for a man. Don't care how much it pays."

Cody frowned. "A man's got to play the cards he's dealt. Wasn't that what you always said?"

"Yeah," Hickok conceded. "So what?"

"Well, maybe I was cut out for the show business. Maybe that's the hand I got dealt."

"Know what I think?"

"What's that?"

"You got a crooked dealer."

A few minutes later they approached the Lyceum Theater. Hickok still got a mild headache every time he saw his name in lights. Cody, on the other hand, was mesmerized by the glitzy display on the marquee. As they turned into the alleyway beside the theater, the dim figures of several men stepped from the shadows. Billy McGlory and four of his thugs blocked their path.

"Far enough," McGlory said in a rough voice. "You broke your word to me, Hickok."

"Hell I did," Hickok said. "I told you Richter would leave the park alive and kickin'. That's just what happened."

"Don't gimme that horseshit! He's gonna hang."

"Why'd you expect anything else, McGlory? He killed them people."

"Well, boyo, you played me for a fool. So now I'm gonna kill you."

"No, you ain't," Hickok said with a tight smile. "I'll drill you before any of your men clear leather. You won't live to see me die."

"That goes double," Cody added. "You'll get my first shot too, McGlory. Guarantee it'll stop your ticker."

McGlory weighed the odds. Something deep and

visceral told him they were telling the truth. They would kill him even though his men would kill them. He thought he'd have to commit suicide in order to commit murder. The price of revenge suddenly seemed too steep.

"There's always another time," he said. "You haven't seen the last of me."

"McGlory," Hickok said.

"What?"

"Don't let me catch you out of the Bowery again. I'll shoot you on sight."

"You don't scare me, Hickok."

"Yeah, I do," Hickok said quietly. "Quit while you're ahead. You'll live longer."

McGlory brushed past him. The four thugs fell in behind and followed their boss from the alley. Cody let out a low whistle.

"That was close," he said. "Why didn't you tell him about Richter?"

Hickok shrugged. "I expect he'll learn soon enough."

Richter had agreed to testify against Leland Stanley. A deal had been struck with the district attorney and Richter would serve life in prison, without parole. Hickok was not keen on the idea, but it ensured the safety of the children. The day Stanley was hanged the threat was removed forever.

"You're not foolin' anybody," Cody said. "You didn't tell McGlory because you wanted to kill him, right?"

"You always was able to see through me, Bill."

"Ever cross your mind you might've got us both killed?"

"Never happen," Hickok said lightly. "We're the Heroes of the Plains."

"You think that makes us bulletproof?"

"I just suspect we're gonna live forever."

Cody was forced to laugh. "You're full of beeswax."

"The show business does that to a man."

They walked off toward the stage door.

The theater was packed. Yet the show was oddly off, plodding along in fits and starts. For the first time since the production began, the children were not backstage that night. Everyone in the cast felt a strange sense of loss.

The audience nonetheless enjoyed themselves. A final curtain call brought a standing ovation for Cody and Hickok. When they walked offstage, they found Charlie Phelan waiting in the wings. He greeted them with a downturned smile.

"Funny thing," he said. "All through the show, I kept looking around for the kids. Doesn't seem the same."

"Guess it'll never be the same," Cody observed. "Gus and Kate got to be part of the family."

"Yeah, I'll miss them," Phelan said. "Things have a way of working out for the best, though. They're better off with their grandmother."

Hickok clapped him on the shoulder. "Charlie, it appears you're out of a job. Got any irons in the fire?"

"Never rains but it pours," Phelan said. "A man walked into the office this afternoon. Hired me to find his wife."

"What happened to her?"

"She ran off with a notions drummer."

"Hell, you'll find her," Hickok said confidently. "You're a prize detective, Charlie. Aces high."

Cody nodded. "We couldn't have done it without you."

"Honor's all mine," Phelan said. "How many detectives get to work with Wild Bill Hickok and Buffalo Bill Cody? Things will seem awful dull after this."

The plainsmen wrung his hand with genuine warmth. Phelan moved off with a cheery wave and went out the stage door. They started toward their dressing room only to be intercepted by Ned Buntline. He held out a telegram to Hickok.

"Western Union for you," he said. "Delivery boy brought it by just before the curtain came down."

Hickok tore open the envelope. His mustache arced in a broad smile as he read the message. He handed the telegram to Cody.

"I'll be jiggered," Cody said, scanning the contents. "Why didn't Sheridan wire me?"

Hickok grinned. "You're on leave of absence with the show business. Gen'rals want somebody they can depend on."

"What is it?" Buntline demanded "What are you talking about?"

"Sioux's on the warpath," Hickok said, reclaiming the telegram. "Sheridan's ordered me to report to Fort Laramie."

"Wyoming Territory!" Buntline screeched. "You can't leave the show."

"Why not? Sheridan needs a scout and there's nothin' here stoppin' me. Duty calls."

"But we need you! Your audience needs you!"

Omohundro and Giuseppina were drawn by Buntline's squalling cries. Cody gave them a troubled look, and Omohundro glanced from one to the other. "What's wrong?"

"Jack, I've been rescued," Hickok said, waving the telegram. "There's a Sioux uprising and Sheridan wired me to come running. I'm headed for Fort Laramie."

"Good God!" Buntline howled. "Will someone talk some sense into him!"

"Ned's right," Cody said. "For your own good, you ought to stick with the show till the season ends. What happens to that marshal's job in Kansas if you're off chasin' Injuns in Wyoming?"

"That don't worry me none," Hickok said. "Couple of months is plenty of time to corral them redsticks. I'll still be wearin' a badge come May."

"Guess I'd be wastin' my breath to argue otherwise."

"Yep, no two ways about it, my mind's made up. I'll catch a train in the mornin'."

"Oh, Beel," Giuseppina cooed softly. "We will miss you so. Must you go?"

"Dove Eye, you're the purtiest Injun gal I ever did see. I'm gonna miss you, too."

"This is madness!" Buntline snapped. "You're throwing away the career of a lifetime. I made you a star!"

"Look here, Ned," Hickok told him. "Jack's ten times the actor I'll ever be. Write him a better part."

Omohundro shook his head. "I'd sooner you stayed with the show, Bill. Wouldn't hardly be the same without you."

"Nope," Hickok declared. "Have Ned put your name in bigger lights. You deserve it."

"Why not sleep on it?" Cody temporized. "Maybe you'll see it different in the mornin'."

Hickok stared at him. "I come East to get them kids settled and the job's done. Time to head West."

Cody knew then it was a lost cause. He'd seen the determined look and that stubborn jawline all too often before. There was nothing more to be said.

Wild Bill Hickok was done with New York.

Grand Central Station was swarming with people. Trains were departing from every gate and passengers scurried to clamber aboard. The main terminal was chaos in motion.

Hickok paused for a last look at the ceiling. Shafts of sunlight from the stained-glass windows played off the azure dome and the celestial span of the zodiac. The sight reminded him of another morning, weeks past, when he'd first arrived in New York. He thought he would never return.

Cody walked beside him through the terminal. Outside, they descended the stairs to a platform beneath the vast iron-roofed railyard. Hickok's train was scheduled to depart at eight o'clock and they were a few minutes early. A cloak of silence enveloped them as they stood in the crush of people waiting to board. Neither of them wanted to be the first to say goodbye.

"Hate to see you go," Cody said, clearing his throat. "You still got time to change your mind."

"Guess not," Hickok said, his war bag clutched in one hand, "You and me both know I wasn't never cut out for the show business. Just ain't where I belong."

"Yeah, I know what you mean. There's times I get a hankerin' for the plains. But then—"

"You hear the applause and them crowds lookin' at you like you just rode in on a white horse. You always was a showboat."

"Goddarnit but it's true," Cody admitted. "Wish

you was more that way yourself. No tellin' where it'd take us."

"Nowhere I'd want to go," Hickok said. "You're welcome to your show business and New York, too. The limelight's not for me, pardner."

Their past lives were a jumble of myths and realities, bits of illusion and shards of truth. Today they sensed a turning point, and a point of no return for all that lay ahead. One was destined to play it out on the stage and the other on the plains.

"Well, don't kill all the Sioux," Cody said with an exaggerated gesture. "Leave some for me on the summer campaign."

"There's likely enough to go around."

Hickok abruptly looked past him. Augustus and Katherine, led by a matronly woman, were moving through the crowd. Cody followed his gaze.

"I asked 'em to come," he said. "They'd never get over it if you left without seeing them. Just wouldn't understand."

"Bill, you know I ain't much on good-byes."

"Then now's a good time to start."

"Wild Bill!"

Augustus hurled himself into Hickok's arms. Katherine was only a step behind, clutching him around the waist, her eyes moonlike. He swallowed hard around a lump in his throat.

"Don't go!" Augustus pleaded. "We want you to stay."

"Yes, please do," Katherine insisted. "Buffalo Bill said you really didn't have to go."

Hickok laughed. "Buffalo Bill's been known to spin a yarn or two."

Elizabeth Stanley moved closer. "I understand you've been called to service by the army, Mr.

Hickok. We want to wish you Godspeed and good
fortune."

"Why thank you, ma'am," Hickok replied. "That's
mighty kind of you to say so."

"Not at all," she said warmly. "Our most heartfelt
gratitude goes with you."

"Wish I was going too!" Augustus exclaimed. "I
want to see all the Wild West!"

Hickok ruffled his hair. "Gus, once you get growed
up, you come on out West. I could use a deputy with
your grit."

"All Aboard!"

The conductor's voice rang out over the station.
People embraced loved ones and murmured their last
good-byes, hurrying to board the train. Katherine
pulled Hickok down and hugged him fiercely around
the neck. Her voice was husky with emotion.

"I will love you forever and ever, Wild Bill. You
will always by my Lancelot."

Hickok again swallowed hard. "Kate, I ain't never
gonna forget you, either. Was I ever to marry, you'd
be my gal."

"Will you wait for me to grow up? Will you, Wild
Bill?"

"Cross my heart I will."

Katherine kissed him soundly, and Augustus snuf-
fled loudly, his eyes wet with tears. Hickok disen-
gaged himself from the children and nodded earnestly
to Elizabeth Stanley. He stuck out his hand to Cody.

"We'll meet somewheres down the trail," he said
gruffly. "The show business ain't got you yet."

Cody clasped his hand. "Look for me when you
see me."

"I ain't never hard to find."

The train lurched forward with a toot from the engineer's whistle. Hickok swung aboard the observation deck on the last passenger coach. He stood tall, shoulders squared, and grandly waved his hat overhead. His mustache curled in a nutcracker grin.

"So long, Kate! So long, Gus!"

"So long, Wild Bill!"

"Soo long, New York!"

**Before the legend,
there was the man . . .**

And a powerful destiny to fulfill.

On October 26, 1881, three outlaws lay dead in
a dusty vacant lot in Tombstone, Arizona.
Standing over them—Colts smoking—were
Wyatt Earp, his two brothers Morgan and
Virgil, and a gun-slinging gambler named
Doc Holliday. The shootout at the O.K. Corral
was over—but for Earp, the fight had just
begun . . .

WYATT EARP

MATT BRAUN

**AVAILABLE WHEREVER BOOKS ARE SOLD
FROM ST. MARTIN'S PAPERBACKS**

WE 7/98

FOR DECADES the Texas plains ran with the blood of natives and settlers, as pioneers carved out ranch land from ancient Indian hunting grounds and the U.S. Army turned the tide of battle. Now the Civil War has begun, and the Army is pulling out of Fort Belknap—giving the Comanches a new chance for victory and revenge.

Led by the remarkable warrior, Little Buffalo, the Comanche and Kiowa are united in a campaign to wipe out the settlers forever. But in their way stand two remarkable men . . .

Allan Johnson is a former plantation owner. Britt Johnson was once his family slave, now a freed man facing a new kind of hatred on the frontier. Together, with a rag-tag volunteer army, they'll stand up for their hopes and dreams in a journey of courage and conscience that will lead to victory . . . or death.

BLACK FOX

A NOVEL BY

MATT BRAUN

BESTSELLING AUTHOR OF
WYATT EARP

AVAILABLE WHEREVER BOOKS ARE SOLD
FROM ST. MARTIN'S PAPERBACKS

BF 11/97

IN 1889, Bill Tilghman joined the historic land rush that transformed a raw frontier into Oklahoma Territory. A lawman by trade, he set aside his badge to make his fortune in the boomtowns. Yet Tilghman was called into service once more, on a bold, relentless journey that would make his name a legend for all time—in an epic confrontation with outlaw Bill Doolin.

OUTLAW KINGDOM

MATT BRAUN

**AVAILABLE WHEREVER BOOKS ARE SOLD
FROM ST. MARTIN'S PAPERBACKS**